Getting a Life

Getting a Life

The tale of an orphan

Raiche Pane

Pearl Press

© Raiche Pane 2011

This book is sold subject to the condition that it shall not, by way of trade or otherwise, be lent, resold, hired out, or otherwise circulated without the publisher's prior consent in any form of binding or cover other than that in which it is published and without a similar condition including this condition being imposed on the subsequent publisher.

The moral right of Raiche Pane has been asserted

First published in Great Britain by Pearl Press
ISBN 978-0-9568688-4-8
Printed and bound by Good News Books, Ongar, Essex, England.

I dedicate this story to my beloved wife Agnes and her family, Sheena and Alan and Alfie and Ellen who, from the outset, treated me as a human being.

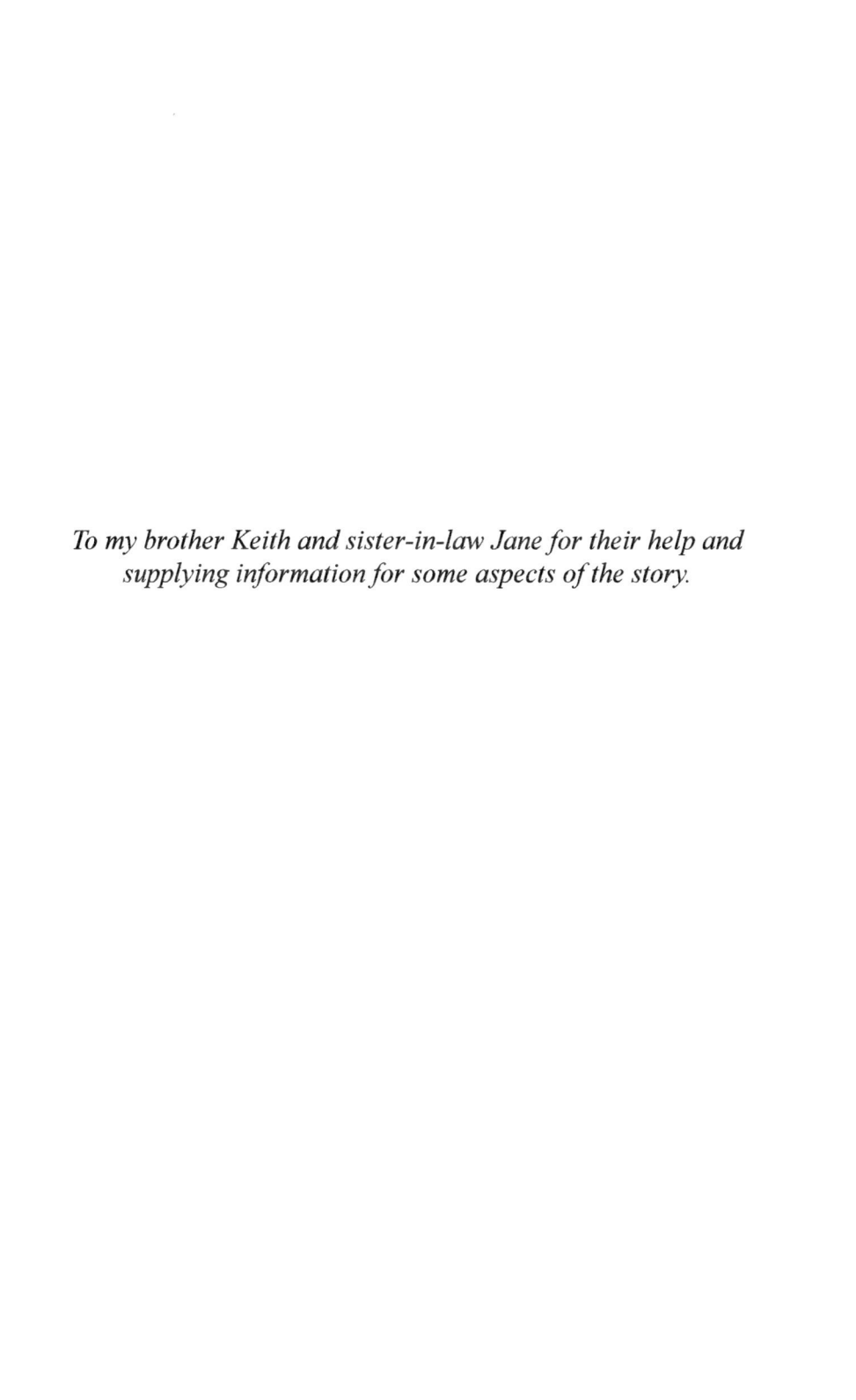

To my brother Keith and sister-in-law Jane for their help and supplying information for some aspects of the story.

CONTENTS

Chapter One	 1
Chapter Two	 9
Chapter Three	 15
Chapter Four	 19
Chapter Five	 23
Chapter Six	 29
Chapter Seven	 33
Chapter Eight	 41
Chapter Nine	 49
Chapter Ten	 53
Chapter Eleven	 67
Chapter Twelve	 71
Chapter Thirteen	 77
Chapter Fourteen	 83
Chapter Fifteen	 91
Chapter Sixteen	 99
Chapter Seventeen	 111
Chapter Eighteen	 117
Chapter Nineteen	 125
Chapter Twenty	 137
Chapter Twenty One	 149
Chapter Twenty Two	 159
Chapter Twenty Three	 169
Chapter Twenty Four	 179
Chapter Twenty Five	 187
Chapter Twenty Six	 195
Chapter Twenty Seven	 203

Chapter Twenty Eight	 211
Chapter Twenty Nine	 219
Chapter Thirty	 225
Chapter Thirty One	 229
Chapter Thirty Two	 235
Chapter Thirty Three	 241
Chapter Thirty Four	 245
Chapter Thirty Five	 261
Chapter Thirty Six	 269

Chapter One

Blood oozed from the gaping wound on his mummy's head. But he was just seven years old and did not understand what was happening. Life was draining from her and then with a long sigh, her head dropped to her shoulder and she died. He shook her, crying, 'Mummy wake up, please mummy, wake up.' He repeated it several times, continuing to cry. Eventually, tiredness overcame him and he lay his head on her other shoulder and fell asleep.

That day had been his seventh birthday. In the afternoon, she had taken him to the pictures after which they went to a Chinese restaurant, where his father joined them for dinner. Upon returning home, his father had a couple of pegs of whisky and then left to play bridge with friends. When it was time for BJ to go to bed, he undressed, changed into his night suit, and said his night prayers with his mother. As she always did, she sat with him a while he fell asleep.

He was woken abruptly by his father's shouting. Through his sleepy haze he heard his mother's distressed voice pleading, 'Please don't.' He got out of bed, rubbing his eyes, and slowly walked into their bedroom. His father was drunk – not for the first time – and was physically abusing his mother. Only this time, she was on the floor against the wall, cowering in great fear, crying. In his raised hand was a long thick bicycle chain lock.

He caught his fathers left arm saying, 'Daddy please don't hit mummy again.' But his father shook his arm free and backhanded him, sending him flying backwards. He hit his head against a cupboard and fell unconscious. Whilst he was still out, his father twice brought the chain down hard on his wife's head. Blood splashed on the wall and her head and face as she slumped further down.

In a flash his father sobered up, sank down on his knees beside her, crying, 'Sweetheart I am sorry.' But it was too late. He had gone too far. Realisation dawned and the magnitude of his action hit him. He cried in anguish, 'What have I done? Oh my God what have I done?' Accepting the hopelessness of his situation, with head bowed and sobbing uncontrollably, he dejectedly walked into the dining room. Taking a chair, he carried it into the sitting room and stood on it. He still had the bloodied chain in his hand and wound it to the ceiling fan. He then used the belt around his waist to loop it to the chain and around his neck. He kicked the chair away and hung himself.

In the space of a few fateful moments, BJ, still unconscious, was orphaned. He started to come around, his head hurting. The lights were still on. It was a while before he was able to fully open and focus his eyes. Seeing his mother slumped against the wall, he crawled to her.

He slept soundly and the hours went by. The sound of banging on the front door woke him. On his way through from the bedroom, he saw his father's hanging body and the overturned chair on the floor. It was the servant, Bimal, at the door. The door opened into the sitting room and he saw the dangling body. Alarmed, he crossed the landing to the next-door neighbour, Darius. A little animatedly, he said, 'Sahib is hanging from the fan.' He and his wife Nina had heard some shouting the previous evening and were now very perturbed.

Following Bimal into the sitting room, Darius saw the lifeless body with its tongue hanging out. He did not touch the chair. He was horrified and had to sit down. He rested his forehead on his hands at a complete and utter loss to make sense of this. But where was Violet, his wife? He felt an overwhelming sense of foreboding.

BJ was crying. His night suit was bloodied, as was his head. Also, his mouth and jaw were slightly swollen and there was blood on his chin. The neighbour asked, 'Bimal please get BJ washed and dressed and then take him to my place. Tell Memsahib to look after him for a while and I will explain later. Come back afterwards please.'

'Yes Sahib.'

He took BJ to the bathroom. He did as instructed, dropped off BJ and returned. They walked into the bedroom. The sight that greeted them drained all blood from their faces, rooting them to where they stood. Darius was forced to look away. It took a few minutes to pull himself together before he had a closer look. The gaping wound, now congealed with blood, told its full story. She was dead. Rigor mortis had set in.

Each apartment had three bedrooms, two bathrooms, a sitting room, a dining room, and a walk-through larder with a sink and a kitchen. The block, which had six apartments, was owned by the River Authority. A gardener maintained the neatly manicured lawns and garden. The neighbour telephoned the Authority Police and told them of the tragedy.

'From what you say, it seems the father killed the mother and then killed himself. How old is the boy?'

'Seven. Yesterday was his birthday.'

'What? His birthday! Poor boy. What a present! It will sully every birthday after this. We will need to talk to him to find out as much as we can. I know it will be difficult but we have no choice as he was the only one there.'

When the police arrived, Bimal went to get BJ and brought him back. He made them tea and offered some breakfast savouries. BJ had already eaten a little in Darius's house but he ate some more. The police and Darius partook using the time to consider the words to use in this tragic situation. But BJ cut across their thoughts: 'Is my mummy dead?'

They looked at the floor and then at each other before the senior officer, an Inspector, nodded. The word 'yes' hardly came out of his mouth, so he had to repeat it only louder. BJ's lips quivered. He bit the lower one but he held back the tears. 'Daddy is dead too, isn't he?' Again the officer nodded this time not even attempting to speak. Silence descended.

The officer said, 'BJ we are very sorry about your mummy and daddy but I have to ask you what happened. Can you tell me?'

BJ nodded and thought for a while. 'I do not know all of it.' He paused put his index finger in his mouth and tilted his head slightly looking at the ceiling, thinking some more.

'What time did you go to bed?'

'I don't know. It was dark when we got home.'

'Got home? From where?'

'Mummy took me to the pictures, then we went to a Chinese

3

restaurant where Daddy met us.'

'What happened when you got home?'

'Daddy had some drinks first and then went to someone's house. I think he was going to play cards for money.'

'BJ your face and mouth are swollen. How did you get hurt?'

'Daddy hit me.'

The Inspector was mindful of how a very young boy may be feeling, so he proceeded in an even gentler tone of voice. 'BJ when did he hit you? And why?'

'Daddy's shouting woke me up. I went to their room. Mummy was on the floor against the wall crying. He was standing over her with a chain. I caught his arm and said, "Don't hurt Mummy." But he hit me.'

Darius said, 'When I got here, BJ was in his night suit, which had blood on it. Do you want to see it? Also there was blood on his mouth and chin.'

They were beginning to piece together the puzzle. There was a bump on the back of BJ's head.

'Then what happened?'

'I must have fallen backwards. When I opened my eyes, I was lying beside the cupboard. I did not see Daddy. My head and mouth were hurting and I saw Mummy on the floor. I crawled to her shaking her to wake up.'

Silence followed again. The police decided they had put BJ through enough. But what was going to happen to him? So they could discuss his future, the Inspector gave Bimal some money. 'Will you take BJ for a bus or tram ride and treat yourselves to ice cream or a milk shake or whatever? But please before you go will you make some more tea?'

The tragedy was beginning to increasingly take its toll on them. They figured they had at least the better part of the morning to get all organised before they left. They had never been in that position before, especially having to deal with an orphan. Life had to continue for BJ with as little disruption as possible. But how? What could they do? They had no immediate answers. So they decided to sound out the local parish priest.

Chapter One

His mother was well known and thought of by her husband's colleagues and neighbours. She was a devout Catholic who had taken BJ to seven o'clock mass Monday to Saturdays and holy days of obligation and eight o'clock on Sundays. She prayed daily. Often she would have her rosary in hand or in her lap as she knitted and BJ played.

His father was also well known, but for the wrong reasons. He had been a merchant seaman until a few months before, and was away a lot of the time. He took to drinking heavily. But he was good at his job and made sure that he was never inebriated while on duty. He also liked gambling on horses and playing cards, usually bridge, for money. He was promoted to Chief Engineer at the age of thirty and became home-based in charge of the dredgers. He had a provident fund, which would pass on to BJ, but he was a minor. The employer would have to create a trust, invest the money and when he was twenty-one, he would inherit the accumulated funds. Normally there would have been a death-in-service benefit but he was unsure whether it would be paid as the death was by suicide. Meanwhile, BJ had to continue his education. There were no known relatives, his grandparents being deceased. And there was BJ, probably inevitably destined for a children's home.

After discussing all this, they felt the best way to proceed would be for the next-door neighbour to take in BJ temporarily. Meanwhile, the Inspector would contact HQ about events. Although the deaths occurred on its property and they had full responsibility for policing, he would also liaise out of courtesy with the local police Inspector. Also the deaths needed to be certified before being taken to the Place of Rest.

The police officers studied the bedroom and sitting room, making notes as they did so. This time, in view of BJ's head injury, they also examined the cupboard. There were indeed traces of blood on the edge lower down.

'That was lucky,' the junior ranking officer said. 'Had he missed it, his head might have hit the floor.' It was concrete with a decorated coating typical in the tropics. They left when they were satisfied they had got all they required.

Nina, seeing the police leave, joined Darius. Both were in shock. Not only had he been a colleague of the deceased, but also a friend who celebrated birthdays, anniversaries and Christmas and New Year's Day together. As it was the tradition, everyone went to the city zoo on Boxing Day, so they had spent the whole day with a host of others picnicking on the grass. They played records on a portable player and the more extrovert among them jived to the music. They were always very enjoyable outings. Now the next one was just about a fortnight away. Poor BJ. What Christmas would he now have? No parents in his young life. How would it affect him?

The medical officer arrived to see the bodies and sign the death certificate. The undertakers arrived shortly afterwards and when the medical officer had finished, the bodies were removed.

Nina and Darius stripped the beds. Underneath the pillow on BJ's bed, Nina found a new white bible. She opened it and saw a photo of his mother, Violet, with a baby that could only be BJ stuck to the inside cover. On the adjacent blank page she had written:

'My beloved son, Bryan.

Happy seventh birthday.

Presently you are too young to understand but I ask you never be without this bible with my photo. Read it especially the words I have underlined on the page I have folded. It will comfort you.

Try to keep the commandments and God will bless you.

Always remember whatever happens, I love you and will be with you no matter where you are and what you are doing.

Mummy.

xxxxxx'

The underlined words on the folded page were from Proverbs 3:

'Let not mercy and truth forsake thee: bind them about thy neck; write them upon the table of thine heart:

So shalt thou find favour and good understanding in the sight of God and man.'

Trust in the LORD with all thine heart; and lean not unto thine own understanding.

Chapter One

In all thy ways acknowledge him, and he shall direct thy paths.'

The final words of her message had now turned out to be prophetic as if she had had a premonition.

In tropical countries without refrigeration, food was spoiled quickly. Fresh food shopping was therefore an early morning daily routine. They collected the non-perishable foods and tins and what perishables that were still edible. Darius took everything to his home while Nina, stayed behind.

Chapter Two

The Police proceeded to the church that Violet attended. They found a priest. 'Good morning Father. Are you the Parish Priest?'

'No, I am not. You want Father O'Shea. Please follow me and I will take you to him.'

They entered a building across a small courtyard. He took them into a lounge. 'Please sit down. I will go and get him.'

A few minutes later, he walked in. 'Good morning. I am Father O'Shea, how can I help you?'

The senior Police Officer said, 'Good morning Father. This is Sergeant Hardy and I am Inspector Marriott of the River Authority Police.

'Father, I have some very bad news. One of your parishioners, Violet Conway, died during the night.'

The priest, visibly shaken, said, 'Oh! My God,' and sat down burying his head in his hands. After a while he recovered his composure and asked, 'What happened? How did she die?'

The officer hesitated before saying, 'Her husband killed her.'

'Excuse me,' he said. 'All this is a big shock; I need to get myself together. Would you like a hot or cold drink?'

They both said, 'Tea please.'

The priest departed and went to the kitchen. He could have rung the hand bell but needed the time to unscramble his thoughts. He asked the servant, 'Please make a pot of tea for three.'

To give himself time to assimilate such horrible news the priest said, 'She was a really devoted and religious person. Often when her husband was at sea, she would bring BJ to morning mass during the week and stay to light a candle and pray. She would kneel at the foot of the Blessed Virgin's statue with her rosary while BJ sat in the pew behind her. As soon as he could understand, she had taught him simple prayers. She had also given him his own rosary, which he would clutch in his hands.

On one occasion I noticed that her lips were swollen and cut, and the side of her face was bruised. She was crying. I felt compelled to interrupt her. She began to sob uncontrollably which set off BJ too. I took them into the vestry for privacy and got her a glass of water. When she had calmed down. I asked what was the matter. She would not reply. I then asked how she had hurt herself. She started to cry again and very haltingly, said, "My husband punched me." There were other times subsequently when I noticed she was bruised but she tried to camouflage it with make-up. I was in a difficult position. I could not intervene.'

He paused a while to drink some tea continuing, 'I gathered over a period of time he was alcoholic and when he was drunk, would physically abuse her. Her greatest fear was that he would hurt BJ so she was very protective of him, bearing the brunt of his anger. But I never thought it would get to this. Was I naïve?'

'Of course not, Father. No one could have foreseen this.'

'You say she is dead. Where his her husband?'

'He is dead too.'

'What? Sorry, pardon?'

'Yes. I am afraid he is dead too. After he killed his wife, he hung himself from a fan.'

'Oh, Blessed Mother of God. And where was BJ during this time? Is he all right?'

'He says he was woken by shouting and saw his father standing over his mother who was on the floor, with a thick chain in his hand. He tried to stop his father but was knocked unconscious. When he awoke he did not realise his mother was dead. He had fallen asleep huddled up against her and was only roused when the servant knocked on the door. It was then he saw his father's hanging body. He is presently out with the servant because I wanted him to be out of the environment immediately. I believe you know Nina and Darius, their neighbours, who also attend your church. She is in the house until they return. She and Darius will be taking BJ in until his future is sorted out. I have never been in this position before

Chapter Two

so any help you can offer will be very much appreciated.'

They all agreed that BJ's future was paramount. They had to make things as easy as possible in the very tragic circumstances.

'Father, do you know if the Church can place him in one of its orphanages?'

'I will find out what I can. I believe he was to have started school in the new year. We must place him by then, which does not leave very much time. But, as you know, we do not have any orphanages in the city. He will be relocated. Please leave it with me and I will start immediately and get back to you as quickly as possible. Can you please leave me your telephone numbers? This is mine. Please ring at any time if I can be help.'

'Thank you Father for your help.'

He sat a while after they had gone to mull over the situation and prayed for guidance. He had to do something, and as he had no appointments that day, decided to explore the possibility of an orphanage taking in BJ.

After telling the servant and the assistant priest he was going out, he took the tram to the city centre, changing to another going out of the city. After some fifteen minutes and a short walk, he arrived at St Philomena's Church. A servant opened the door of the presbytery. 'Salaam Sahib.'

'Salaam. May I see Father Fernandez please?'

The servant went to get him. When he saw who was at the door he smiled broadly. 'Good morning, Father. It is good to see you again. How are you?' But he saw that his fellow priest was grim-faced. He took him into a lounge and both sat down. 'Something seems to be wrong. Is that why you are here?'

Father O'Shea told him about that morning's news. 'I need to place BJ in St George's orphanage upcountry. The Brothers stay in the annex during the holidays. Is the Principal here?'

'As a matter of fact he is down, but I do not know whether he is in.' He rang a hand bell and the servant appeared at the door. 'Yes Sahib?'

'Please see if Brother Angelo is in and ask him if he can come here. Someone wishes to speak to him.'

The servant left. Father Fernandez asked what happened and before Father O'Shea could finish the story, Brother Angelo walked in.

'Good morning Brother Angelo, this is Father O'Shea from Our Lady of Mount Carmel. Father this is Brother Angelo.' They shook hands.

'What can I do for you Father?'

'One of my more devout parishioners and her husband died tragically during the night orphaning their only child, a boy, aged seven. Please can you accept him into your orphanage?'

Seeing the priest's face and hearing such news especially so close to Christmas, the Principal was sensitive enough not to ask any questions. He was only too willing to help.

'Yes, we will take him. However, there is not a lot of time as the new year starts on Monday, the twenty-second of January. The boarders will be returning on the Saturday and Sunday. I, in fact, go back on Saturday, the sixth of January. Can you have him ready by then and bring him to the station? The train leaves at ten past eleven in the morning. I will meet you there and he can travel with us to school. The matron and her husband who run the orphanage are very nice people and they will try as they always do to help him settle in to the routine, especially as he is so young. Can you please excuse me a few minutes? I will get a prospectus for you.'

He returned after a few minutes. 'Can you please complete the application form so I have all the details for the register? I will contact the matron so she can get a bed and locker ready.'

The priest said, 'I do not know all his details and will have to find out. I have only known him as BJ and he was to start in the First Standard next year. I will have to get his baptism certificate too. Is it all right if I posted you the form? Or I could send the house servant to deliver it personally?'

'Whatever is convenient. If you post it, send it to the school. The address is on the form. The prospectus tells you about the school and there is a list of the boarder's kit. The uniform is basic khaki, and for outings, whites. I appreciate he has just been orphaned but will it be possible to provide as much as possible please? It would help the orphanage's resources because it relies on the goodwill of parents and private donations.'

'The Legion of Mary has a contingency fund and I will speak to the President.'

'Brother, I am so very grateful. I was concerned about what would happen to BJ. He is a lovely natured boy. He and his mother were daily at mass. It is such a pity that a gentle and loving woman should die in such circumstances, orphaning a boy like him.'

Chapter Three

When he got back to the presbytery, he read the prospectus. The list of essentials consisted of:

Three khaki pants and shirts, three white pants and shirts, three night suits, four bed sheets, a blanket in season, one pillow, one mosquito net in season, three towels, underpants (as necessary), singlets (as necessary), swimming trunks, socks, sports socks, shoes, slippers, white canvas sports shoes, hockey stick (first term), football boots (second term), toothbrush, toothpaste, soap and towels.

He spent some more time meditating and praying for BJ and his future.

That evening, he visited the President of the Legion of Mary.[1]

'Hello Father, come in.'

'Good evening, John, Margaret. God bless you both.'

'Can I get you a drink?'

'Tea please.'

'How has your day been?'

'Not too bad, thanks.'

Margaret returned with the teas and some Indian sweets. When she was settled in her chair, he said, 'John, in your capacity as President of the Legion of Mary, I have to make an urgent request. But first I have some bad news to tell you. I think you know who Violet Conway was.

---

[1] *The Legion of Mary is an apostolic organisation of lay people in the Catholic Church. Members are volunteers whose works include door-to-door evangelism, visiting the poor, sick and needy and prisoners, mentoring new converts and generally meeting the spiritual needs of the community.*

It also builds up the members spiritually through weekly meetings for prayer, planning and discussions in a family setting. The members give a report on their work task taken from the previous week's meeting so that by sharing their experiences they can learn from each other. Tasks depend on the needs of the parish. A new member would work with an experienced one who had done the work before so that they could demonstrate how to make the approach and handle the visit.

She and her husband died last night, orphaning their son, BJ. You may have seen him in church with her.'

They merely nodded, overcome with shock and surprise.

'He has no other relatives and is presently with his neighbours, Nina and Darius, who you may also have seen at mass. But as they have three children, two of school age, they cannot afford to look after him permanently. He was to start in the first standard next year. I have therefore arranged for him to go to an orphanage upstate and the Principal will be taking him on Saturday, the sixth of January. As the orphanage relies on the goodwill donations from parents and other organizations, the Principal asked if I could provide as much as possible of the essentials listed in the prospectus.' He passed it to John, who read through it. 'Oh yes, he will need a suitcase and a hold-all for the bedding.'

While John went through the list, Father and Margaret drank their tea. When John looked up, the priest said, 'Please, will the Legion consider buying as much as it can out of the contingency fund?'

'I am shocked by the news. What a time for it to happen, just two weeks before Christmas. More importantly, how must BJ feel? How old is he?'

'As he was to start in the first standard, he must be seven. In fact I think it was his birthday yesterday.'

'Yesterday? And his parents died on the same day? What a tragedy. Poor boy.'

'It is two weeks to Christmas for you too and I am very sorry to bring this to you. But I want to help the orphanage help BJ, and we do not have a lot of time.'

'We understand Father.'

'Thank you, I will leave it with you.'

On Sunday, at each mass, he announced the death of Violet Conway and her husband during the week, orphaning their seven-year-old son.

At the meeting on Monday, Father did not feel it necessary to go into detail about the tragedy. But he did emphasise that BJ was going to an orphanage upstate and the Principal had requested assistance. 'I urge you please do what you can. This is what the Legion stands for. I will leave you to consider it.' And he left.

There was a heavy silence for a while. John broke it. 'This is the list of essentials,' and read them out. 'As Father said the Principal asks for as much as possible to defray the orphanage's costs. What do you think?'

'We should get everything. Can we make not make a small donation individually? We can make up the balance from the contingency fund,' the Treasurer, Fred said. There was a general murmur of approval.

'I gather from that we mostly agree. Does anyone have any reservations?' No one answered.

'Can I take it we are unanimous?'

'Yes,' they answered collectively.

'Good. Thank you for agreeing to help. Before we proceed, we will spend some time in prayer for the souls of Violet and her husband and also for BJ. I cannot imagine how he feels. Let us pray that he will not be emotionally and psychologically damaged in any way.'

After the meeting, the treasurer got one of the collection bags from a drawer and put some money in it. He left it on top of the chest in the corner and said, 'I will leave it here so you can make your donations privately. As it is an emergency collection, you can contribute something next week if it is more convenient.'

Chapter Four

BJ never returned to the apartment. Within a couple of days, it was stripped. There was a well-known weekly auction in the city centre and everything was sold including his mother's jewelry. A music shop bought his father's guitar. However, they felt it appropriate to retain a few photos of his parents, including one on their wedding day, and one of his mother and him. They retained all baptism and marriage and education certificates.

Bimal was in tears as he was paid off. He respected the mother, who he said was the best person he had ever worked for. She did not treat him as a servant but a human being and was generous to him.

BJ was a quiet boy but he seemed especially subdued at Nina's and Darius'. He was at his best playing with other boys and girls. He seemed to relax. They did wonder if he was subdued because he was in their house.

Christmas was celebrated in the usual manner, with special food and drink and regular visitors. Presents were opened and the children enjoyed playing with them. BJ got a Meccano set and they spent time building the crane. When finished, he was quite excited with it.

On Boxing Day, the Anglo-Indians traditionally visited the zoo. They took their portable gramophones and jived to records. They played games, they had fun and there was a great party atmosphere. BJ loved seeing the animals. He was absolutely fascinated by the lions, tigers and other big cats and the otters. Visitors bought small live fish that they threw into the water so they could chase and catch them. As they wanted him to enjoy his last days, they had deliberately not told him he was being sent to an orphanage. Father O'Shea intended to visit and tell him himself while they were present.

It was the second of January. So that he would not dwell and fret over the news throughout the day, the priest thought it best to tell BJ in the evening not long before he would go to bed. That time had arrived and they sat down. 'Can I get you a drink Father?'

'Tea please, thank you. How are you BJ?'

'OK, Father. Aunty and Uncle have looked after me very well.'

'Good, I am glad. BJ, unfortunately, you cannot stay with them forever. You were to start in the first standard at school this month, and your fees must be paid. Aunty and uncle cannot afford to pay them. They have Lisa's and Jason's to pay. The church is sending you to a school where you will be well looked after. They will teach you, give you food and clothes. You will have your own bed and will be with other boys who do not have mummies and daddies like you. The school also has boarders and you will all be taught together.'

'What are boarders?'

'They are boys who live together in school and only go home for the school holidays. Their parents pay fees for teaching and food. But they buy their clothes. We have got you everything you will need and I will take you to the station on Saturday. The Principal will be there and he will travel with you by train.'

All the time he was talking, Father was watching BJ's face for any reaction. Similar to the days since the tragic demise of his parents, he did not show any emotion. However, his eyes clearly betrayed his great sadness and fear.

'Is there anything you want to ask me?'

He paused a while to think. 'No, Father. I just want to thank aunty and uncle for looking after me, and you too for sending me to a place to stay and learn. But I am very frightened.'

'You will be in a good place with good people in charge of the boys and you will have everything. You will play games and all kinds of sports.'

BJ, still fearful, nodded saying, 'Thank you. Can I go now please?' He joined the other children on the floor who were playing snakes and ladders.

After a while, Father got up to leave. 'Bye everyone, bye BJ. I will see you on Saturday. Aunty and uncle will bring you to the church where I have your suitcase.'

'Cheerio Father.'

Chapter Four

BJ continued to play for a while and then Nina said, 'Right children. Time for bed.'

'Goodnight Aunty and Uncle.'

'Goodnight Mummy, Daddy.'

Chapter Five

The day for BJ to go to the orphanage arrived. He was very quiet and Nina and Darius were sensitive not to engage him unnecessarily. Later in the morning they walked to the church. The servant answered the door but Father O'Shea, who had been expecting them, had heard the knocking and was on his way down the stairs. 'Hello Darius and Nina. Hello BJ.'

'Good morning Father,' they said in unison.

Nina crouched down to give him a hug and a kiss. 'Good luck and God bless you son.'

Darius also crouched down. 'Yes son, be good and God bless you.'

'Good-bye Father.'

'Good-bye. I will see you at mass on Sunday as usual, no doubt.'

With that, they left. They felt a pang of sadness. As nice a boy as he was, they just could not afford to take on the responsibility. And cruel though it seemed, they would never be able to feel the same way about him as they did for their own children. All things considered, it was the best thing to do for BJ.

'BJ, come in. There is still some time to go. Mahmud, please get some cold lime juice for us.'

And to BJ, he said as they entered the sitting and meeting room, 'Sit down BJ.'

When they were both seated, he said, 'Today is a big day for you. You are going away but I want you to know that I will pray for you. Always remember that. I knew your mother. She was a gentle and kind woman. Think of her in all that you do and you will not go wrong.'

BJ merely nodded. The last three weeks or so had obviously traumatised him. From having his parents and a home to live in, now he had nothing. He was going away, but he had no idea how far or where it was. Awaiting him was a new place to live and with people he did not know. He was frightened.

Mahmud arrived with the drinks and some biscuits. He also brought the packed lunch for BJ. It had some sandwiches, savouries and a couple of sweets. He had removed the metal top from a coca cola bottle and replaced it with a cork so it would be easy for BJ to take out, even if he had to use his teeth.

Father said, 'Help yourself.'

'Thank you Father,' he said, and took a couple of biscuits.

The priest himself took a couple. 'I want to tell you what is now going to happen. Shortly, I will take you by taxi to the station. There, we will meet the Principal of the school you are going to. His name is Brother Angelo but all the pupils call the Brothers "sir".'

'What is a Brother? Is it like brothers and sisters?'

'No. They are like me. Only I am a priest and say mass. The Brothers also devote their lives to God. They do not have any money, wear white cassocks like me, but they teach.'

BJ nodded.

The priest rang a bell.

'Yes Sahib.'

'Please get a taxi for us.'

Mahmud left to walk to the main road about 150 yards away. It was not long before one appeared. He stepped to the edge of the pavement and waved it to a stop.

'Please go to the church to pick up a priest and a boy. They are going to the main railway station.' On arriving at the church, BJ and the priest were waiting at the gate. The driver put the suitcase and hold-all in the boot and they got into the taxi.

'The main station please.'

'Yes Sahib.'

The journey was in silence. BJ looked out of the window throughout the journey, seeing buildings and areas he had not seen before. He wondered if he would ever come this way again. He was still frightened. He was leaving everything he was familiar with. He had been so dependent on his mother and now she was not there. But he still did not cry. It was as if his tear ducts had stopped functioning.

They got to the station and walked onto the platform where the train was standing. Father's white cassock stood out in the crowd, as did those of the Principal and two other Brothers. The Principal spotted them and walked towards them. 'Good morning Father.' And looking at BJ he said, 'You are BJ. Good morning. I am the Principal Brother Angelo.'

'Good morning sir.'

'Good morning Brother.'

Father now turned to BJ. 'Remember what I told you. God Bless you.' He placed his hand on his head for a while, said a silent prayer and then he was gone.

The Principal and BJ walked to the other two Brothers and said to them, 'This BJ Conway. BJ this is Brother Francis and Brother Hackney.'

'Good morning sirs.'

'Shall we go in? Brother Francis took BJ's suitcase and they entered a carriage and sat down. He said, 'We bought you some comics,' and handed them to him.

'Thank you sir.' One comic was the Beano, one was the Dandy and the third was the Lone Ranger.

The train left at ten past eleven. It was the first time he had been on a train. He looked out of the window at the rolling countryside. He saw fields with people working on them. There were carts being pulled by cows. And as the train continued rumbling along with a steady rhythmic noise he began to read a comic. All this time the Brothers engaged in general chitchat, read the newspaper or were wrapped in their own thoughts.

They arrived and Brother Francis got hold of BJ's suitcase, Brother Hackney taking the hold-all. They went through the ticket barrier out into the car, bus and taxi park. They got into a taxi. Fifteen minutes later, they turned into large grounds. There was a playing field on the right and trees on the left. They passed two tennis courts and there it was: a huge building with playing fields in front of it. The taxi stopped and they climbed out. BJ was overwhelmed. He was in a strange place and he was fearful of what lay ahead of him. He felt very alone and vulnerable.

Matron was waiting in the Brothers' and teachers' lounge in the main building and heard the taxi arrive. She went out and the Principal said, 'Matron, this is BJ Conway.'

'Good afternoon Miss.'

'Hello, BJ. I am Mrs Collins. Please come with me and I will take you to the orphanage.' She picked up his suitcase. They walked about 100 yards to another two-storied building and went up the stairs.

She was a woman full of human warmth, her face and manner exuding kindness. It had a reassuring affect on him and he was beginning to feel more relaxed and less frightened.

'This is Alan and his brother Cyril Hacker. They came here last year, and later, they will show you where the lockers and bathrooms are and tell you about everything. This is your bed. Theirs are the other side of yours.' As they were the youngest, the beds were in the front row.

The orphanage was divided in two small dormitories, sleeping about thirty orphans up to age sixteen. Matron was in charge of the juniors up to age eleven who slept in one, and the seniors were in the other in the charge of her husband.

'Alan and Cyril, show BJ his locker and the bathrooms.'

At the other end of the orphanage, through swing doors, was a large area with the lockers one side for the juniors and the other side for the seniors. Beyond them were the long sinks, and the showers were on the opposite wall. Also there were good-sized water barrels and plastic jugs and taps to fill them. Some younger boys used them at times.

'These are the spare lockers so you can choose any one.'

They helped him unpack. It was not long before the bell rang for their afternoon tea. The orphans had a separate long table in the corner of the refectory. BJ was about to sit down but in time noticed the others remained standing and became very quiet. The matron started and they joined in, saying the grace before meals. 'Bless us, O Lord, and these Thy gifts, which we are about to receive from Thy bounty, through Christ our Lord. Amen.'

There were three small slices of bread with a smattering of butter on the plate sufficient to thinly coat one slice. They dipped the other two slices in a weak cup of tea. After about fifteen minutes, the matron clapped her hands. They fell silent and stood up. She started the grace after meals. 'We give Thee thanks, O Almighty God, for these Thy benefits Who lives and reigns, world without end. Amen.'

As they left the refectory, Alan and Cyril said, 'When the boarders are here, we would begin our games time. But during the holidays, we play our own games if we want to. Sometimes Mr Collins will take us swimming but as matron did not say anything we won't be today.' Instead Alan and Cyril showed him round the school grounds.

'Matron said you are seven and will be in the first standard. This was their room last year so it may be the same.' On the same floor of the block was the second standard room and the science laboratory. 'The Science lab is for boys from the seventh standard.' The school hall with stage at one end took up the whole of the upper floor.

They showed him the other buildings. The biggest one had the chapel at one end of the ground floor. Classrooms, the Brothers' dining room, the teachers' lounge, the Principal's and secretary's offices were on the first floor and the Brothers' bedrooms and senior dormitory were on the second floor. A second double-storey building had the kitchens and refectory on the ground floor and the junior dormitory on the upper. A third largish building contained separate junior and senior dormitories' lockers and showers.

A fourth building housed the hospital on the lower level and the nurse's quarters and guest rooms above. There was a medium sized open-air swimming pool.

'When the boarders are here, we cannot swim. But on Saturday evenings, when they go for their walks and during holidays when they have gone home, we can, as long as Mr Collins can supervise us.'

There were several playing fields but only five were used. Fifth field was for the youngest and as the boys grew bigger or became good players, they were moved up.

They killed time joining some others in rounders. BJ had never played it before, so he had to be told what to do. At least he succeeded in hitting the ball and getting to first base. And his fielding was not bad, considering it was his first time. The bell rang at and they returned to the orphanage to shower and change. They then gathered in chapel to say the rosary.

Schedules were very flexible, since only the orphans and a few Brothers were on the premises. Until dinner, they were allowed to go to their bed to read or play board games. The bell rang when dinner was ready. They dined on the staple diet of curry and rice, downed with a glass of water. Then, they went to their beds.

Before they undressed, they knelt by their beds and said The Lord's Prayer, three Hail Marys and the Glory be to The Father. Only then did they change. Some played board games, others read comics. Eventually, the lights dimmed and all went quiet as they tucked into bed.

Chapter Six

That first night the sky was clear and all was quiet. The wind was blowing in the direction of the school and despite the perimeter of the jungle being a couple of miles away, the roar of the big cats carried in the wind. The silence of the night amplified the volume and woke BJ. His childish imagination played tricks on him and he thought they were coming into the dormitory. He was overwhelmingly frightened and covered his head with the sheet and blanket. It was sometime before sleep overcame him. During the night he wet the bed.

He was awakened by the sound of a tinkling bell. It was the matron ringing the wake-up alarm. He climbed out of bed and realised his night suit was wet. It was the first time in years that he could remember wetting the bed. He was frightened about what the matron would say and the other boys would think.

After morning prayers, as the other orphans started to get dressed and make their beds, BJ held up his hand.

The matron was near to him. 'Yes Conway?'

'Matron, I am sorry but I heard the lions roaring and I was frightened. I wet the bed.'

The matron had experienced this with other new young orphans so it was no surprise. BJ was not the first and he would not be the last.

'Do not worry. And do not be frightened. The jungle is far away and the lions do not go outside of it. Take off the sheets and I will give you clean ones for tonight.'

'Beadle! Please take this mattress onto the balcony.' With temperatures peaking at around 80 degrees, apart from the inevitable stain, it would be dry in no time and would also be aired to get rid of the smell. The boys washed and went to mass at seven in the morning. They had breakfast at half past seven. It was the same food as afternoon tea the previous day.

The rest of the day was their own. However they were allowed a couple of hours in the pool. Mr Collins asked, 'Conway do you know how to swim?'

'No sir, I have never been.'

When they got to the pool, Mr Collins said, 'Stay at the shallow end with me. You can stand up in the water. Now spread your body. Don't worry, I will keep you up. Just hold your hands out and keep your legs and body straight.'

He supported him under the stomach. It was a while before BJ was able to float on his own. Then came the splashing and thrashing of legs and arms to move him through the water. It was untidy but after a lot of patience from Mr Collins, BJ was able to swim after a fashion and remained closely supervised because clearly he was not confident. But he found he enjoyed being in the water.

Lunch was the same as dinner.

As the day went by, he became a little less frightened. He was into the holiday routine and getting to know other orphans. Just as well because when the boarders returned all would change. Times would be strictly adhered to and the discipline very strict.

The day arrived for the boarders to return. It was a Sunday. A few from other parts of the state drifted in, the younger ones with one or both parents.

Then, at about teatime, the hired buses started to arrive with the boys from the city. The suitcases and hold-alls were unloaded from the backs of lorries and juniors and seniors headed for their respective locker rooms. They began to catch up with each other. Initially they were interested in exam results and what position was achieved. A few were kept back in the same standards as they had not attained the marks required to justify promotion. Standards were high as BJ was to find out. Then they told each other what they had done during the holidays, especially how many pictures they had seen. With about seven cinemas, each showing a different film weekly, there was a wide choice.

Dinnertime that evening was much louder. But as soon as the Brother in charge clapped his hands silence descended. Once all were standing, one could hear a pin drop.

Chapter Six

Now that the boarders were in, the daily routine was:

6.00: Rise and wash.
6.30: Mass
7.00: Breakfast
7.30 - 8.30: Study
9.00: Lessons
11.30 - 12.00: Catechism
12.00: Lunch
12.45: Lessons
3.15: Tea
3.45 - 5.00: Sport
5.00: Shower
5.30: Evening prayers - rosary/benediction
6.00 - 7.00: Study
7.00: Dinner for juniors
7.30: Bedtime for juniors
8.00: Lights out for juniors
7.00 - 8.00: Study seniors
8.00: Dinner for seniors
8.20: Night prayers in the chapel
8.35: Bedtime
9.00: Lights out

On Saturdays after tea at quarter to three, the boarders went to their classes to write letters home. At a quarter past four, they showered, and at a quarter to five the juniors in the charge of another Brother went for a walk in the countryside, sometimes through the lanes linking small villages, and other times through the woods. The seniors walked to the shops with a Brother in charge. They stopped in front of a small hotel and then would go their own way. Those with pocket money used to go to the restaurants for savoury snacks. Those whose pocket money had run out, just walked around the shops and all met back at the hotel at a quarter past six. From seven to eight instead of study, they read their library books.

The orphans, instead of writing, would get showered and dressed and go for a walk, juniors with Matron, seniors with her husband in a separate direction to the junior boarders. Sometimes, while the boarders were away, they went swimming instead.

Chapter Seven

BJ fell into the routine and applied himself to lessons. He was a quiet and conscientious pupil showing above average intelligence being particularly good at arithmetic and spelling. However, one boy sitting beside him became jealous, as he was not quite as quick on the uptake.

The boys were seated at long desks divided into five compartments with a bench seat attached. BJ was sitting at the end and one morning his rubber fell onto the ground. He leaned over to pick it up and the boy beside him pushed him off the seat. There was a noise and the teacher who was writing on the blackboard turned around. BJ looked rather sheepish but some of the boys seated immediately behind him looked at the back of the head of the culprit who was acting innocent.

'What happened, Conway?'

'My rubber dropped on the floor. As I was picking it up, I fell off.' His mother had taught him not to lie. But also he knew he could not tattle. So in saying what he did, while it was not the whole truth, it was not a lie either.

But the teacher had seen the pupils pointedly looking at the back of the head of the culprit. 'Horder, did you push him over?'

'No miss.'

'Are you sure? Is that the truth?'

'Yes miss.'

Not having seen anything, she knew better than to ask any boy what actually happened. She therefore continued with the lesson.

The morning session ended and they went to lunch. Later, as they were enjoying leisure and play time, BJ saw Horder head for the bathrooms. They were at the end of the classroom block. He followed him and saw him at the urinal. BJ pushed him hard against it and as he turned round, clumsily punched him several times in the stomach. It happened so quickly, the victim was caught completely by surprise. And the punches hurt. BJ may have been only seven-years-old, but he could hit. And when several came in a cluster they hurt even more.

'Don't you ever do that to me again, you liar.' And BJ left him slightly bent over clutching his stomach. His fly was still undone and the front of his pants was wet.

As the weeks became months, he earned good marks in the frequent tests and in the first end of term exams in all subjects, he averaged 71% being placed fourth. He maintained that place in the final exams and was promoted to the second standard.

During a lunch break early in his second year, BJ saw a third standard boy hitting a smaller one around the head making him cry. 'Give me back my marbles.'

'No! I won them fair and square.'

Without hesitation, BJ ran and with his knees bent, jumped on the back of the bully knocking him to the ground. He pulled his hair back and said, 'Pick on someone your own size, you bully. Leave him alone.'

He climbed off him but was ready in case the other wanted to continue the fight. He did not.

'Why were you hitting him? He is much smaller than you.'

No answer.

The bullied one was a new boy, who, together with his parents, had only started this year. His name was Li Cheung. His mother was a teacher and his father was the new physical trainer. He had been the Thai and then South East Asia welterweight boxing champion. Mrs Leung was an Anglo-Indian who had been teaching English in Bangkok and that was how they met. They married and continued to live there. But they were forced to move back to India because her father fell ill and her mother, also elderly, was unable to cope on her own.

Li said, 'We were playing marbles and I won all of his. He wanted them back and I would not give them to him. So he started to hit me.'

By this time, the bully who was named Stewart, had decided to slink away. BJ shouted, 'Don't you bully him again.'

BJ asked, 'Are you ok now?'

Li nodded. BJ walked away.

Chapter Seven

Over a period of time they became close friends. One day, Li offered BJ an Indian sweet. BJ was very tempted. He had not had one since he came to the orphanage. But he refused saying, 'I can't'

'Don't you like sweets?'

Like them? He loved them, especially the kind being offered. But again BJ said, 'Yes I do, but I can't.'

'Why?'

After some hesitation, he replied, 'You have only just started school and may not know I live in the orphanage. The boarders call us poor boys.'

'Poor boys?' Li interrupted.

'Yes, poor boys. We do not get any pocket money. We wear mostly old clothes and shoes that the boarders get too big for. We do not go to the pictures because we cannot pay. I can't take a sweet because I can never give you one of my own.'

'It does not matter. Take it. Please.'

'Thank you, but I can't. If one day we fight you will say you gave me sweets and I did not give you any back.'

'I won't say that.'

'You do not know. I have heard what the other boys say to each other. Let us just be friends. You don't need to give me anything.'

Their friendship developed and they became very close.

The following year, a new Principal took over. One day he overheard a boy say, 'The poor boys.'

'Hockley come here,' he said.

'Who are the poor boys?'

'The free boys, sir.'

Strangely put, but the Principal knew he was referring to the orphans.

'Why are they poor boys?'

'Because they do not pay for anything or get pocket money. Also they wear our old clothes and all.'

The Principal was surprised by this discrimination. It was contrary to the school's principles.

35

'OK, you can go now.'

That evening he decided he would take charge of both dinner sittings. After they had eaten, he clapped his hands but told them to remain seated.

'I have only just arrived and until today was unaware of how you boarders saw the orphans. You call them poor boys because they get free schooling and all else. They wear the clothes you have grown too big for and when you are promoted to the next class your textbooks are passed down to them. You boarders are lucky to have parents, brothers and sisters and a home that you go to for the holidays. You get pocket money every month. I wonder how you would like not having all that. And then being called a poor boy. Now that all stops and it stops now.

If I hear anyone saying that again, I will cane them and write to their parents. If anyone keeps calling them poor boys I will expel them. The school has standards and looking down on those less fortunate than yourselves will not be tolerated.'

At the monthly teachers' and Brothers' meeting, they decided to stop the discrimination against the orphans. Also the school would bear the cost of all going to the pictures. They came to an arrangement with the town's community centre to pay a fixed price for the whole school. As there would be special showings on Sunday afternoons a good deal was agreed upon.

The following morning at breakfast the Principal again took charge. The boys knew something was up.

As before, after they had eaten, he told them to remain seated.

'Two weeks ago I told you that I would not tolerate anyone calling the orphans poor boys. Last night the Brothers and teachers held their monthly meeting. We decided that from Sunday, no one needs to pay to go to the pictures. The orphans and those boarders who may sometimes not be able to pay because they have used up their pocket money will now not have to stay behind. Also, though you boarders have parents who pay your fees and expenses, the school, helped by the church and private donations pay for the orphans. Up to now they have not been allowed to use the swimming pool at the same time as you boarders. That too changes. All boys will swim together. All facilities are available to all.'

Chapter Seven

Turning to the table at which the higher standard boys sat, he continued, 'In the pool, when a teacher or Brother is not available, you boys will look after the younger ones. And finally, there will be no separate table for the orphans. They will mix in with all according to the standard they are in. Make room for them now so they will know where they are sitting for lunch.'

The boarders moved over as the orphans joined their classmates. When all were settled, the Principal said, 'Now stand to say the grace.'

And that was that. The Principal had decreed and things changed. No more them and us, no more segregation.

One day it was raining heavily. As BJ's classroom was now in the main building, he had to use the bathroom block about 50 yards away. As he was about to run back, another boy swept rain water from a big puddle with his foot. BJ tried to go past him but again he had water swept against him. But he got away.

A Brother had observed this and called the two of them as they arrived back.

'Have you been playing in the puddles?'

Harris got in first. 'Conway kicked water against me sir. Also he picked up an earthworm broke it in two and threw it at me.'

BJ's face filled with horror. But the schoolboy code was that you did not sneak on others. So he kept quiet.

'Actually, I saw what happened. You are lying. It was you that kicked water. And there was no earthworm. Conway did nothing. Wait outside the Principal's office and I will see you there.'

To BJ he said, 'You can go now.'

'Thank you sir.'

The offender was strapped on the palms of his hands.

Another day, BJ found an envelope addressed to one of the boys whose name he did not recognise. He handed it to his teacher who passed it to the Principal. The Principal called BJ to his office. 'Where did you find the envelope?'

'In a long bog, sir.'

37

'Did you open it?'

'No sir, I did not open it. It was not mine to open. I found it and gave it to my miss. I did not know the boy's name.'

'Was there any money in it?'

'Sir, I did not open it. I did not know there was anything in it. My mummy told me before she was killed....'

The Principal thought, killed? Was that a child's slip of the tongue? Was she really killed? How? Perhaps she was run over. That must be it.

'....I must always tell the truth. I was to be like George Washington. She said I was too young to understand but if I did what she said, as I grew up I would. Also people would believe me. Sir I am not lying.'

All the time, BJ, with his head tilted slightly and looking up innocently, continued to unwaveringly look the Principal straight in the eye.

The Principal noted the eye contact and believed him. He was amazed by his honesty and childish innocence.

'OK, I believe you. You can go now.'

As it happened, the boy who was a senior, had not realised he had lost the letter. The Principal called for him. 'This is yours.'

Instinctively, he put his hands in his pockets and it was not there. 'I only got it today.' All letters were handed out at lunch in the refectory.

He opened it as his mother had sent him Rs5 extra pocket money. It was still there.

The Principal noticed the money and was glad he had believed BJ.

The weeks passed. Because all boys were now allowed to go to the pictures, BJ saw a Western that Li and his parents had seen at an earlier showing. The main character, a cowboy who was a cavalry scout, and the Indian chief had come to trust one another and become friends. Swearing their allegiance and loyalty to each other, they cut their thumbs and pressed them together so their blood mixed. It made them blood brothers. Li suggested that he and BJ should do the same. He agreed.

The next free day, Li brought one of his father's shaving razor blades. It was not unusual as they used it to sharpen their pencils. Each nicked their thumbs and pressed them together. Li said, 'Now we are not just good friends, we are blood brothers.'

Chapter Eight

At the beginning of the second term, during a physical recreation session after school one day, there was boxing training for those who were interested. Not all were. BJ sat among those outside the ring. Two were sparring. One boy who was the one who had pushed BJ off the bench the first year, was there, and was more aggressive than the other. After a short while, the weaker one began to cry. The gloves were taken off and the trainer asked, 'Anyone else?'

BJ put up his hand. He got into the ring and was gloved up. The trainer said, 'Box.' Before BJ could put his guard up, he was punched in the face. Though caught unawares, he did not stumble.

The trainer asked, 'Are you OK?'

'Yes sir.'

BJ put up his hands in a southpaw stance and waded in. He kept his eyes on his opponent and punched fast with both hands to the stomach. He was clumsy but effective. His opponent's face did not escape either. Though BJ took a few blows, he rained several more. It only lasted about a minute but it was clear who was the victor.

The trainer called 'stop,' signaling time. He had seen enough. BJ was a raw talent and would need nurturing to fulfill his full potential. He was surprised by the southpaw stance.

BJ became a regular sparring partner to any boy of the same weight. The trainer taught them basic technique and how to punch cleanly and effectively. BJ and other young ones continued to be rather unorthodox but they improved as time passed.

In August, the school held its annual boxing championship. BJ was in the first fight as it was at the lightest weight: 3 stones, 7lbs and under. After three one minute rounds, he was a clear winner. All winners received a medal. Winners at each weight from the one above BJ's represented the school in the inter school championships in September during the Indian Puja holidays.

The following year, BJ came into his own academically and as a boxer. Again he won his fight at his weight, therefore qualifying to represent his school in the inter school championships. He won in the final, and with three other winners in the junior division, the school won the championship.

Now he was beginning to win over his peers and the teachers even more. He was one of the least troublesome boys, though sometimes he got into childish mischief.

His boxing and academic achievements were consistent each passing year. But he never bragged or changed. He remained quiet and unassuming obeying the rules and despite being called chicken at times, was brave enough to withdraw when others misbehaved. Also he started to show promise in athletics and some field sports.

During the school holidays, when the boarders were away, he trained and read his textbooks. He determined to do the best he could in everything. But as he grew up and began to think more rationally, he knew it was the right thing to do if he was to give himself the best chance in life in the outside world.

The first day of class of the final year, the Brothers told them they had to choose the subjects they would sit the exams for. English Language was compulsory and had to be passed or they would not qualify for a certificate. Further, they needed to get a credit to get a First or Second. Passes in five other subjects were also needed with a minimum number of points. However, it was advisable they do two optional subjects.

BJ had not dropped Hindi and Bengali, which he could have done in the previous year. He chose all the other seven subjects also: English Literature, Elementary Mathematics (Arithmetic, Algebra and Geometry), Additional Mathematics (Trigonometry, Dynamics, Statistics, Advanced Algebra), Physics, Chemistry, Geography and English History.

The Brother in charge asked, 'Are you sure you want to sit ten subjects?'

'Sir, as you know I am an orphan. I won't be able to go to college so I need to give myself the best chance I can to compete for work. Anglo

Chapter Eight

Indians are leaving for England in droves and I will need Hindi and Bengali to survive in India.'

'Can you then not drop English History? You won't need it here.'

'I like it sir and I know I will get a good credit. It is just increasing my knowledge. Also I will have the summer holidays to study.'

That evening, as in previous years after afternoon tea, they prepared for their annual sports day. It was held at the beginning of the year so it did not interfere with studies for all classes' final exams. As in previous years, he won trophies that year, coming second in the javelin, long jump and hop, skip and jump and first in the high jump. The finals in the field events were held prior to sports day. BJ was a middle distance specialist and came third in the 400 yards and first in the 800 yards and one mile races.

In the final race, he was to run the anchor leg in the 4 by 400 yards relay. The third leg runner tripped and fell about 35 yards away and BJ ran back to make sure he was ok. Apart from feeling a little embarrassed, he was. A couple of other boys had come to his aid and helped him off the course. BJ took the baton and resumed the race getting to the finishing line a hopeless last, to loud applause from all the parents and guests.

The guest of honour, a local dignitary, turned to the Principal. 'What is that boy's name?'

'BJ Conway. He is one of our orphans and a model student.'

'Seeing what he just did, I am not surprised.'

At the presentation, she opened her speech saying, 'On October 29, 1941, in the midst of World War II, Winston Churchill, then Prime Minister of Britain said, 'This is the lesson: never give in, never give in, never give in, never, never, never, never—in nothing, great or small, large or petty—never give in.' Often, this can be very difficult to do. But so long as you remember, no matter what, never give in, you will go far. I had not planned to say this. But seeing BJ Conway run back in the relay to make sure his fellow runner was ok and then picking up the baton to resume the race, despite being so far behind, brought it to mind. BJ please come up here.'

BJ was embarrassed and she sensed his discomfort. 'Don't be

embarrassed. You taught me, indeed all of us, a salutary lesson. We are never to give up.'

She extended her hand to shake his saying, 'I commend you for what you did. Your immediate concern was for your fellow runner but despite the delay and the hopelessness of the position you still finished the race. It showed a single-mindedness and determination to complete the task. Keep it up and you will succeed in whatever you do.'

There was loud and enthusiastic applause, particularly from the nuns and Brothers and other guests.

In September for the sixth consecutive year, he represented the school in the Inter-School Boxing tournament. After all this time never having lost, he had built up an aura that sometimes defeated his opponents in their minds even before they climbed into the ring. The previous year he had fought at 9 stones and under. But he had developed physically since and was in the heaviest weight, 10 stones and under. So he was now up against another undefeated opponent who had fought at the weight above him previously. To add to the tension, BJ needed to win the last fight of the night so his school would win the senior championship.

There was a buzz as they entered the ring. The air was expectant. As he stood in the corner he went into a trance momentarily. BJ saw a vision of his mother. She was smiling encouragingly and said 'come on my son. You will win.'

Mr Leung noticing the hardening of BJ's face and eyes, asked, 'Are you OK?'

'Sir I will win this. For the school, for you and for myself. Also, I want the other orphans to believe they can do it too if they want, not just the boarders.'

The announcer introduced them and to add to the sense of anticipation, mentioned each was undefeated at different weights in the championship for some years.

The bell rang for round one. The referee called them to the centre of the ring, made them touch gloves and said, 'Box'.

BJ had not taken his eye of his opponent. Immediately, he planted his feet and with his right hand jabbed him on the point of the nose, followed again and again in the area around the nose and mouth. He had snapped out the jabs. The first punch drew blood and the others drew more. In a flash, a left cross to the bloodied face caused the opponent to raise his hands to protect it. But this exposed his midriff and BJ shot a short right to it and a quick left uppercut to the side just under the ribcage. It was clinical in its execution.

The opponent went down on his left side clutching the other where the uppercut had landed. There was a deathly silence. It was just a few seconds into the fight. Those on the blind side were unsure what had happened. He was clearly in discomfort and the referee stopped the fight without bothering to count. BJ ran from the neutral corner to his opponent. He placed a glove on his shoulder and said, 'I am sorry. Are you OK?' He nodded saying, 'No hard feelings. You won fair and square.'

His defeated opponent's trainer said, 'Well done, boy. You have always been a good boxer and you were certainly very sharp this year, particularly tonight.'

'Thank you sir.' And BJ went to his corner.

After a while his opponent got up and, helped by his trainer, walked back to his corner and sat on the stool. The trainer had used a sponge to wipe the blood away and now he rinsed him with water and toweled him off. Blood still seeped from his nose and his cut lip. The referee called them to the centre of the ring. His opponent came and raised BJ's arm aloft with one hand while patting him on the back with the other. He then walked round to the other side of the referee who announced BJ as the winner on a TKO. Again the opponent came around, put his arm round BJ's shoulder and walked to the ropes where he pressed down the middle one with his leg while holding up the top one with his gloved hand so he could climb through. He was applauded for his sportsmanship.

His school was champion again and for the third year running, BJ won 'Boxer of the tournament.'

The next major event was the school's annual concert. His late father had played guitar very well when he was not drunk. Though his instrument was too big for BJ, he taught him how to tune it, the notes of each string and the scales. BJ used to lay the guitar flat on the bed, use his left hand fingers to place over the strings and plucked them with the fingers of his right.

In the orphanage, Mr Collins had two guitars. The better of them he kept for himself; the other he used to teach those that were truly interested and showed some potential. BJ obviously did and as he grew older he learned to play chords holding the instrument properly. Mr Collins encouraged him to improvise and introduced him to the blues and country and western music. Some gospel was also played and a particular favourite became 'Just a closer walk with thee', the words of which were:

'Just a closer walk with Thee,
Grant it, Jesus, is my plea,
Daily walking close to Thee,
Let it be, dear Lord, let it be.

I am weak, but Thou art strong,
Jesus, keep me from all wrong,
I'll be satisfied as long
As I walk, let me walk close to Thee.

Through this world of toil and snares,
If I falter, Lord, who cares?
Who with me my burden shares?
None but Thee, dear Lord, none but Thee.

When my feeble life is o'er,
Time for me will be no more,
Guide me gently, safely o'er
To Thy kingdom's shore, to Thy shore.

Chapter Eight

*Just a closer walk with Thee,
Grant it, Jesus, is my plea,
Daily walking close to Thee,
Let it be, dear Lord, let it be.'*

The more BJ played and sang it, the better it sounded, especially when his voice broke.

Sometimes Mr Collins and he entertained the other boys during the holidays and Sundays. Inevitably news spread in the school and a conversation with the music teacher resulted in BJ being asked to perform it at the school's annual concert. The teacher scored the arrangement and they rehearsed it regularly. The performance would close the evening.

The moment came and most of the lights were switched off. The Principal went on stage.

'Ladies and gentleman, for reasons that will become obvious, please remove all handbags and anything else obstructing the centre aisle. Thank you.'

The hall was then plunged into darkness except for the stars outside. Two trumpeters started to play the song in a slow march time as they walked in step along the aisle to the stage. They had rehearsed it so that by the time they finished the first verse they would be at the front. As the drummer increased the beat slightly for a few bars the trumpeters had time to get back in their seats with the orchestra. It started to play and a voice was heard from behind the opening curtains. There was BJ in white with a red sash around his waist with just a portable spot light on him.

The drummer again increased the beat for a few bars and now there was a Dixieland flavour to the third verse and then there was an instrumental interlude. The music teacher Mr Carroll played the clarinet solo and the audience began to applaud. In that vein BJ sang the last verse.

The drummer slowed down the beat as the first verse was repeated. To finish, the beat reverted to the slow march, the trumpeters got up and marched to where they started. As they did so the curtains shut and the lights were switched on to great applause and shouts of 'encore', 'more'

47

and 'again.' Several ladies were dabbing their eyes because of the emotional delivery and arrangement of the song. It lasted a while and eventually the Principal signaled they should perform it again. It went down as well as the first rendition and received equally enthusiastic applause.

Chapter Nine

The final year boys now had the last few weeks of term to study for their exams. BJ became increasingly nervous because he knew he had to do well. But he also had a quiet confidence that he had prepared as well as he could. He just hoped his memory would not fail him.

It did not, and he was happy with what he submitted. Time would tell whether his confidence was misplaced.

The last exam was on Wednesday. On the Thursday when the rest of the school was in classes, BJ heard his name being called by one of the final year boys, 'Princie wants to see you.'

BJ thought it was to talk about him leaving the orphanage. He knocked on the office door although it was open. 'Come in, BJ. Sit down.'

'Thank you and good morning, sir.'

'BJ, the exams are over. How do you think you did?'

'I am confident I will get a good first.'

'And we have no doubt you will; we never did.'

He continued, 'Some months ago, we spoke about your future after you left the orphanage. I told you not to worry, as I wanted you to concentrate on your studies. I would try and arrange something and I have. You have been a model pupil and everyone who has taught you since you first came here speaks highly of you. Their comments are reflected in your reports, which you have seen. Do you remember the church you used to go to before you came here?'

'Yes sir, it was Our Lady of Mount Carmel.'

'You will be going to live there. Father O'Shea, who arranged for you to come here, is still the parish priest. The school wrote to him at the end of each year to tell him of your progress and achievements.'

BJ was surprised and his face showed it.

'You look surprised.'

'Yes sir I am.'

'We try to help our orphans when they leave. Usually a lot have to go to Catholic hostels. But on Saturday when all the other boarders leave on the train you will go with Mr and Mrs Chueng and Li. They will take you from the station to the church where Father O'Shea will be expecting you. Mr Collins will give you a suitcase to take what clothes and personal belongings you have. It will go with all the boarders' suitcases on Friday evening to be loaded on the train as usual.'

He opened a drawer and pulled out two envelopes. 'You have never received any pocket money, so this is a little to get you started, handing BJ the first envelope. The teachers have contributed some and the school has topped it up. It should help you until you find a job.'

'Thank you and the teachers, sir. Thank you very much.' His hand was shaking as he reached out to take it.

The Principal then passed over the second envelope. 'This contains all your school reports and your school leaving certificate.'

As he took it BJ asked, 'What is that sir?'

'It is my certificate as Principal describing you as a person, your achievements and contributions to school life. It is also a character reference. Everything I have written is excellent and deservingly so.'

'Sir, thank you for accepting me into the orphanage and teaching and developing me. I know I made mistakes as I grew up and I am sorry. But as I grew older, coming to the final exams, I realised more and more how valuable the education was. It means a lot to me and my future life. I do not know what it holds but I hope I will be a good ambassador.'

The Principal thought, what a mature attitude. But he did say, 'I - we all wish you the very best in life. If there is anyone who deserves it, you do. I will keep the envelopes safe for you until tomorrow. Then you can put them in your suitcase. After breakfast on Saturday you will leave with the boarders for the station.'

'Thank you sir.'

He left the office with his heart racing. He had been apprehensive about his future but now he was somewhat excited about the prospect of

Chapter Nine

stepping out into the world yonder.

He returned to the dormitory to sort out his belongings. He was not sure what he would be allowed to take with him, so he went to Mr Collins's office. He knocked on the door.

'Come in...BJ, sit down. What can I do for you?'

'Good morning sir. I have just seen the Principal. I am travelling with the boarders on Saturday. I am allowed to take some clothes with me. But I do not know what. Also he said you would have a suitcase for me.'

'Yes that is right. I have it ready here for you with some better whites and shoes. Also in the suitcase are your many trophies.'

'What about the other shoes and sports shorts and other items sir? Shall I leave them in the locker. The clothes will need washing.'

'Take everything apart from the khakis and the football boots. On Saturday, when you wake up, please strip the bed. Leave the linen and clothes you do not take on the bed for the dhobi.'[2]

'Thank you sir.' He took the suitcase and went and put it under his bed. He would finish packing tomorrow.

Saturday occupied his mind. The imminence of leaving the orphanage exercised him somewhat because of the unknown. He knew he was going to live in the church that he used to go to with his mother. But that was when he was a child and accompanied. Now he would be going there to live as a sixteen-year-old seeking a job. A job? How hard would it be to find one? He had no experience. And yet how was he to gain that if not given an opportunity? He thought of his mother and wished she was around to support him emotionally and encourage him.

---

[2] *The washerman.*

Chapter Ten

And then it was Saturday. BJ was leaving the security of the orphanage to enter the real world and he had mixed emotions. He was excited and apprehensive. He thought, this is it, I am no longer a schoolboy. Something within him told him not to be afraid. All would be well. A new life awaited him. He must grab all opportunities that came his way.

He stripped his bed and folded the linen. After washing and dressing, he emptied the remaining items from his locker. They were already folded. And these too he placed on the bed. He put the boots under it.

After breakfast he went to see Mr and Mrs Collins. 'Goodbye matron and sir. Thank you for everything.' They each extended their hand to shake his. 'Good luck.'

He left the dormitory for the last time and headed for the station with the others. There, Li and his parents met him.

BJ thought about the journey in the reverse direction. He was older now but he was still somewhat apprehensive. Though he was assured of somewhere to stay he was concerned about finding a job.

Approaching the destination, the boys started cheering until the train stopped. Parents and boys milled around searching for each other.

Li, his parents and BJ caught a taxi to take them to the church. There, My Cheung said, 'Driver please wait a while.' He retrieved BJ's suitcase from the boot and walked into the courtyard. Bimal opened the door. He and BJ were surprised to see each other. Father O'Shea said, 'You remember Bimal, don't you?'

'Yes, Father. My mother really trusted him. One day she dropped her purse. Bimal found it and returned it to her. She had not known she had dropped it. Not a rupee or anna was missing. Father, this is Mr Leung. Mr Leung, Father O'Shea.'

'Pleased to meet you. The Principal told me you would be dropping

BJ off. Thank you.'

Mr Leung said to BJ, 'It is now half past twelve. I will call back for you at about four o'clock. Is that ok?'

'Yes sir.'

Bimal carried the suitcase and followed Father O'Shea up the stairs to a room at the far end of the house, away from the main road. It was a side road anyway so there was not a lot traffic. It was mostly cyclists, walkers and some cars or taxis. On the other side of the road was a medium sized park with flowerbeds and lawns.

'This is your room BJ. Bimal will bring you your meals here. Breakfast is usually at about half-past seven after the seven o'clock mass Monday to Saturday. On Sundays it is at about nine o'clock, after the first mass at eight o'clock. At four o'clock we have lassi or lime juice or tea or coffee and some cakes or sandwiches or savouries. Lunch is at one o'clock and dinner at seven o'clock every day.' He put his hand inside his cassock and brought out an envelope.

'This is a gift from the Legion of Mary to get you started. You will need to buy clothes and other essentials.

In the previous January, Father had attended the first meeting of the year. All fourteen members were present, the youngest was twenty-five and the oldest fifty-two. She was in fact the President. Several others had been attending the church for more than ten years.

After the opening prayer, the President said 'Father is here because he has something to share.'

'Good evening. And a very happy new year to you all. Several of you will remember a tragedy in December 1950, when a seven-year-old boy was orphaned. The Legion helped kit him out with all he needed to go to an orphanage upstate.'

Several murmured and nodded their heads at the memory.

'I have kept you abreast with his progress in school and you have annually made a donation for me to send to the orphanage. Because he was a free scholar the money could not go directly to him but went into a common fund for the orphans' needs. This will be his last year; he does his final exams in December after which he will have to leave. As you will appreciate, he has no money. Because of the circumstances in which he was orphaned, and his mother's strong links with the church, the church is acting as his guardian. He will come to live with us temporarily. But all he will have are the school clothes. He needs suitable attire to search for a job. I urge you not as your parish priest but as a human being, to consider to what extent you feel able to contribute to a fund for him. A few rupees from each of you every month will soon mount up. What I would ask is that you do not fix a limit. Please give as much as you feel able to. I will not check on progress and I do not even need to know how much you have donated collectively. In November just put it in an envelope and I will give it to him when he arrives. The exams finish in the first week of December and he will come here as soon as school closes for the year.'

Upon being handed the envelope, BJ said, 'Thank you Father. I will thank the Legion of Mary personally. But what is it?'

'There is time for that. I will tell you in due course. Meanwhile I just want you to settle in. This is now your home.'

'Father, how much must I pay you for the room and food?'

The priest smiled and said, 'Do not worry about that. The church has no income and therefore does not charge for living here. Besides, you are still a minor. In a manner of speaking the church is your guardian. However, that will cease when you become eighteen and unfortunately you will not be able to live here any longer. But you do not have to worry about that now. You still have two years to go. I just want you to settle and be happy. Your Principal has spoken very highly of you. Continue in the same way and you will do well.'

'But Father, I cannot take advantage of you and the church. You are allowing me to live here for two years and will feed me also. Is there not a way I can give something to the church?'

'If you really want to contribute, you can put money into the collection on Sundays. That is the church's income.'

'Father, I will do that but how much should I put in? I have no idea what I would pay outside. In fact I do not know what anything costs. Also

I do not know how hard it is or how soon I will be able to find a job.'

'God will provide, just trust in Him.'

'Thank you Father.'

'Now just relax. This is your home, now. Bimal and I are here to help at any time. He will bring you lunch shortly.'

The priest left and BJ was on his own.

The room was austerely furnished. It had a bed against one wall, a three foot cupboard with a hanging rail and shelves, a small chest of drawers, a single easy chair and at the far end under the window was a small table and one chair. Above the bed was a crucifix.

He unpacked the few clothes and personal bathroom essentials from the orphanage. He spent a few minutes looking out of the window at the park just taking it all in when there was a knock on the door. It was Bimal with a plate and tiffin carrier containing his lunch. Bimal laid out everything on the table and asked BJ in Hindi, 'Shall I put it on the plate?'

'Yes please Bimal. My I have some cold water? Do you have any ice?'

'No Sahib but the water will be cold as we keep bottles in the fridge.'

He sat at the table, gave thanks, as was the discipline in school and ate his first meal outside it. Somehow it tasted more appetising. There was curry, rice and dal. He had not had dal since he went to the orphanage.

Bimal returned with a small jug filled with cold water and a slice of lime and a glass.

When finished, he continued to sit at the table for a while wrapped up in his own thoughts. He was assailed by all kinds of them; of his parents, the orphanage, what he had achieved in school and wondered about tomorrow and all the future tomorrows. The reverie was broken by the hall wall clock striking the half hour. It must be a half past one.

He opened the envelope Father had given him from the Legion of Mary. He could not believe what he was seeing. There was a wad of large notes. As there was a breeze blowing through the window, he went and sat on the bed to avoid any being blown away. He counted and he counted. There were Rs325. He counted again as he could not believe there was so much money. He had no concept of its value anyway never having had any before.

Chapter Ten

He remembered the envelope from the Principal. He got it from the suitcase and opened it. There were Rs65. He now had a total of Rs390. He took his rosary from his pocket, knelt by the bed and prayed.

'Father God, I have a lot to learn about life. My mother taught me to be grateful for all we had and to remember those less fortunate than ourselves. I do not have my parents anymore and now I am here having left the comfort of the orphanage to make my way in the world. Please help me not to get into bad company or habits. I do not want to sin. Please help me find a job soon, a good job, and one with prospects. Thank you for the money I have been given. Bless Li and his parents, the orphans still in the orphanage, Father O'Shea, Bimal and all those in the Legion of Mary that gave me money. Please help me to save and not waste it. Amen.'

He stayed on his knees in silence for a while. He had been worried about where he would live, how he would cope with no money until he found a job and here he was. He had a home and he had money.

He stood up and took 25 of the Rs65 from the envelope and slipped it into his pants pocket. He went downstairs and quietly called, 'Bimal?'

'Yes Sahib?' And Bimal appeared.

'Where is the kitchen?'

Bimal led the way through a door. The opposite side was another door that was open to let out the cooking heat and provide some fresh air.

'What is outside?'

They walked out into a small grassy area bordered by flowerbeds.

'Are you busy?'

'No Sahib. I was sitting on the step and having a break and a beedie.[3] In the afternoons everything after lunch is quiet as people usually have a siesta because of the heat.'

'Shall we sit down?'

When they had done so side by side, BJ said, 'I was surprised to see you. How are you?

'I am very well Sahib. And you?'

---

[3] *An Indian cigarette.*

'I was well looked after in school. Everyone has been very good to me. I did not know what I would do afterwards but Father and the school arranged for me to come here. Now I have to find work.' After a while he asked, 'How long have you been working here?'

'When your parents died I was without a job. But Father had to replace the previous servant who was moving to another city closer to his village. He asked me to work here and I have been here since then.'

'Nine years? Father must like you. But then my mother did. I remember she said you were very honest and a good cook. Also you looked after me.'

'Sahib, she was a kind and quiet woman. She always gave me a little extra money every month.'

They chatted generally about the area and transport so BJ would know how to get around.

'Does a dhobi[4] come every week?'

'Yes Sahib'

'Will he do mine separately? I will pay him myself.'

'I am sure he will do. He comes every Monday. I will ask him. I give him the dirty clothes and linen and take the washed and ironed ones. I will tell him that from next week you will have a bundle for him for which you will pay separately.'

'Good I will give you the money each week.'

Bimal then asked, 'Do you still like bhakakhanis[5] and fried eggs?'

'I have not had any since I went away. I hope to buy some. Is there somewhere where I can get them close by?'

'And dal purees?[6] Puree[7] bhaji?[8]'

BJ nodded his head. 'Them too.'

---

[4] *Laundryman.*

[5] *A bhakakhani is a fried Indian bread made out of corn flour.*

[6] *Spicy lentil fried flat bread.*

[7] *Fried flat bread.*

[8] *Spicy potatoes.*

Chapter Ten

'For breakfast tomorrow we will have bhakakhanis and fried eggs. Fathers usually have it on Sundays. Other days it is dal purees or puree bhaji. Sometimes it is eggs and toast. It is not the same every day.'

'I cannot wait to have them again. All we had in school were three small slices of bread with a little butter to spread thinly on one slice.'

Time passed. As he did not have a watch, BJ asked, 'What is the time?' Bimal did not have a watch either but he remembered hearing the hall clock striking earlier. They walked to it and it was (thirty-five to three), which meant they had been chatting over an hour.

BJ reached into his pocket and brought out the money. He unfolded it to reveal two ten and a five rupee notes. He handed it to Bimal. 'This is for you.'

'Sahib. You will need this until you get a job.'

'Bimal, it is ok. Please take it. Before my parents died you looked after us. You said my mother gave you extra every month. That is because you were a good man.'

'Thank you sahib.'

'Now, please tell me where the bathroom is. I need to wash and get ready. Mr Leung who brought me here is coming back for me at four o'clock.'

Bimal walked him upstairs and showed him where it was. There were two bathrooms, both with showers and running water.

'Thank you Bimal.' And Bimal left to return to the kitchen.

BJ showered. Completely refreshed, he put on clean whites. At about half past three, Bimal knocked on the door. He had a cup of tea and some Indian cakes. He savoured them.

Just before four o'clock, he went downstairs and into the kitchen giving Bimal the empty cup and plate. 'I will be back for dinner.'

He went outside and walked to the gate. He wanted to see the area and looked up and down the road. He had not waited long when Mr Leung came into sight. BJ walked towards him and when he was close enough to be heard said ' Good evening sir.'

'Good evening BJ. Have you settled in ok?'

'Yes sir.'

They walked to the shopping hub. As they did so, Mr Leung said, 'BJ, Li told me all about you at the very beginning. How you saved him from being bullied. You became friends and as in the cowboy and Indian pictures became blood brothers. Most importantly, when he first offered you a sweet, you refused because you could not do the same for him. I know that he offered sweets again and also to pay for you to go the pictures. You refused every time. You are not in school now. You will find a job and then you can give us all the sweets you care to. We will be able to do things for each other.'

BJ kept a respectful silence.

Mr Leung continued, 'Now we want to buy you some good clothes. You will need them to go to interviews for jobs and for when you start work. Here we are.'

They entered a gents' tailors.

'Salaam Sahibs,' a salesman said in Hindi.

'Salaam. I would like to see some shirts and pants for the boy.'

The salesman measured BJ's waist, inside leg and neck measurements. He then went to the shelves and hanging rail and returned with a choice laying them on the counter.

'Sahib, ties also?'

'Oh yes please.'

The assistant went to the tie rack and brought several different patterns and colours.

Mr Leung said, 'What would you like? Choose three pants, shirts and ties.'

BJ had no idea of price and simply said 'the cheapest.' Mr Leung looked at him. Knowing BJ as he did, the reply did not surprise him. 'Don't worry about that. Choose what you want.'

BJ had already decided as soon as he saw them. He chose light-blue, mid-blue and light-grey pants and white, pale blue and turquoise long-sleeved shirts. He sorted three ties that would go with any combination of pants and shirts.

Chapter Ten

'Oh, I forgot. BJ you will need a coat and a jumper,' and turning to the assistant, he said, 'Also a coat and a jumper please.'

The assistant measured BJ's chest and walked to another rack and some drawers. He returned with a choice of coats and jumpers.

'Which coat do you like?'

'Sir I like the mid-blue one but it will clash with the trousers. May I change it for a dark blue one please? The coat can then be worn with any of the pants.'

'Of course. Choose what you want.'

Having chosen, Mr Cheung asked, 'How much?'

The assistant looked at the price tags, totted it up as he went along. 'Rs15 each for the pants, 8 for each shirt, 3 for a tie, 20 for the coat and 14 for the jumper. Rs112 but to you Sahib, an old customer, 105.'

'Come on, you always do this,' Mr Leung said, smiling. 'Rs83.'

'Sahib, sahib. How will I live?' He too was smiling, 'alright, 100.'

'90.' He opened his wallet and counted out the notes. '20, 20, 20, 20, 10; 90.' He extended them and after a moment's hesitation, the salesman reached out and took them.

'Sahib you are a hard man.' But he was still smiling; he had got a good sale. He got brown paper from a roll under the counter, cut a few lengths and wrapped the pants, shirts, coat and jumper separately. And then again in one big package securing it with thick twine.

He passed it to Mr Leung, who then handed it to BJ.

'Thank you very much sir. You are very kind.'

'We are glad to be able to do this.'

They walked out of the tailors and after a while they came to an ice cream parlour. They entered and Mr Leung led them to a table in the corner.

'What would you like? A cold or hot drink, a milkshake or ice cream.'

He had not had the last two for years. 'May I have a milkshake please?'

'Would you like a cake or a bun?'

61

'No thank you sir, just a milkshake will do, thank you.'

The waiter came and took the order. While waiting, Mr Leung said, 'Now Mrs Leung, Li and I want to do something else for you. He reached into his pocket as he was talking and handed BJ an envelope. I know that the Principal gave you some money from the teachers and the school. This is some more money from the three of us. You will need it until you find a job. If you think anything of Li and us, please take it.'

BJ could not believe what was happening. Three envelopes containing money in two days! He sat transfixed and at a loss for words. The waiter brought their orders, which gave him time to catch his voice. They were both having milkshakes.

'Sir I do not know what to say. I am lost for words. But thank you again.'

'That is all you need to say. We did it because we wanted to. Now don't give it another thought, please. Alright?'

'Yes sir.'

'We are flying to Bangkok on Monday. Until then we are staying at my brother's house. Tomorrow we would like you to have lunch and spend the afternoon with us.'

BJ nodded saying, 'Thank you.'

They finished their shakes, paid and left.

'Do you remember any of the shops or the area?'

Not the shops particularly but I do remember a little of this area.

'I will take you back to the church.'

They made idle chitchat as they walked, and BJ observed the shops along the way. Before long, they were at the church.

'I will call for you at noon.'

'Thank you again sir for your kindness and good night.'

'Good night.'

He walked round to the kitchen back door, which was still open. Bimal saw him and said, 'Salaam sahib.'

'Salaam Bimal. That smells good what is it?'

'Pork vindaloo. I remember you and your mother used to like it.'

'Oh, smashing! Can't wait. Is there a newspaper here?'

'It may be in the sitting room,' he said and headed there with BJ following. 'Here it is.'

'Will it have advertisements for jobs?'

'I do not know sahib. I cannot read English.'

'I am sorry.'

Bimal smiled, 'It is ok sahib.'

'Thank you for the paper. If Father wants it tell me.' And he went to his room leaving the door open. He undid the twine and laid out the items on the bed. He got some hangers from the cupboard and hung up the pants and shirts. He put the folded jumper on a shelf.

He sat on the bed with his feet up and his back against the wall. He opened the envelope. There were Rs50. He closed his eyes and silently gave thanks.

He opened the paper and searched for the job advertisements. But as he scanned them, apart from getting an idea of what the salaries were, there were none for a school leaver. He did not know what to think.

He turned back to the front page and avidly read the articles. He was wising up to the world outside school and the orphanage. In the sports section, he came across a few names of former schoolboys who were now playing football in the amateur league. And on the last page there were all the listings of what the cinemas were showing.

He had barely finished when he heard footsteps approaching. He got off the bed expecting it to be Father but it was Bimal with his dinner.

He savoured it, enjoying every mouthful. As the lunch earlier it smelled nice—literally making his mouth water. He thought the food in the orphanage was adequate but compared to this, hardly appetising. He did not leave a grain of rice on the plate. He sat for a while, savouring the taste of it in his mouth. Only after his saliva had washed it away, did he drink some cold water.

What a day, he thought. In the morning he was in the orphanage without a single rupee and now, he was here with money and new clothes.

He had eaten like he had not done since his parents died. And as he thought of them, sadness overcame him.

He got the bible his mother had given him with her photo stuck to the inside cover. As often before, he felt her presence. And he spoke to her as if she was in the room with him.

'Mummy, I remembered what you wrote and taught me. I tried to see and listen twice as much as I talked. I hope I learned a lot more because of it. Also because of you bringing me to mass every day, Father O'Shea is allowing me to live here. Bimal is here too. He remembers you as a kind person. I will be kind to him also. Others have been very good to me and I cannot believe how things have turned out. Now I just have to find work, not just any work, but a good one with prospects. I have to save as much as I can as I have to leave here when I am eighteen.'

He sat in silence for a while. He picked up everything, intending to take them to the kitchen, but Bimal appeared at the door. 'Thank you Bimal. The vindaloo was delicious. Now I cannot wait for breakfast tomorrow.'

Bimal smiled and said, 'Salaam,' and putting the palms of his hands together, touched them to his forehead in respect and gratitude. After he had left, BJ decided to take a walk.

He took Rs5 and went downstairs to the kitchen. 'Bimal I am going for a walk. I won't be long. What time do you go home?'

'I do not go away. I live in a room attached to the church hall,' he said, pointing through the open back door to the building at the end of the courtyard garden. 'If Father is out, I wait for him before I lock up and leave. When Father leaves for mass in the morning he opens the back door so I can get in.'

'But is there a bathroom in there?'

'There is a bathroom inside the hall but the hall is locked. I use the outside bathroom like all the other visitors.'

'What time do you leave?'

'As I live here it does not matter. If everyone is in and I have finished my work in the kitchen I go. But you go for your walk. I will wait.'

Chapter Ten

'Thank you. I won't go far as I do not know the area very well. Is there a bookshop close by?'

'Yes. There are two or three and several other shops. As you leave the gates, instead of turning left to the main road, turn right and you will come to another road. It has all sorts of small shops and restaurants. That is where I get the bakakanis, puree bhaji and dal purees.'

'Thank you.'

He found the shops and noted what they were. He entered a small bookshop and browsed through the westerns section. A lot of the books were second hand. He remembered his father reading them. He turned to the back of some to read the synopses.

Speaking in Hindi, he said, 'How much is each book please.'

'75 paisa each or three for Rs2.'

He chose three, paid and left. He walked up and down the road, bought Bimal a bundle of beedies[9] and headed back to the church.

As earlier, he went in through the back door. He gave Bimal the beedies, who expressed his thanks. He was touched by the boy's kindness and thought, just like his mother.

They said good night to each other and BJ went upstairs. He locked the door and undressed. He put on his night suit and lay on the bed. After reading the passage in the bible his mother had underlined and praying, he randomly selected one of the books to read. It was sometime before he went to sleep.

---

[9] *An Indian cigarette.*

Chapter Eleven

The following morning, BJ went to mass, sitting at the back by the side aisle. The church was full so that communion took several minutes even with two priests serving. Just before noon, he told Bimal he was going out and went to the gate to meet Mr Leung. A car pulled up. Mr Leung was in the front passenger seat. He got out and opened the rear door for BJ. Inside he said, 'BJ this is my brother. It is his house we are going to.'

'Pleased to meet you sir.'

'Likewise BJ.'

Li and Mrs Cheung were already there. He was introduced to the other Mrs Cheung and their son and daughter. The hospitality was excellent and he thoroughly enjoyed the Thai food. The two brothers then took BJ into another room where they were served with cold drinks.

The host went straight to the point. 'BJ do you know what work you want to do?'

'I will do anything. But if I had a choice I would like to work in an office.'

'A bank perhaps?'

'I would love that but I have only just finished school. It will want experience.'

'Suppose I told you I am the General Manager of the city branch of the Oriental Bank?'

BJ was surprised but in his naiveté, was unsure where this was going. However, he now began to understand a little why only the three of them were in the room.

Mr Leung Senior continued. 'My brother and his family think very highly of you and I know that you did well in school. They are sure you will get a good First.'

'I hope so sir.'

'I understand you did Elementary and Additional Maths, English Language and Literature, Physics and Chemistry and four other subjects.'

'Yes sir.'

'How would you like to work for my bank starting tomorrow?'

BJ was dumbfounded. His face was a picture. He opened his mouth to say thank you but he just blew air. Eventually he muttered, 'I don't know what to say; I am stunned.'

His hands were shaking so he paused to take a drink to get himself together. When he had calmed down he said, 'Sir, I would like nothing better. A bank job? I can't believe it. Thank you. Thank you very much.'

'My brother has every confidence in you and I trust his judgement. As you are a school leaver expected to get a school certificate, I will treat you as a qualified person and take you on as a trainee. Your starting pay will be 250 rupees a month and I will review it every six months as you gain experience.'

BJ nodded saying, 'Thank you sir.'

'The bank is not far from here and my brother will show you where it is when he takes you home. We start at quarter to nine in the morning, and finish at quarter after five. But on Saturday we finish at a quarter to one. Ask for me when you arrive.'

'I will not let you down sir.'

'I know. I trust my brother but having met you, I am confident you will do well.'

'Thank you sir.'

They returned to join the others and BJ's face spoke volumes. Li asked, 'Happy?'

'Very much! All of you have set me off to a good start. I left school and the orphanage on Saturday worried about what was ahead of me. Now I have new clothes, money and a job. Unbelievable!'

Mr Leung Junior said, 'You deserve it. Your parents would be proud if they could see you now.'

BJ's felt pangs of sadness. As he was growing up he realised his mother had left him her own unique legacy; herself, her character and the values by which she had lived. As she wrote in the bible he was too young to understand at the time but he now knew what she meant. There was a Divine Hand orchestrating the events in his life.

The rest of the day was a blur as he was so filled with euphoria.

Alone in his room he lay on the bed with his back leaning against the wall. He could not believe what was happening. It must be a dream, he thought, I will wake up and it will be the day after my final exam. I never had any money, now I have so much. Until yesterday afternoon, I did not know its value, what I could buy and how much anything cost.

A day after leaving school he had a place to stay, his meals all for free and the next day he would start his first job at a salary of Rs250 a month. He sat in silence for some time.

He read a bit but his mind was everywhere other than on what he was reading. He decided what to wear the next day, and got his papers together. Satisfied, he read the bible, said his prayers and went to sleep.

Chapter Twelve

On Monday morning, as had often happened in the past, he was assailed by all kinds of emotions. Apprehension, nerves and excitement vied with each other. He left earlier than he should have done, as he felt the need to settle himself down. But he need not have worried. Preparations had been made to make him feel comfortable and the oriental culture of courtesy and good manners helped even more.

The week unfolded and he was happy with his initial steps into the outside world.

After lunch on Saturday, he went to the pictures. He was spending very little money; his only expenses being his working day lunches.

On Sunday afternoon BJ walked to the hub to familiarise himself with the shops, restaurants and cinemas. In a covered shopping area, a young boy and a man were walking towards him. The boy said, 'Daddy, that's BJ Conway who you saw boxing and heard singing at the concert. You said you liked his voice.' And yes, he had. The boy's name was Alan Carter and caught BJ's eye saying, 'Hello.'

He introduced his father who said, 'I saw you box in September and a couple of times before that. You were very good. I was also at the concert in October and heard you close the show. I manage a nightclub and restaurant and also organise a few local talent shows throughout the year. How would you like to audition to sing at the club and on the shows?' BJ was taken aback and hesitated as he searched for the right words.

The man saw this and said, 'The club is not far from here and the band will be rehearsing. Why don't we go there and you can sing a few songs?'

At the club, the manager said, 'Good afternoon all. This is BJ who I told you about after the school concert last October. You have said that you would add a new dimension to your performances if you had a male vocalist to complement Rita.'

'BJ, Nick is the drummer, Bob the double bassist, Len the lead guitarist, Alex the saxophonist who also plays guitar, Leo the pianist and Rita is Leo's wife. Now don't be nervous. What would you like to sing?'

'May I use that spare guitar please? Also do you have a plectrum?' This surprised them, as they had not thought he could play. They had only been told he was a good singer. He stood facing the others, held the plectrum between his thumb and index finger and using it and his other three fingers, gently plucked the strings as he got the feel of it. He ran through the scale and improvised. The group members looked at each other approvingly but also with some surprise at the unusual way he used the plectrum and his fingers.

He did a slow country and western song, after which there were encouraging words from all and he was asked to sing a fast song.

He played the intro and sang. He also played the riff, impressing all. They joined in the vocal accompaniment and seemed to enjoy themselves.

The manager said, 'Keep singing what you want, the others will join in.'

'Sir you know I have only just left the orphanage. There was limited opportunity to listen to and learn new songs. I do not know very many. But I will learn as the group plays them.'

The manager said, 'Sing what you know.'

So he sang his heart out, slow and fast songs. Afterwards the manager said, 'I would like to speak privately with the band. You carry on playing and singing and we will go into my office.'

Some minutes later they reappeared. The manager said, 'We think you are very good and would like you to rehearse every Sunday with the band. The talent shows are held at one of the cinemas. How do you feel about opening the next one? We will pay you 15 rupees. From time to time after that, as you learn new songs, you will make guest appearances at the club.' He was convinced he would go down well and would be a regular act on future shows.

Before they finished, Leo the pianist who seemed to be the leader, said, 'BJ, we meet every Wednesday to chat, listen to records to see if we can add them to our repertoire. I have a piano and the others bring their guitars. Would you like to join us? We will bring a spare guitar for you.'

Chapter Twelve

BJ nodded, 'Yes, OK. Thanks for asking.'

'Here is my address,' he said, writing it down on a sheet of paper. He gave him directions from the church. 'Shall we say seven in the evening?'

'We have dinner at seven. May I come after that please?'

'Come when you are ready.'

That first get-together, BJ took it all in. Len handed him a spare guitar and during a lull, as Rita made drinks, he softly played the blues finger picking the strings. The others looked at each other impressed. Len asked, 'Where did you learn that?'

'The teacher in charge of the orphanage played guitar, taught me chords and introduced me to the blues. During the holidays when the boarders had gone home, I practiced nearly every day trying to improve and develop my technique.'

'No wonder you play so well. We have talked about the blues and adding it to our repertoire. Do you know any blues songs?'

'Not especially blues but I sing and play songs with a bluesy feel.'

'Sing one.'

And he started to do so. It was a song they knew and they joined in. Very soon they had gelled and come up with a very good rendition.

Rita returned saying, 'That was good. Why don't you do it at the club?'

'Alex is not here. The sax will add to the sound. I think we should rehearse it more and make sure all of us are comfortable. Also one will not stand by itself; we will need a selection of blues songs.'

Before the session ended, there was no doubt he would be an asset to the group. However, they also knew that with a front man like BJ they would have to revise their set.

After BJ had gone Rita suggested, 'We must do more vocal harmony to accompany him. It will show off his tone, interpretation and demonstrate an array of nuances that will be expected from us if we are to develop beyond being just a club resident group. I can join in the vocal backing and let him take the lead. I will only do the female songs. I think it will work well because it is better to have a lead male vocalist.'

It was not long before BJ was encouraged to sing a few songs on Saturdays. Then it was the talent show. Mr Carter was the Master of Ceremonies and as the lights dimmed slowly and went off he walked to the centre of the stage.

'Good afternoon ladies and gentlemen, boys and girls. Welcome to this first show of the New Year. We have as usual an excellent line up of local talent including two new acts. One is a singer. I first heard him at my son's school concert last year. He received very enthusiastic applause and had to sing again. Some of you will have heard him at the Empire the last few Saturdays. Please give him a warm welcome. BJ Conway, with the club's resident group.'

As the curtains were being slowly drawn, the group played a short instrumental to wolf whistles and loud clapping. And then BJ began to play the guitar intro to a fast song, which was instantly recognized, eliciting further clapping.

They had rehearsed it and sung it at the club. The audience appreciated it. They did a blues song, which showed off BJ's finger picking. The applause was deafening with shouts of 'More, more!' as the curtains closed.

It was some time before the Master of Ceremonies was able to speak and then only after holding up his hands, signalling silence. 'I see you liked that.' The audience responded positively. 'We have to move on with the show.'

After the concert, Mr Carter and the group asked BJ to join the group permanently. He had been paid Rs10 each time he had sung at the club and because the show was in a cinema taking more money, instead of being paid the Rs15 promised at the outset, Mr Carter paid him the same as each of the other members: Rs20.

'Thank you sir, thank you all for letting me join you.'

And so the weeks went by. BJ gained in confidence and made suggestions about the arrangements. Increasingly, he was allowed to play first lead guitar. Fortunately there was no discord and he and the joint lead guitar worked very well. They shared the riffs sometimes doubling up for effect and the group developed their own sound and delivery.

They were more than happy to work around him as front man. Vocal accompaniment and harmony became integral to their performances enabling them to embrace a wider audience. In the course of the year, they progressed to closing the first part and then the whole talent show. At the club, they played every Thursday, Friday and Saturday and on Christmas and New Years Eve, if they fell on other days of the week.

Their popularity grew and they started getting bookings to perform at special events in hotels and then nightclub cabarets. As Mr Carter was also responsible for the bookings, he had to get in a reserve group to fill in so they could fulfill other engagements. To present themselves better in the hotels and cabaret, they wore matching waistcoats and bow ties adapting their sets to suit the venue accordingly.

BJ earned a lot of money, which he banked. His only luxuries were the pictures and clothes. He led a full life because when he had time he went swimming, trained in the martial arts and played badminton. He filled out bodily and became very fit.

Chapter Thirteen

A few months before his eighteenth birthday, he started to look in earnest for affordable accommodation. But the adverts were for two or three bedroom flats. One day he told the band members he needed to move out of the presbytery at the end of the year.

Leo and Rita discussed the matter at home and were prepared to offer him a room with them temporarily but were unsure the arrangement would suit BJ. Fortunately not long afterwards they learned a bachelor neighbour who lived in a one room flat with a bathroom across the courtyard, was moving out. But there was no kitchen only a Primus stove to boil water for hot drinks. There were kitchens and cheap restaurants liberally scattered around the area, so he could bring in food or eat out as he wished. They mentioned it to BJ, who immediately asked to see it. He was happy because it was clean and quite spacious. He thought he could buy some second hand furniture and make it comfortable. Leo and Rita said, 'As you can see, there is no kitchen but you can eat with us if you want. Or we can bring you the food in a tiffin carrier if you prefer to eat privately.'

The group members helped him settle in. He bought a bed, a cupboard, a small dining table and two chairs, a small sofa, two easy chairs and a coffee table. Things were looking up for him. He had his own flat, a job that paid well and the extra money he got for singing. Yet he had shut himself off emotionally.

Bimal was sad to see him leave but BJ made it a point to say hello to and spend some time with him after each mass. He also never stopped giving some money every month and buying him a pack or two of beedies.

The next three years he consolidated his position in the group and his reputation as a performer spread. More bookings followed, as their popularity increased but he remained ever humble and unassuming. The only time he showed any assertiveness was when he was rehearsing and arranging the songs. But the others had come to trust his judgement and were very amenable.

Just before Christmas after his twenty-first birthday, he received a life changing surprise. Father O'Shea saw him after mass. 'BJ I have something for you. Can you come into the sitting room please?'

Inside he said, 'Please sit down as I need to go to my room to get it.' Returning, he handed him an envelope.

'Thank you Father,' he said, and not thinking it important put it in his pocket.

'How is everything?'

'God is good. You know I have a very good job, am well paid and I earn extra with the group.'

Father knew about it because other parishioners had suggested they be booked to perform at church socials and dances.

The priest left and once alone, BJ opened the envelope. It was a letter from the River Authorities, his late father's employers. Money due to him on death had been held in trust for BJ until he attained the age of majority. There was a cheque for Rs3875 and 56 paise. On seeing the figure, his hands started to shake and his mind was scrambled. He went back into the church and sat in a corner. After a while, he got up and lit three candles in front of The Blessed Virgin Mary's statue and prayed. He walked to the other side to the statue of The Scared Heart of Jesus and did the same thing.

On leaving, he took out almost all of the money he had in his wallet and went to see Bimal. He gave it to him. He was surprised, as only three weeks earlier BJ had given him some anyway.

Life took on a new meaning for BJ and then one night as he said his night prayers, a thought came to him and would not go away. It haunted him through the night infiltrating his sleep. In the morning he knew what he was going to do. Most of the Anglo Indians were going to England all for a good reason: to better themselves and their lives. He would emigrate. He had no one in his life to keep him in India. Although his father had in one crazed drunken stupor deprived him of family life, his money could give him a fresh start.

That Sunday, during a break in rehearsal he asked to see Mr Carter privately.

Chapter Thirteen

'Sir, you know I have always been grateful for giving me a start. You also know I was orphaned when I was seven. To my surprise, before Christmas I inherited my father's back salary and provident fund. I want to make a fresh start in England. I am sorry I will have to leave as soon as I get a passport and a sailing trip booked. I will understand if you want me to leave immediately.'

The manager was very surprised. 'BJ I am shocked and disappointed; I never expected this. But I understand. I am sorry to lose you and I am sure the group will be too. Audiences and members have consistently spoken very highly of you all. I myself have noticed the vast improvement in the group's performances since you joined. Stay as long as you like. But as soon as you are notified of a sailing let me know. Shall we tell the others now?'

'I think so.'

They went out and the group saw BJ's and the manager's sombre faces. 'Would you like to tell them or shall I?'

'I will sir,' BJ said, and proceeded to tell them his intention. 'I have very much enjoyed being a part of the group and I hope you will not begrudge me this opportunity to make a fresh start.'

They were silent a while as the news sank in. Leo was the first to speak. 'I am disappointed but for purely selfish reasons. I have enjoyed you being with us. You have taken us to a new level and got us more bookings and we have earned more money as a result. But I understand your sentiments. I will be sorry to lose you but Rita and I wish you the very best of luck.'

The others said, 'Hear hear!'

And to break the tension, Len said jokingly, 'When you go, I will then have to do all the hard work again playing first lead!' But the laughter was somewhat strained. They were thinking that he would be hard to replace and without his input they would lose a lot of their impact.

The manager said, 'Unless any of you feel strongly otherwise, I have told BJ he can say as long as he likes. He has to get a passport and then book a sailing. As a lot of people are emigrating it could be a while. I will leave you to carry on rehearsing.'

But their disappointment hung like a pall and their practice lacked oomph. They decided to cut it short.

'I am sorry. Please do not hold it against me. You all have families. I don't. I was orphaned here. I need to burn my boats.'

'We understand.'

He decided to speak to Mr Cheung also. The next day he went to see him filled with trepidation afraid he might be asked to leave immediately.

'Good morning BJ. Take a seat.'

'Good morning sir.'

'What's on your mind?'

'I appreciate you giving me a job and I have been very happy here. After I turned twenty-one, surprisingly, I inherited my late father's back salary and provident fund. One evening it occurred to me that I should emigrate to the UK. The more I thought about it the more I felt comfortable. As you know I have no family to keep me here. Now I just want to make a fresh start. I hope you will not hold it against me.'

'Of course not. Do have any idea when?'

'No sir. I still have to get my passport and then a visa. Only then will I be able to try for a sailing.'

'I understand. I am obviously sorry you will be leaving but I wish you every happiness. We will talk further later as I will have to give you a reference. And it will be a very good one as you have been an asset to the bank having earned the respect of all your colleagues and managers.'

'May I stay on please?'

'Of course you can. When you get a ship, tell me immediately and we will sort things out for you.'

'Thank you sir.'

The group met as usual on Wednesday, by which time they had each been able to assimilate the news. The evening was relaxed and the weeks went by. The manager had put him in touch with various people who were able to help BJ. He applied for his passport and saw an official from the Emigrants to the UK Association who liaised with others to expedite its issue so he could apply for a visa. But there was still the matter of a

Chapter Thirteen

sailing. As BJ was a lone traveler initially, the travel agent suggested he wait for a cancellation.

No sooner had his passport come through, than BJ got home from work to find a note pushed under his door. It was from the travel agent. There was a late cancellation. Could he leave in five weeks time? BJ's heart was racing. So this is it, he thought. Yet he was sure it was what he wanted. He left immediately, walked to the main road and hailed a taxi. The agents were open for business until half past six in the evening to deal with the exodus to England. He accepted the booking, which was for the cheapest fare he had asked for. He would have a berth in a cabin for three. Also, the agent had to reserve a sleeping berth on the boat train to the docks. Because of times, he would have to spend another night there before embarking.

BJ ate in a restaurant before returning home. He pondered on events trying to plan his course of action. He would need to tell his boss, Mr Carter and the group members. Also he would have to let the landlord know. Fortunately he lived next door in a much larger flat.

The next day he spoke to Mr Cheung. 'My passport has only just come through and with the mass emigration taking place I did not expect to get a passage for months yet. But yesterday I was offered a cancellation to leave in five weeks time.'

'We only need one month's notice so five weeks is ample. I will get all sorted and transfer your account to our English branch.'

'Talking about money I need to withdraw Rs2000 immediately please to pay my fare and buy essentials.'

He wrote a note authorising the withdrawal of such a large sum and handed it to BJ. 'Here. Take this to the cashier. At the end of the day it will be ready for you to collect.'

He got up, extending his hand to BJ. 'Thank you for letting me know so promptly. Best of luck. Tell Mr Chang to come and see me.' Mr Chang was BJ's manager.

And that was it. Now his preparations started.

After work, he went to the travel agents to pay the money. From there,

81

he went to the shops to check what suitcases were available. He looked at several, making notes of prices and quality. He ate and headed home. He was tempted to go and tell Rita and Leo that he would be sailing in a few weeks but decided against it. Out of courtesy he felt he should tell Mr Carter first. Indoors, he started to list what he had to do to facilitate his move.

Time flew by. As news spread in the club and at the office, plans were made to give him a send off. The office affair was sedate compared to the club. Mr Carter did BJ proud speaking very highly of him.

BJ had a few days free to finalise everything. The last night, he slept on the floor as he had sold all his furniture. The final morning, he gave Rita and Leo all his bedding. His worldly possessions were now in two large leather suitcases. And there was his prized guitar. He spent the day with Rita and Leo until it was time to leave for the station to catch the boat train.

He settled into his compartment. There were three other travelers. They exchanged pleasantries politely but otherwise were wrapped up in their own thoughts. The only sound amplified in the darkness was the rattling of the train along the rails.

BJ thought of his first journey to the orphanage all those years ago. Then he did not know what lay ahead of him. Now he felt a sense of déjà vu. Only now he was going to a new country across the seas. He decided not to anticipate anything. He would have plenty of time in the days ahead while at sea to do that so he determined to just take each day as it came.

At the journey's end, one of Mr Carter's friends, Jake Summers met him. He would be staying at his home overnight, as the ship did not sail until half past two in the afternoon, with embarkation from half past ten in the morning.

The following morning, Jake took him to the docks, dropping him off where the ship was berthed. With his suitcases on the pavement and his guitar case slung over his shoulders and back, BJ shook hands, 'Thank you for everything. Until we meet again.'

'Good-bye and best of luck.'

Chapter Fourteen

As he turned, he saw a European man trip and fall on his knees next to him. BJ went to help and asked a coolie to get some cold water, preferably ice. Helping the man to his feet, he helped him to a bench and asked, 'Do you mind if I roll up your pants leg?' The man nodded. BJ did so and took a clean hankie from his shoulder bag. The coolie returned hurriedly with a small lump of ice. BJ took a Rs5 note from his wallet and gave it to the coolie. He wrapped the ice in the hankie and placed it over the knee.

While he was engrossed treating the man, he did not notice a girl approach. She was his daughter. She placed her hand on his shoulder asking, 'What happened Daddy? Are you alright?'

He nodded. Then, she looked down at the boy tending him and gasped. She recognised BJ and dug her nails into his shoulder and with her other hand grasped his upper arm. Her father heard the gasp and glanced up at her. Her face was red. But it was not just her face. It was her eyes and her demeanour that surprised him. She wiped perspiration beads from her nose and forehead. She patted her hair into place. But BJ was so engrossed with what he was doing, he did not see or hear her.

As the ice melted, he squeezed out the water and when there was nothing left, he continued to press the cold folded hankie to the knee. After a while, he used another hankie to dry it and pulled the man's pants leg down.

BJ asked, 'How does it feel now sir? Is it any easier?' he said, looking up as he spoke.

'Much better thank you.' It was only then that BJ noticed the young woman standing with her hands gripping the man again.

Realisation dawned. His face changed from sheer amazement to beaming pleasure as he said, 'Anna! Anna McLeod! I never imagined I would meet you.' And he thought, this must be her father. He said, 'then

83

you must be Major General McLeod?'

The Major replied, 'Yes. You two obviously know each other.'

Anna answered, 'BJ went to the boys' school in the same town as the convent. The students went to each other's concerts, special events and sports days. BJ boxed in the inter school tournaments, won several trophies at the sports and appeared in the concerts. So the girls got to know him by name and sight.'

The Major was now feeling a lot less discomfort and started to rise but grimaced as he put weight on his knee. BJ asked, 'Can I give you a hand?'

The Major said, 'Yes please.'

'If you remain seated, I will take your luggage into the customs area and come back.' They each had one and he took both away. He returned and said, 'Would you mind waiting while I take my own?' Having done so, he again returned to them and helped the Major to his feet. 'Put your arm around my shoulder and I will take the weight.'

Anna said, 'Let me carry your guitar. It will be easier.' Without waiting for an answer she lifted it off his neck and followed.

They went through the formalities of checking in and then identifying their luggage. The Major again put his arm round BJ's shoulder as they walked towards and up the gangplank into the reception area of the ship. The discomfort had eased appreciably and the Major took his arm away saying, 'Thank you very much. I think I can walk myself now.'

Anna handed back the guitar case and went to the side of her father. BJ respectfully hung back.

They were required to register their preference for the first or second sittings for meals. Anna tugged her father's sleeve and as he leaned his head down towards her she whispered, 'Daddy please ask BJ to join us at our table for the first sitting.'

He nodded sensing there was a very good reason. He turned to BJ who was standing a few feet behind them. 'BJ, we intend to have our meals at the earlier sitting. Would you like to join us at our table?'

BJ looked at Anna and then at the Major. 'If it is ok with Anna, then yes, thank you.'

Chapter Fourteen

'Of course it is.'

They registered and the Major said, 'We will see you in due course.' They parted as he and Anna had a suite on an upper deck and BJ was on the cheaper lower deck.

In their suite, the Major said, 'What a nice man. Even when he spoke to the coolies, he was polite, saying please and thank you.'

She said, 'He was an orphan and the fee paying scholars used to call them poor boys yet those girls who had brothers in the school learned that apart from his boxing and sports successes he was also very clever. A new Principal stopped them being called poor boys and integrated them with the boarders at meals. Before they were segregated and sat at a separate table.'

She then took his breath away when she said, 'Daddy, you and Mummy fell in love at first sight. Would you have BJ as a son-in-law?'

'I saw your reaction when you recognised him. Your eyes lit up and you dug your nails into my shoulder and arm. I also saw his face when he saw you. How do you know he is the one for you?'

'Something happened at our sports day in my final year. It was BJ's final year also. A few weeks earlier we had seen him box and win on a TKO. He had represented the school for seven years and was undefeated. Also he closed his annual concert with a gospel song, which was the talk of the girls as we walked back to the convent. Even the nuns were moved by the way he sang it. So he was fresh in all the girls' memories.

A few of us were walking by the stalls when one of them said, "There's BJ." He was with a friend who was also a boxer. In fact his father was the trainer. One of the girls giggled and said "Hello BJ." BJ looked at the giggling one first and then our eyes met. I know I went red but I did not look away. We walked past. But then I turned round and as it happened he also did. Again our eyes met. I blushed, we smiled at each other and then that was it. I never saw him again until today.

But I realise now why I was never interested in going out with boys let alone getting serious. I had thought about BJ often but I did not think we would ever meet; he was an orphan and would stay in India and I was in England. And now here he is. For the next fifteen days we will see each other often. Please Daddy, would you have him as a son-in-law?'

'Of course, if he is the one you want to marry. All I want is for you to be happy. Actually because of what he did when I tripped, I was thinking of having him join us for a drink so I can thank him properly. Maybe after we freshen up you can go looking for him.'

BJ, meanwhile, had gone down to his own cabin. It was a three bunked one. Bunk A, which was his was against one side and the other two were tiered on the opposite side. There was a cupboard, a dressing table and in a recess, a sink. Towels were neatly placed on each bunk.

He took off his tea shirt and had a wash. He damped a hand towel under the cold water tap and wiped his upper body. It felt good. He cupped a hand and drank some.

He then sat on the bed for a while. He thought about Anna. He could not believe he had seen her. And not just seen her, she was on the ship and for the next fifteen days or so he would be in her company daily at meal times at least. What if she does not like me, he thought. Beyond that, he refused to think any further.

The ship was due to leave at half past two. His watch showed a quarter after two. All the passengers' suitcases must be on board and it would be some while before his arrived in the cabin. The other two passengers had not come to the cabin while he was there. He decided to go to the promenade deck and watch as he left India behind. However, when he got to the promenade deck there was already quite a crowd at the railing. Rather than squeeze into any gap, he decided to go higher up. He went to the games and swimming pool deck. There were a few passengers there so he was able to stand away from them on his own. He looked at the quayside. It was a hive of activity as workers shouted and hurried about doing their jobs. The gangplank was lowered and pulled away. He looked out over the tops of the buildings. The heat shimmered above the roofs as if India was waving goodbye to him. The hawsers were lifted off and wound up onto the ship.

The tugs on the water side strained against the ship's inertia. Imperceptibly at first, the ship moved away from the quayside. Then it gathered momentum until eventually, it was turned so the bow was facing open water. The tugs released the hawsers. He walked to the stern so he

Chapter Fourteen

could see land receding into the distance. He was wrapped up in his thoughts staying there until it disappeared beyond the horizon.

That's it, he thought. I have burned my boats. The land of my parents and my birth is behind me. And he prayed in his mind, Lord here I am on my way to a new life in a new country. I do not know what the future holds for me. I do not expect it to be easy. I just ask You will give me strength and courage to face up to the new challenges. Help me to find a job so I can live. Thank you, Lord.

He turned around and there was Anna. She had been there a while positioned at the railing in such a way that it was not obvious to another passenger that she was watching him. As it happened, the others had all departed some time ago once the ship was in open water.

'Anna!' That she was there at all filled him with pleasure. His face lit up.

'I have been looking all over for you.'

'For me? Is something wrong with the Major? Is his knee ok?'

'He is fine. He wants you to join us in the lounge for a drink so he can thank you properly.'

As they walked she asked, 'How is your cabin?'

'It is the cheapest one on the lowest deck and has all I need. It is a three bunked one but I have not met the other two passengers yet. However there is a porthole so I can see the ocean. I do not know what the more expensive cabins are like.' She did not say anything as she and her father were in fact in a top grade suite with a balcony.

They got to the lounge, which by then was fairly crowded. The Major was sitting at a table in the corner at the far end and saw them as they entered. He stood up and waved to attract Anna's attention. She waved back saying, 'There he is.'

They got to the table and the Major was still standing. He held out his hand to shake BJ's. As they did so, he thought, Hmm a good strong handshake.

'Please sit down. What would you like to drink?'

'Sir, thank you but I do not drink.'

'Have a cold or hot one then.'

BJ hesitated, fidgeted in his chair and then said, 'Sir I am embarrassed by this.'

'Why? I do not want you to be.'

He looked at the Major, then at Anna. She had her chin resting on her thumb and her first finger up the side of her face. The other three fingers were curled towards her palm. She was studying his face for the first time.

He had thick black hair that needed no styling. She saw the kinks in the side, his sideburns and noted the way his hair at the back curled slightly. She thought that if she ran her fingers through his hair or it was windblown it would still look neat. He had brown eyes and a dimple in his chin. She had heard somewhere that it indicated the person was a flirt. And she was slightly jealous.

He looked back at the Major and said, 'Sir I am an Anglo Indian travelling on an Indian passport. I was only allowed to bring out Rs75, which I think is £3, 15s. I have to make it last until what little savings I have are transferred and I find work. I appreciate your offer but I cannot afford to return the favour.'

'Rs75 and you gave the coolie 5?'

'Sir you saw how concerned he was for you. Rs5 is perhaps what he earns in maybe a few days with luck. His need is greater than mine. I still have Rs70 left.'

The Major looked at Anna and then at BJ. 'Anna and I want you to spend as much time as you want with us and we will buy you drinks. But we do not want you to feel obligated in any way. We are doing it because we want to. After all did you not spend Rs5 because of me? If I had not tripped you would still have that money. Now please have a drink.'

Not wanting to offend, he said, 'A coca cola or vimto with ice please.'

'Anna has told me a little about you. You went to the orphanage in the same town as her convent. Would you like to tell us more?'

Again he fidgeted. He looked at Anna and back at the Major. He took some time to answer.

'I went to an orphanage when I was seven. After my exams I went to live in the church my mother used to take me to. I lived there for two

Chapter Fourteen

years until I was eighteen and then I had to leave. The physical trainer in school was the father of my best friend. He had a brother who was a bank manager. He gave me a job and it was the only one I had. I never thought of emigrating. In any case I could not have afforded the fare.

When I became twenty-one, surprisingly I inherited some money. My father's provident fund had been held in trust for me. That made me decide to make a fresh start. I had no family and nothing to keep me in India. The Emigrants to the UK Association helped and advised me considerably. Then there was a late cancellation and I had to leave in five weeks. But now I have burned my boats and here I am. I do not know what lies ahead of me. But then I did not know what lay ahead of me when I was orphaned or left school either.'

'What are your plans when you get to England?'

'Nothing specific sir, I do not know what the work situation is like.'

'What sort of job are you after?'

'I would like to use my experience in banking. But I will take any work to earn some money and pay my way until I find a suitable job. If necessary, I have been advised to join the RAF and make it a career.'

'Where are you going to live?'

'All I have is the name and address of another Anglo Indian. He is going to meet me at the docks.'

'Who arranged that for you?'

'The Association. It is part of what they do. It puts you in touch with another emigrant who gives you a home and helps you settle in.'

'Can you remember the address?'

'No sir. But I think it is in Kington or something like that. As I am being met I did not take a lot of notice.'

Anna and the Major glanced at each other but neither said anything. There was East and West Kington and they lived in East.

'What's his name?'

'Mr Andy Sullivan.'

The Major was not sure of this arrangement but appreciated it was

89

not he who was emigrating from India. If that was the way then who was he to question it? He just did not feel comfortable.

BJ had made an immediate impression on him. He liked his humility and humaneness. He liked how he fidgeted when having to talk about himself. Quite simply he liked him.

BJ felt quite shy being in Anna's company. She was the first English girl he had spoken to. After a while he said, 'Sir, Anna, I do not mean to be rude but please will you excuse me. I would like to unpack some clothes, have a shower and get ready for dinner.'

'Not at all. You carry on.'

'Thank you for the drink. Thank you also for inviting me to share your table.'

'Nice boy. I couldn't help but notice his eyes when he looked directly at you. He likes you but is somewhat shy, perhaps embarrassed he cannot afford to buy us any drinks.'

Anna blushed a little but was pleased.

Chapter Fifteen

The announcement was made that the first sitting was in five minutes. BJ headed for the dining room and caught Anna's eye at the entrance as she looked around for him. As the Major led them to a table by the window, they heard a girl say, 'There's BJ Conway.' BJ turned and looked in the direction of the voice. She was with a middle-aged couple who were looking at BJ. The fourth person at the table was a male who had his back to him but had started to turn round. As he did so they recognised each other. His name was Barry and had been two classes lower in school than BJ.

They shook hands warmly smiling with obvious pleasure. 'This is a surprise. I knew you were going to Blighty but I did not know it would be this sailing.'

'It all happened very quickly. There was a late cancellation and I had to leave in five weeks. We have not seen each other in that time.'

'Will you be singing on the ship?'

BJ looked at the Major and Anna whose faces showed a lot of interest. Anna said, 'Singing? I remember you singing at the school concert. Also, I remember now you were carrying a guitar when we boarded.'

Barry looked at Anna and recognised her. 'You went to the convent. You are Anna McLeod. We saw you winning your races and appearing in your concerts.'

Addressing her he said, 'My family and I went to the amateur talent shows at which he sang and also saw him at the Empire club where he was a singer guitarist in the resident group. They appeared in cabaret and hotels and other nightclubs. He became well-known and popular locally, especially with the girls.' He smiled mischievously looking at BJ. Anna felt pangs of jealousy wondering how many girlfriends he may have had.

'BJ, this is my mother, my father and my sister Julie.' Addressing his family he said, 'You have seen and heard him, now you have met him formally.'

BJ said, 'Pleased to meet you all.'

The father rose from his chair and shook BJ's hand, 'Pleased to meet you too.'

'No doubt I will see you around BJ. Let's hope you can sing for us. I am sure there must be other passengers who will recognise you.'

The Major, Anna and he proceeded to their table and sat down. The Major remarked to both generally, 'Interesting, you are wearing the same colours.' She wore a dark blue dress and a matching velvet choker with a small gold cross round her neck. As she had a naturally rosy complexion she had no need for makeup apart from a trace of pink lipstick. Her shampooed chestnut brown hair had a right parting and now hung down to her shoulders. She had grey eyes, a wide mouth and her face lit up when she smiled accentuating the dimples in her cheeks. And she had this endearing way of lifting her left shoulder slightly and tilting her head towards it when she did.

BJ wore almost the same colour dark blue pants and shirt with a light blue jacket and tie. In his breast pocket he had a dark blue hankie. Each had immediately noticed their similarly coloured attire but as the Major mentioned it, they simply exchanged glances.

'By any chance is this what you wore when you performed?'

'Yes sir. Originally we dressed simply but as we got other bookings we had to present ourselves more appropriately because of the guests and diners.'

They looked at the menus. BJ was surprised at the choice. There were starter, main and dessert courses. The first two included Indian and western dishes. Some of the western items he had never come across before like prawn cocktails, consommé, steak Diane, cod, French fries. Also some of the desserts had funny names. He decided to stick with what he knew.

The waiter came to take their orders.

'What would you like?' the Major asked BJ.

'After Anna and you please,' BJ replied respectfully.

They did so and he asked for an egg salad starter, and the beef Madras curry with pilau rice and dhal.

'Popadoms sir?'

'Yes please.'

There was a jug of water with ice and some lime slices in a small bowl on the table. The Major poured water in each of their glasses. BJ waited a while but as neither took a lime slice he did and put it in his glass and drank a little.

The Major said, 'Tell us more about your singing. Anna told me about your gospel song at the school concert. You had a very favourable impact on her friends and the girls generally. Even the nuns were impressed by the sensitivity and your talent which they said belied your age.'

BJ fidgeted in his chair looking at each in turn. He was clearly uncomfortable.

'Don't be shy,' said the Major.

BJ took a few sips of water, settled himself down and swallowed hard before he spoke slowly and deliberately.

'I was lucky sir, very lucky. One of the boarder's parents was at the school concert. On the second Sunday after I left school I was walking around the shops and this boy and his father saw me. The father introduced himself saying he had heard me sing. He was the manager of the Empire club where its resident group was rehearsing. He asked me to audition. Having been in the orphanage, I did not know a lot of songs. At the end they invited me to practice with them every Sunday and join them on Wednesdays when they met in the pianist's house to listen to records and learn new songs. They invited me to perform occasionally and after a few weeks I became a permanent member. It took off and we started to perform at other venues and the talent shows.'

'The diners and the audience must have enjoyed it for you to be in demand at the various venues,' the Major opined.

BJ did not answer, just fidgeted.

'Well as your friend said earlier, let's hope we get an opportunity to hear you.'

The starters arrived and they were silent for a while.

93

Because it was the first evening at sea there was no live entertainment in the main area. Instead, the Entertainments Organiser explained to the passengers the itinerary; the ports of call and the quizzes and other events planned for the sail. On one evening there would be a talent concert and the last night would be a gala evening.

The evening closed with a quiz on general knowledge. The questions were a mixture of British and Asian. They did not score the highest but they were up there. It certainly broke the ice for them and BJ felt himself relaxing a little, though he still felt out of place in their company.

After a while, as he did not want to overstay his welcome, he said, 'Thank you for your company. I have enjoyed our time together. Please excuse me. Good night Anna. Good night sir.'

'We have enjoyed your company too. Good night.'

He went to his cabin and there was still no sign of the other occupants.

He was up at six o'clock. The other bunks had not been slept in, there was no luggage and he concluded he had the cabin to himself. He did wonder how they were not taken up, as he understood there was a demand for berths by the Anglo Indians anxious to go to Blighty. But he was happy to be alone in the cabin. Fate was again being kind to him.

He had a wash and put on his swimming trunks and running clothes. Grabbing a large towel, he went onto the promenade deck. There was a yellow line all the way around and eight circuits was a mile. He placed the towel on a deck chair and started to run. He maintained a brisk pace not bothering to count the number of circuits. After some thirty minutes, he collected his towel and went up to the games deck, heading for the swimming pool. There was no one in it. He placed the folded towel on a deck chair and taking off his watch, put it on top. No splashing or diving was allowed so he used the steps to climb in at the 6 foot deep-end. The pool was 30 feet by 15 feet and despite it being in the open the water, was comfortably warm.

He swam up and down, up and down again and again not counting the lengths. After a while, he got out to check his watch. There was still time, so he got back in and floated on his back feeling the morning sun's warmth on his wet front. He resumed swimming. It was just after 7 o'clock when he toweled himself and put his running clothes back on. He tied the towel around his waist so the wet trunks would not show through and went to his cabin.

He got a clean shirt, underpants and pants and went to the men's bathrooms. There were several curtained shower enclosures and a couple of other passengers were already there. He did love his showers perhaps because of the daily ones in the orphanage. After rinsing himself, he remained under the water allowing it to refresh and invigorate him especially after the early morning run and swim. He felt good.

Because of his early start and routine, he was bright-eyed and alert. On his way up to the dining room, he met Anna and they greeted each other warmly. They walked on together and she asked, 'Sleep well?'

'Yes. I don't have a problem sleeping. And you?'

'Yes thanks.' Just before they got to the dining room she said, 'BJ, Daddy and I felt you were a bit tense yesterday with us. You don't have to be. Don't you want to share our table and spend time with me?' Instantly she realised what she had said and hastily added, 'and Daddy too.' She was fishing anxiously to find out if he wanted to be with her.

He stopped, turned and looked directly at her. 'Anna I am just afraid I will say or do the wrong thing and you will change your mind. I have not had your upbringing and am not in your social class.'

'Don't be silly. Please trust us and relax.'

The Major was already at the table when they entered. 'Good morning BJ.'

'Good morning sir.'

After breakfast the Major asked, 'Do you play draughts?'

'Yes sir.' His father, when not drunk, taught him the rudiments of the game and what pieces to keep in certain positions for a good defence. It stood him in good stead in the orphanage and afterwards.

'Would you like a game?'

The Major thought after a few moves that BJ had built up a very strong defence and clearly was very good. He would have to work at breaking it down if he was to win. But he knew it would not be easy.

BJ himself later felt that he could win but thought it best to let it slip while making it difficult. But as the game progressed the Major was astute enough to discern he was being handed the game.

That evening there was a live band. BJ wanted to dance with Anna but was scared to ask. And she was waiting for him to do so! The Major teased BJ, 'Come on son, why don't you dance with the girl. You know you want to.'

BJ blushed and fidgeted. But he looked at Anna, 'Would you mind?'

Instead of answering, she got up and they walked onto the floor. He gingerly put his arm around her waist and held her hand trying to keep a modest distance between their bodies. But with other couples on the floor it was not easy. The song ended but everyone stayed where they were. Two other songs in the same tempo followed and neither spoke yet enjoying being together. There was a silent communication between them.

After the third song, the vocalist said, 'Thank you. The next dance will be the jive. So unless you are over one hundred-years-old, I expect you to be on the floor.

Anna asked, 'Jive?'

'Yes.'

They immediately had an understanding and matched each other move for move, step for step. It was innovative and the other dancers created space for them on the floor. But they were oblivious to it. At the end of the three songs, he said, 'Thank you. I enjoyed that.'

'Thank you too for asking me to dance. Don't be so reluctant in future,' she said, beaming a warm smile at him in her inimitable way with lifted shoulder and tilted head.

The three of them stayed together till the end of the evening and BJ felt a lot more at ease. Anna and the Major were bringing him out of his shell. What he did not know but the Major noticed was the change in Anna. It was in her general demeanour.

The next morning the Major was up early. He went on the promenade deck to breathe in the morning fresh sea air. He sat on a deck chair and thought about his late wife Senga. Yes, it was love at first sight for them.

Chapter Fifteen

They married in 1941. He wondered what she would have thought of BJ and how Anna had been affected on first seeing him. After some time reminiscing, he walked around a couple of times, wrapped up in his own thoughts. He stopped and stood at the rail staring at the horizon. He saw a pod of porpoises playfully jumping in the wake of the ship. And then they were gone. It was not long before he heard, 'Good morning, Mr McLeod.'

The Major turned to see Barry. 'Good morning to you too. How are you this morning?'

'Fine sir.'

'Let's sit awhile. I want to ask you something.'

'Barry isn't it?'

Barry nodded.

'The other night you seemed particularly pleased to see BJ. Were you good friends in school?'

'No, but I would like to think that after he left the orphanage we were. I like and respect him as a person.'

'How did it start?'

'He was in the orphanage and I was a boarder. I was two classes lower than him. I was only in school a few days and I was homesick. BJ saw me crying and came and put his arm around my shoulders asking had a boy hit me? I told him I missed my mum and dad and wanted to go home. He told me not to cry and asked if I had brothers and sisters. He said, "They must miss and want you home too especially your mum. I miss my mum and dad too but they are dead. I have no family. You will get letters and pocket money and will go home for the holidays." We talked a little and I stopped crying. After that for some while afterwards whenever he saw me, he asked how I was.'

'That was very nice considering he was an orphan and very young himself.'

'Yes sir. When I thought about it as I grew older I realised how profound those words were.'

He thought a while and continued, 'BJ not only became the school's best boxer but he was also good at all field sports and running. But he remained humble. Boys respected him because he was especially protective of us younger ones. If anyone bullied us we only had to tell him and he would speak to the bullies and warn them. No one challenged him. They were scared to. I want to keep in touch with him in England. He is a valuable friend.'

'Thank you for telling me that. You see, when we were about to embark I tripped and fell on my knee. He helped. He was very polite to the coolies that he asked to get some ice or iced water. He carried our suitcases, helped us on board and has been very respectful.'

'That is typical of him. In school we were taught to respect our elders and authority. But BJ respected the young too even the cooks and refectory servants. I never heard him say a nasty thing about anyone. I imagine you know that children, being children, give each other nasty nicknames sometimes. There was a boy who had a big head and we used to call him big head. Another boy had big ears that stuck out and we called him elephant ears. Names like that. But I never heard BJ use those names. He always used their proper names.

Even in the club where he sang, he was never big headed. He was popular and the girls liked and flirted with him. He could have gone out with any of them but he never seemed interested. I am sure he never had a girlfriend. Unfortunately, some boys were jealous. Because he showed no romantic interest in girls they used to say he was homosexual. But they did not dare say it to his face. BJ took up martial arts and could have taken care of himself but he would not have needed to. He was such a nice person that others would have intervened.'

'All you have said confirms my own opinion after just two days. However you have told me a lot more so thank you.'

'Will you excuse me please sir as I want to find my family. It will be breakfast time soon.'

'Of course son. You go ahead.'

Chapter Sixteen

Two nights later, as usual, they were in the lounge. Anna had gone to the bathroom. Approaching the table an inebriated passenger grabbed hold of her arm. She tried to shake it free but he persisted.

'Leave me alone.'

Major said, 'BJ. Anna needs help.'

He got up and took a few strides towards them. He stepped in saying, 'Excuse me please.' The man was taken unawares and released his grip. BJ put his arm around the back of her shoulders and held her upper arm. She leaned against him resting her head on his shoulder. As they walked away he swore at BJ, 'Don't turn your back on me!' punching him in the back, finishing with an insult to BJ's mother.

'Aw come on man,' some exclaimed. Others muttered disapprovingly.

But BJ's priority was Anna. They sat down and he took his clean breast pocket hankie, dipped it in his glass of water squeezed out the excess and gently dabbed her forehead, nose and cheeks. 'Are you alright?'

She first nodded and after a few seconds said, 'Yes, I am now. Thank you.'

'Are you sure?'

'Yes.'

'Excuse me a while please.'

His face changed from tender concern to granite. He got up and walked towards the drunk who had waited momentarily before turning around to stagger away smirking. But seeing BJ a passenger said to him, 'Mr, you're in trouble. The man you abused is after you.'

The drunk turned around and did not like the look on BJ's face. There was a steely glint to his eyes. He went ashen. He stepped back and would have fallen into the lap of a woman had she not quickly got up. He fell into the chair expecting the worst.

BJ said to another passenger, 'May I borrow your chair please?'

He pulled it over and sat down. Leaning forward looking the drunk straight and hard in the eye he said, 'My parents died when I was seven years old, nine years after they were married. 'Before my mother died she told me that people who got drunk were basically cowards who found false courage in grog.' Some passengers laughed but the drunk was oblivious to it. He was concentrating on BJ who continued, 'Now before you apologise to me, you will apologise to the lady who you manhandled. In upsetting her, you upset her father and you upset me. I do not like that.'

Without waiting for an answer, BJ got up and so did the drunk meekly following him. They went to Anna and the Major.

'I am sorry ma'am. I was wrong and there is no excuse.'

'Thank you. I appreciate it.'

Turning to BJ he said, ' I am sorry I insulted your late mother and you. I truly am.'

BJ extended his hand to shake his. 'Tomorrow is another day. We are several more from our destination and we will bump into each other often. No hard feelings.'

The Major was flabbergasted by his graciousness but very impressed.

With that, BJ sat down and the drunk left. On his way, Barry said to him, 'Mister, you're lucky. That guy is an undefeated boxer and a martial arts exponent.'

He said nothing but thought, 'Yes I was lucky. I saw the look in his eye.' That incident taught him a salutary lesson and was the catalyst that made him stop drinking.

BJ drank some water but his hands were now shaking a little. He asked Anna, 'Are you feeling better?

'Yes, I am glad its over.'

BJ, still upset by the insult of his mother said, 'The reference to my mother cut to the heart. I am churning inside. Please excuse me. I need to splash some cold water on my face and get some fresh air to calm down. I won't be long.'

He had barely set off before Anna said, 'Daddy I must go and make sure he is ok. He is upset.'

She followed him and waited outside the gents' bathroom entrance. He came out, surprised to see her. 'Anna what are you doing here?'

'You were clearly upset and I wanted to be with you.'

On deck they walked in silence for a while. Seeing a ship going in the opposite direction, they walked to the railings. He stood beside an upright and she was close to him shoulder to shoulder.

He felt her presence. He was glad his other shoulder was against the upright, as he could not move even if he wanted to. But he was not inclined to. It was nice. He was pleased that she seemed to be comfortable with their physical closeness. They watched the ship recede into the distance and disappear beyond the horizon. He became a little sombre and sensing it she asked, 'Any regrets about leaving India?'

'None. There was nothing for me there. I was just thinking about my parents especially my mum to whom I was very close. Now I am going to a country where I don't know anyone and have to find a job. At least I have someone meeting me who will put me up.'

'But you know me. And Daddy. Also there is Barry.' After a while she continued, 'I was close to my mum too.' He noted the 'was' but discretion prevailed. He did not pursue the matter. And then they heard a mature female voice say, 'Shame such a pretty girl is getting up close to and friendly with an Indian.'

They both heard it and immediately Anna turned around and said, 'I beg your pardon. What did you say?' By the time she had finished, she had stepped in front of the couple who were taken aback. BJ said, 'Anna it's OK.'

'No, it's not OK.'

The woman gulped a couple of times. She had not expected this. Whether her husband agreed or not was not known, because he had lost his tongue gripped in silence. Then haltingly the woman said, 'I - I - I did not mean anything.'

'How could you not have meant it? Whatever is in your heart determines what you say. You thought it and as you said it you must have meant it. Now apologise please to BJ. That is his name. And to me for insulting us both. He has more character and integrity in the tip of his little finger than both of you put together.'

'How dare you speak to me like that. I will tell your father.'

'How dare you say what you did. Anyway my father does not like small-minded people like you. We will go and see him now. Coming?'

But they were not going anywhere. 'I will see him when I am ready not when you tell me to.' And they walked off.

BJ said, 'Thank you for defending me. But she is right in a way. You are English and pretty and I am an Indian.'

'Yes, but she meant it in a derogatory way and that is what made me unhappy. You are a human being. And us being friendly has nothing to do with anyone else. People can think what they want so long as they do not insult us particularly you.'

BJ felt they had been gone a while so he said, 'I do not want to upset the Major. Let's go back.'

The Major was still at the table but he was not alone. When Anna had followed BJ out after the incident with the drunk, Barry and his family who had witnessed the episode asked, 'May we join you for a while please?'

'Please do.'

They sat. Barry's father asked, 'May I buy you a drink?'

'Thank you. I still have one to finish so a soda will do fine.'

Barry said, 'Just like in school. He was always protective of and considerate towards the weaker ones.'

The Major said, 'The way he handled himself showed a lot of maturity. I am not sure I would have been as self-disciplined and in control. I first saw the drunk manhandling Anna and although she is my daughter somehow, something in me just made me say. "BJ, a drunk is upsetting Anna."'

The mother said, 'I hope you do not mind my saying so but what happened has brought them very close together. I was touched by his tenderness towards your daughter and the way she responded to him. There is a chemistry between them.'

Chapter Sixteen

The Major agreed in his heart but simply said, 'No I do not mind,' and left it at that.

'Where are they now?'

'BJ was obviously concerned about Anna but when he was sure she was ok the insult to him and his mother hit him hard and he just felt he needed to get some fresh air and calm down. I guess he just wanted to be alone with his thoughts for a while. I know he was orphaned when he was seven and he was very close to his mother.'

They chatted generally, getting to know each other better.

The Major saw the expression on Anna's face as she and BJ approached. Something had upset her. And it was not BJ. When they got to the table Barry and his family got up. The father said, 'Excuse us please. It was nice getting to know you.'

But the Major said, 'You do not have to leave. Please stay.'

Barry and his father got a couple of unoccupied chairs.

'What happened?'

Anna told him everything. 'Why are people so unkind? First, a drunk not only upsets me but insults BJ and his mother. And then for no reason at all, someone talks of him being an Indian as if he is a second-class human being, an untouchable. Didn't Gandhi fight against the class system?'

The Major asked BJ, 'Are you alright?'

'I am now. But what I did not want was to cause you and Anna any embarrassment or trouble.'

'It is the others that have embarrassed themselves. Both of you are upset. Now go and spend as much time alone together. I have company and I will be ok. Now please go.'

BJ said, 'you sure you do not mind?'

'I suggested it did I not? Now go. I do not feel the same way as that woman that insulted the two of you. I am happy for both of you to be together.'

Mindful of the conversation the first afternoon on board, the true meaning was not lost to Anna, but was to BJ.

'Thank you Daddy.'

'Thank you sir.' And with that they left and went out onto deck. They walked round for a while each enjoying the silence. It was not an awkward silence; it was intimate. It was warm and comforting. They were in each other's company. From time to time they simultaneously looked at each other and smiled. They were in a cocoon and oblivious to anything and anyone around.

They went to the railing and stood looking out at the reflections of the ship's lights dancing on the water and beyond as they waltzed into the darkness. After a while turning his head to her he said, 'I do not want to offend you but can I ask you something personal?'

'I know that you would not deliberately offend me. Or Daddy. So you can ask me anything.'

He hesitated momentarily and then blurted out, 'I have no right to ask you this but do you have a boyfriend waiting for you when you get home?'

Her heart stirred. He must like me, she thought, why would he ask otherwise?

'No there is no one. I have never had a boyfriend.'

'But you must have a lot of admirers and dated several. You are so attractive.'

'I did not have my first date until I was eighteen. I did like the boy and we went to an office dance. But he was a bit too forceful and pulled me too close to him the first time we danced.'

BJ interrupted, 'I hope I did not pull you too close and were not uncomfortable when we danced.'

She thought, I had wished you had pulled me closer than you did, but instead said, 'No I was not. Anyway, I had to break away and tell him not to do that. He seemed to be OK about it but later he tried to kiss me when I did not want him to. I never dated again after that. I have been asked out many times but I was not interested in going out with boys just for the sake of it. I see myself as a real relationship girl. I will only spend time with someone I trusted, could grow fond of and was sure he felt the same way.'

She had spoken spontaneously and realised as soon as she had said it why she was alone with BJ.

BJ had picked up on what she said too. His heart stirred but still he was cautious and would not allow his imagination to run away with him.

She continued, 'My friends and girls I work with are always talking about boys and who they go out with. What about you?

'I have not got a boyfriend either,' he said mischievously. She laughed nudging him in the ribs.

'You know what I mean. Did you have a girlfriend in India? Maybe because you were a popular singer you had lots of girlfriends.'

'No, I did not have a girlfriend. I was never interested in getting involved.'

Both pleased with each others responses they basked in that knowledge for a while and then Anna said, 'Let's go up on the games deck.'

He did not demur. He was just pleased to be in her company knowing she was comfortable with him too.

When they got there, it was relatively deserted. Being exposed to the night sky, passengers were not interested in games choosing to enjoy the dancing and relaxing in the lounges to where the music was piped anyway. A few passengers ambled along.

They walked to the pool, which was lit up with different coloured lights underwater. No one was swimming.

'I wonder if the water is warm.'

Unwittingly he said, 'It is.'

'Have you been in it?' She was wondering when he could have done so as they had spent most of their time together.

'I have swum every morning before breakfast.'

'Before breakfast? What time did you swim?'

'About half past six.'

'That early? What time do you wake then?'

'Six o'clock. I run for about half an hour and then swim for the next half hour or so.'

She did not say anything then but she knew she would be joining him tomorrow morning.

'Let's have a dip. I have not been able to before as it was the time of the month.'

It threw him. He had a quizzical look and innocently he asked, 'Why did the time of the month stop you?'

Fortunately there was no one within earshot otherwise they will have thought him really stupid and naïve. Well he was not stupid but he genuinely did not know. In fact Anna was pleased because it meant he had no experience of women. She knew he genuinely did not know what she meant.

She started to explain feeling no embarrassment whatsoever. As she spoke he became horrified. First the blood drained from his face and then almost immediately it went red. He was acutely embarrassed. Stuttering he said, 'Anna I am so sorry. I had never heard that expression before. I am sorry. I hope you are not angry with me. I did not mean to be personal or to offend or embarrass you.'

'Don't be silly. You asked me earlier if you could ask me something personal. Can you remember what I said?'

'I could ask you anything.'

'Well then. I do not mind nor was I embarrassed. You asked. I started to tell you.'

Being sensitive to his feelings she changed the subject. 'Let's go and get our costumes and towels.'

They parted at the stairs. 'I will see you back here shortly,' she said. 'I won't be long.'

'My cabin is much lower down and will take longer for me to get there and back. I will be ready as soon as I can.'

She was back first. She had changed into jeans and a blouse over her costume.

'Sorry to have kept you waiting. Hope I have not been too long.'

Chapter Sixteen

'Don't worry.'

His towel was slung over his left shoulder. They went up to the pool, which was still unoccupied but there were still a few passengers strolling and enjoying the sea air. It was pleasantly cooler because of the gentle sea breeze.

He pulled a deck chair closer to the pool. They took off their outer clothes and placed them neatly on it. As he stood up he looked at her. She was attractive. She had on a black modestly-cut costume that accentuated her curves. He had been to several swimming galas and had swum regularly but he had not noticed the women in the way he was noticing Anna now. She was different. She was not just another woman or girl. It was Anna. She was special. And he liked what he was seeing.

She too was noticing him. He had on square-cut trunks and the lights created highlights on his finely honed torso. Bare-chested she saw how muscular he was especially his upper arms and shoulders. The veins stood out prominently and there was not an ounce of superfluous flesh on him.

'Let's go in.' And they did so. As she felt the water she said, 'You are right. It is comfortably warm despite it being exposed to the elements as it is.'

They set off together doing the breaststroke side by side for several lengths. After a while, she stopped. She placed the back of her arms on the side of the pool dangling her legs in the water. He did the same beside her. Neither spoke. After a while she said, 'I enjoyed that. Let's swim some more.'

Now they did the crawl and the breast and back strokes. They were good swimmers. The odd couple of passengers stopped as they strolled by to watch them. One was the couple that Anna had had the confrontation with, but neither she nor BJ saw them.

It was some while before they decided they had been in the water long enough. They had lost track of time and they were now on their own on the deck. They climbed out wrapped their towels around their shoulders and sat on deck chairs facing out to sea.

The reflection of the ship's lights still danced on the water. Anna said, 'I really enjoyed that. I love swimming and being in the water. What about you?'

'I too love swimming. Fortunately the bank where I worked had an arrangement with a hotel they did business with and staff were allowed to use their pool. So I swam regularly at least once a week. I also went to swimming galas.'

'No wonder you swim so well. You are like a fish in the water.'

'You swim well too. You don't splash the water like most swimmers do.'

They went silent. The only sounds were that of the wake created by the ship as it cut through the water, the sound of the propellers and the drone of its engines. He eventually glanced at her. Her head faced him but her eyes were closed. He did not say anything at first but as he continued to look at her, it was clear she had dozed off. The emotional ups and downs of the evening, the long time in the water and the sea air had lulled her to sleep.

He did not move, fearing he would disturb her. But he studied her face. She was indeed very attractive. He could not believe that the girl on that sports day over five years ago was here beside him on a ship in the middle of the Arabian Sea. He wondered what would happen when they docked. Would she want to keep in touch? He certainly wanted to. But where did she live? Would it be near to where he was going? All these thoughts went through his head. And then she stirred.

She opened her eyes and realised she had nodded off. 'I am sorry. That was rude.'

'No it was not. Come it's late. Let's go.'

They went to the bathrooms to dry off and change into their outer clothes. As they walked down to the stairs to the point where they would have to go their own ways, both were disappointed that the evening had come to an end.

'I have really enjoyed this evening apart from the insults. But in a way I am grateful because we have spent time together as a result.'

'I too have enjoyed being with you very much. I just hope your dad does not regret what he said as we have been away a long time.'

'I would not worry about that. He likes and trusts you. You must know that. He will not have allowed us to be alone otherwise.'

They arrived at the stairs. They looked at each other and she said, 'Goodnight BJ and thank you.'

'Good night Anna.'

That was it. He thought, what an evening! He got to his cabin, stripped off and lay on the bunk with his hands under the back of his head. Savouring the tender moments between them he fell asleep. He roused and went under the covers.

Chapter Seventeen

The next morning he woke at the usual time. He kept to his routine and went on to promenade deck and started running.

Anna too was up early. She had not packed running shorts. But she put on an old pair of jeans and a blouse. She did have Keds, which she put on and grabbing the towel, still damp from the previous night, she went down. Going on deck, she saw the back of BJ as he ran away from her. She walked through to the other side and this time he approached, but running backwards so he did not see her. He kept looking over his left shoulder and as he was running anti clockwise his face was towards the sea. He turned around to run normally and seeing Anna, ran to her and stopped.

'Anna!'

'I have come to run and swim with you. This is your routine, isn't it?'

'Yes.'

'Let's run then but where is your towel?'

'It's the other side,' he said, and they set off.

When they ran around the stern end of the ship, BJ said, 'There is my towel.'

Without stopping, she threw hers with her damp costume in a plastic bag wrapped within on top of his and they continued. Having been a runner in school and a regular swimmer, she was fit so they were able to maintain a very steady pace neither speaking. Their breathing was rhythmic with their strides.

As if he had a built in clock, BJ looked at his watch and it showed just after half past six.

'It's time for a swim now. Is that OK? Or do you want to run some more?'

'Let's swim. After last night, I cannot wait. But my costume was still damp from last night so I will need to go to the bathroom to change. What about you?'

'I have another pair on. I alternate them to allow them to dry. I will have to take them to the laundry later to wash them however. I have other clothes to wash also.'

'Have you used the machines before?'

'No not yet.'

'Daddy is hoping to play bridge this morning. While he does, we can do the laundry together and I will show you.'

They retrieved their towels. He waited as she went to the bathroom to put it on under her outer clothing.

When they got to the pool, the deck was deserted. They took off their outer clothes and laid them on a deck chair with their towels. The breeze was gentle but it was still warm despite the hour.

They swam as they had last night but for a shorter time. 'This is a nice way to start the day. Before I was on my own in the water.'

'Well you won't be alone again. I will be joining you.'

'You will?'

'Yes, don't you want me to?'

'Of course I do. You should know that.'

At the stairs she said, 'I will see you at breakfast.' And they went their own ways.

He took his time getting showered and dressed, pleased that this morning had continued from where they had left off the previous evening. He knew he more than liked her and she liked him too. He looked forward to enjoying her company while they were on the ship and hoped for the better when they docked.

The night before the talent show, the Entertainments Officer said, 'As announced the first evening, tomorrow is the passengers' talent night. So that we can schedule the evening I need to know who wants to appear. Tomorrow at 10 a.m., we will be auditioning here in the lounge. I already have one name on my list. A number of you have told me and other members of the band there is a passenger who was the front man in a club

Chapter Seventeen

resident group that also appeared in cabaret and hotels. BJ Conway where are you? Come up sir.'

BJ was caught completely unawares. The Major said, 'Show them what you are made of son.'

'We have a spare guitar for you. Sing some songs please.'

He took the guitar and adjusted the height of the mic. 'Thank you everyone.'

He chose to do a song the band had played so they would be able to accompany him. He improvised on the guitar to get the feel of it and led into the intro when he was ready. Passengers went on to the floor in numbers. He was well received and the Master of Ceremonies said from the floor, 'Carry on singing.'

He sang songs in different genres. The band were professionals and so they fit in comfortably following BJ's lead and promptings.

As the Master of Ceremonies returned to the stage, there was generous applause. He shook BJ's hand saying, 'Thank you sir.' And turning to the floor said, 'Ladies and gentleman that is a sample of what you will hear tomorrow. Only we will get Mr Conway to sing a few more songs and close the show.'

As he sat down he said, 'I did not expect that.'

Anna put her hand over his. 'You are very good.'

'Yes, son. You are good.'

'Thank you.'

The next morning at ten, BJ and Anna went to the auditions. There were a few others there. The Master of Ceremonies called each name and they did their bit. Some were allowed to go on longer than others. When only BJ was left the Master of Ceremonies said, 'I know what you can do. As I said last night you will close the show and we will give you twenty to twenty-five minutes. Perhaps you can get together with the band now to sort out the songs you will perform. The rest of you I will see outside please. Unfortunately some will not be on the show tonight.'

That evening, the band played for about thirty minutes and then the passenger acts did their turns. One was a particularly good comic dressed up as an old woman. It was a fun night but they were merely the warm ups for BJ who came on after the interval. As on the previous night, he went down well. Even the band and Master of Ceremonies applauded.

Anna smiled at him warmly as he took his seat squeezing his hand. 'You look very comfortable on stage. You seem to assume a different personae when you perform.'

'The club manager once said the same thing. But I am not conscious of it; I just get wrapped in performing.'

As the ship left the Mediterranean and entered the Atlantic Ocean, the sea became choppier. By the time they got to the Bay of Biscay the waves were huge. The ship was like a cork bobbing sideways and forward and backwards. The average speed was now down to just 4 knots per hour and at times the bow dipped under the waves causing the propellers to partly churn the surface of the sea and air. BJ began to feel queasy as the day went on. The evening's entertainment was cancelled which was just as well. He got worse during the night and slept restlessly. At six o'clock he was in no fit state to run and swim. He worried about not being able to tell Anna and hoped she would surmise something was wrong.

She had gone down to do the usual but BJ did not turn up. After a few minutes she went to his cabin and knocked on the door. He knew it was Anna.

'BJ it's me. Are you OK?'

'Hang on please.' Unsteadily he put on his pants and a shirt and opened the door.

'You did not come on deck and I was worried about you. I am glad I was. You look very unwell.'

'I feel awful.'

'The choppiness has made you seasick. I will go and tell Daddy.' Shortly afterwards, the Major knocked and entered.

'Good morning sir.'

'Good morning son. I have spoken to the Purser and he is arranging for the ship's doctor to come and see you. He may give you some medication or a fast working injection.'

Chapter Seventeen

BJ's face showed anxiety and guessing why he added, 'Don't worry. Anna insisted she will pay for the doctor.'

BJ was embarrassed. 'I am sorry to be a nuisance.'

'Don't think that, please. You must know by now we care for you.'

All he could say was, 'Thank you.' But it did make him feel good.

Anna had showered and dressed and came to the cabin. The Major said, 'Get into bed until the doctor arrives. It won't be until after breakfast anyway. I will leave the two of you alone now.'

Anna drew up the chair and sat beside him. 'Were you able to sleep at all?'

'Not really. I kept waking up as I was sick.'

When the announcement for the first sitting was made, she left. 'I will be back after breakfast,' and squeezed his hand.

While he was alone he dozed, awaking at a knock on the door. It was the doctor. 'I hear you are seasick. I will give you a fast acting injection and you will be ok in about three, four hours time. Rest in the meantime.'

He had just finished when the Major and Anna arrived.

The doctor said, 'All done. I have given him an injection. He will be back up and about by lunchtime. The Purser tells me my fee is being added to your bill.'

'Yes.'

'Enjoy the rest of the sail Mr Conway. You'll be ok.'

'Thank you doctor.'

Anna said, 'I brought you a couple of ham rolls. You can eat them later when you feel better. You rest now. Shall I take your key? I will pop by now and again to check on you. Leave the catch off so I don't disturb you.'

She took it out of the door and they left. 'I'll see you later.'

He thought a while. They care for me. And then he was asleep.

The injection started to work. He slept and did not hear Anna quietly look in a few times. She could not relax worrying about him.

He roused the fifth time she opened the door. 'You're awake. How do you feel? You certainly look a lot better.'

115

'I feel better, thanks. You and your father have been extremely kind since we met. And now you are paying the doctor's fee for me. Thank you.'

'Think no more about it. I will do anything for you. You go and get showered and dressed and I will come back for you in half an hour.'

Events and the time spent together had drawn them very close and BJ began to feel loved and wanted. Yet he was afraid it would not last. Just like his parents were taken from him, he was afraid they would be too. So he determined he would enjoy them while they were on the ship and hope for the best afterwards.

Chapter Eighteen

The last evening arrived and it was the gala event. Deep down, BJ felt some sadness. As he danced with Anna, the mood was somewhat sombre. They both sensed it and because of the trust that was now between them, she looked up at him and said, 'BJ you are not yourself. What's on your mind?'

'Can we go outside please?'

They walked in silence for a while and then he said, 'Anna I have very much enjoyed being with you and your dad. You and I especially have done a lot together but it now ends. May I keep in touch with you please?'

'Oh no BJ! Did you think I would not want to? Tomorrow the sail ends but not our relationship. Both Daddy and I want to keep in touch with you. We will see each other again. I want to very much.'

'Thank you.' But he was still scared that back in her own environment, as time passed, she would forget him.

Seeing the doubt on his face, she took off her gold bangle and handed it to him. 'This was my mother's and means a lot to me. Keep it for me. When you have any doubts or fears hold it and think of us.'

He put in his pocket, lost for words.

'Come let's go back in.'

The Major too was feeling the atmosphere. Being mature and more experienced, he did not have to strain his brain to figure out why. He had seen the way Anna had opened up during the last fortnight. Now she was not herself.

When they returned, he was discreet enough not to comment. 'Daddy do you have a pen and paper please?'

'No. Why?'

'I want to give BJ our address and telephone number so we can keep in touch with each other.'

'We can sort that out tomorrow. BJ, give us Mr Sullivan's address.' But he had already considered things and knew what he was going to do. He would talk to Anna alone.

BJ felt somewhat reassured but sadness lingered. They made the most of being together as they would not be able to go running and swimming in the morning. They had to pack their suitcases.

Alone in their suite, Anna used the cabin's notepad to write down their details and slipped it into her handbag.

The Major rang the bell for the cabin boy and ordered Horlicks and biscuits. As they drank he said, 'I have not changed my mind about having BJ as a son-in-law. You have come out of yourself a lot and it is very noticeable you are good for each other.'

'We were both sad tonight that the sail was ending. I told him it did not mean the end of our relationship; that I wanted us to keep in touch. To reassure him I gave him mummy's bangle to keep for me so he could think of us.'

Somehow he was not surprised. He knew what that bangle meant to her.

'Anna, I have been uneasy about the arrangement that he would be met at the docks. So many things can go wrong and he could be stranded. We will make sure he is met and all is OK. If not he will come to stay with us.'

'Daddy! You would do that?'

'Why not? I am very fond of him. And I know you would like that.'

She started to cry, 'Thank you Daddy. I would like nothing better.'

'Let's see what happens tomorrow.'

The ship docked during the night.

Again there was a sombre mood at breakfast. Anna gave him the note and asked for his details. Looking at the address she added, 'We will not be far from each other.'

'Really?' And he was all smiles.

After breakfast they had to while away the time until the luggage was unloaded.

When they disembarked, they proceeded into the immigration area. As the Major and Anna were British passport holders they went through

Chapter Eighteen

without undue delay. The queues for foreign passport holders were longer and therefore slower. BJ was anxious that the Major and Anna would be kept waiting as they had agreed to make sure he was met as promised. In time, he was cleared. 'Sorry to have kept you waiting.'

'You don't have to appologise. We expected you to be delayed.'

They went into the customs hall to identify their suitcases. Customs officials paraded along them and questioned some passengers. One stopped BJ.

'Have you got any cigarettes or alcohol?'

'No sir. I do not drink or smoke.'

'I did not ask if you drank or smoked. You could be bringing them in for friends or family,' he said peremptorily. BJ was a little taken aback.

'No sir. I do not have any cigarettes or alcohol.'

'Open your suitcases and the guitar case.'

BJ was unnerved and did as he was asked. The official looked into and under some clothes. He looked in the guitar case. Clearly there were none so he said, 'OK you can go.'

BJ closed and locked everything, picked them up and turned to walk away. He had not noticed the Major and Anna had been behind and close by him throughout.

'You seem unsettled. You OK, son?'

'No, sir. That unnerved me. I was not prepared for it. Thank you for waiting. I will be OK in a while.'

They went into the arrivals hall. BJ looked around anxiously but did not know who he was looking for.

The Major saw his very good friend. 'Harry, good to see you. Trust you and the family are well.'

'Alfie, good to see you back. And you Anna. How was the wedding and the sail?'

'Excellent. There is a lot to tell you. This is our friend BJ that I told you about. BJ, this is our friend Harry King.'

'Pleased to meet you BJ,' and extended his hand.

119

'Likewise sir,' and shook hands. Harry thought, hmm, firm grip.

'Harry, as I explained when we talked, someone is supposed to be meeting BJ. Would you mind if I just make sure he is OK?'

'Not at all. You go ahead and do what you have to.'

Turning to BJ, the Major said, 'Let's go to the Information Desk and see if Mr Sullivan is there. If not we will ask them to put a call out on the loudspeaker.'

Approaching the desk, there was no sign of anyone that may be meeting a passenger.

BJ spoke. 'Good morning. Can you please put a call out for Mr Neil Sullivan?'

'Your name is?'

'BJ Conway.'

She announced, 'This is a call for Mr Neil Sullivan meeting passenger Mr BJ Conway. Will you please come to the Information desk. Mr Neil Sullivan, please come to the Information desk.'

The minutes ticked by. Nothing. No one appeared.

After a while, the Major asked, 'Can you try again please?'

Still nothing.

A look of concern betrayed BJ's feelings and he was panic stricken.

The Major had had a bad feeling about this from the outset. And now he was being proved right. But he did not want BJ to worry so did his best to speak reassuringly.

'Son, don't worry. I anticipated this. We will go to Harry's then later we will take you to the address you have just in case Mr Sullivan was held up or for some other reason was unable to meet you.' But he knew his words had a hollow ring, as deep down he doubted them.

The four of them proceeded to the car park. Three weeks earlier, the Major and Anna had driven to Harry's place, picked him up and then headed for the airport. After they said their farewells, Harry had taken the car to his house to keep. Now the Major loaded the suitcases into its cavernous boot. He opened the rear door for Anna and BJ and then got

Chapter Eighteen

into the drivers seat. Harry got into the passenger side.

BJ was very quiet and looked out of the window. England. How different the buildings were to those in India. And the cars too. He noticed the road and traffic signs—something he had not seen in India.

He thought of the taxi and train journeys to and from the orphanage. He did not know what he was going to and what lay ahead of him. Now the same feelings overcame him. He was still worried about where he was going to live. He did not have any money to go into an hotel. And he had no idea what it would cost anyway.

Anna glanced at him and saw that his face was grim. He was clenching his teeth and she saw it in his taut face muscles. Sensing his concern she put her hand over his saying, 'Everything will be OK. Daddy and I will not desert you. We have already discussed it and will look after you.'

He looked at her in surprise. 'You have?'

She nodded squeezing his hand.

'Thank you. But you know how I feel. I am of a different culture and am not in your social class. I do not want to be a burden or an embarrassment.'

The Major uttered, 'BJ do not think like that. We have enjoyed your company during the sail and we are doing what we are because we want to. Otherwise we will not have bothered. While we were at sea, I contacted Harry on the ship to shore telephone and briefed him on the position. That is why we are going to his house now. So please relax. As Anna said we will not desert you.'

'Thank you sir. Thank you all.'

Harry thought about how the Major had described BJ over the phone. He was seeing why they were drawn to him.

BJ noticed all the houses were almost the same with gardens, some with garages in front of which stood cars. They turned into the drive of a big house. As they got out the front door opened and a woman approached them. 'Alfie lovely to see you again.' She gave him a hug and a kiss on the cheek.

She then turned to Anna and greeted her similarly. She knew possibly they would have a friend with them so she turned to BJ, 'You must be BJ.

I am Ruth. Pleased to meet you.'

'Pleased to meet you too ma'am.'

'Let's go inside.'

The house was different to any BJ had been in before. The furniture was different. Everything was different. And there was a television.

'Sit down BJ. Make yourself comfortable. Would you like something to drink? A beer?'

'No thank you ma'am. I do not drink. I will have whatever anyone else is having, hot or cold.'

'Please call me Ruth.'

'The Major said I will just have a hot drink, tea or coffee whatever is convenient. Is that OK for you Anna? And BJ?'

Each concurred.

BJ was not sure where to sit. There was a long sofa, a shorter one and three single chairs. He went to sit on a single but Anna said, 'Come and sit here with me'. She sat on the shorter sofa and BJ sat at the other end.

The drinks arrived and Harry and Alfie made small talk while Anna and BJ listened, sometimes being drawn into the conversation. After a while Ruth called, 'Lunch is ready.'

Harry, followed by the Major, Anna and BJ, went into another room. There was a dining table and six chairs and a large sideboard. Ruth said, 'Anna you and BJ sit there, Alfie and Harry can sit the other side and I will sit at the end by the door so I can get in to the kitchen easily.' There was fruit juice in a jug and Anna poured some into BJ's glass. Lunch was a warm chicken salad.

When they had finished eating, Harry said, 'Let's go into the sitting room.' They sat in the seats they had been in before and Harry said to BJ, 'I noticed you had a guitar case. How long have you been playing the guitar?'

'I first started when I was about five.'

'Five?'

'My father played and he taught me how to tune it. My fingers were too small to play chords so I used to lay it on my knees or the bed and

Chapter Eighteen

just play the notes practicing the scales on all strings and up the fret board. After a while, I used to be able to play some simple songs. In school a teacher taught me more.'

Anna said, 'He not only plays the guitar very well now but he sings too.'

The Major said, 'He is too modest to make a point of it but we learned on the ship he was in a club's resident group and they performed at hotels and in cabaret.'

BJ was by now doing his usual fidgeting when embarrassed. Anna put a reassuring hand over his and squeezed it saying, 'Don't be embarrassed. You are among friends.'

She continued, 'A number of passengers who recognised him told the Entertainments Officer and members of the band about him. He was asked to perform and was received very well.'

Ruth came in with the drinks, which BJ was grateful for. It was a very welcome interruption because the focus was no more on him. BJ got up respectfully as a lady had entered. She said, 'Don't stand up. I am not used to it. You are showing the men up.'

The men laughed.

They settled into general conversation mostly conducted by the older ones. BJ was happy just to listen to them and enjoy the banter.

Time went by and the Major got up saying, 'We will have to be on our way. Thanks for your hospitality and for looking after the car.'

'You're welcome.'

'Nice to see you Anna and to meet you BJ. We will meet again no doubt.'

BJ thought, 'No doubt? I hope so. I really hope so.' He did say, 'And you too. Thank you for your hospitality.'

They all walked out to the car. Harry opened the passenger door for Anna but she said, 'Thank you but I will sit in the back with BJ.'

The Major reversed out of the drive and all waved goodbye.

BJ was very apprehensive.

The Major asked, 'What is Sullivan's address?'

Anna said, '75 Stones Avenue, West Kington.'

The Major had to stop and ask where the road was. There they all got out and the Major said, 'Let's see if he is in first.'

He led the way to the front door and knocked. Not a sound was heard from inside. He knocked again. Still no answer.

He said, 'Let's speak to the neighbour and see if they know anything.'

He went next door and knocked. Immediately, a man came to the door. 'Mr Sullivan from next door was supposed to meet a passenger at the docks but did not turn up. Does he still live there?'

'Yes. But he and his brother flew back to India two days ago. They received a cablegram telling them their father was seriously ill in hospital and was in an oxygen tent. He was not expected to live long.'

'Thank you,' they said and they turned and walked back to the car.

They got in but the Major did not start the car. He turned around looked at BJ and said, 'In a way we are glad it has turned out like this because we want you to come and live with us.'

BJ was initially speechless. He struggled to compose himself and with a quivering voice said, 'But sir, that woman on the ship said it was a shame that Anna was getting friendly with an Indian. What about your neighbours? What will they think?'

'I would be surprised if they were that small minded and thought unkindly. Besides those that we are friendly with know I was based in India and Anna went to school there. I do not anticipate a problem. Even if I am mistaken about them, it will make no difference. We want you with us. On the ship, Anna and I had already talked about you coming to live with us sooner or later.'

'On the ship?'

'Yes. From the outset we were uncomfortable about the arrangement you had but we knew that because you are a man of principle you would want to keep to it. Now you are released from any obligation to Mr Sullivan.'

BJ merely nodded saying, 'Thank you sir, thank you Anna.' Anna squeezed his hand. The Major started the engine and headed off.

Chapter Nineteen

Some fifteen to twenty minutes later, they were on a road running alongside a river. They turned into a wide tree-lined avenue and halfway down the road, they turned into a wide graveled drive. The house was about seventy-five feet back from the road with flower borders and lawn. A dog started to bark. The sound told BJ it was a big one. There was a high hedge affording privacy from the road.

Anna went to the double garage and opened it. There was a small white car on one side. The Major drove in and himself got out and opened the boot. The dog was now barking excitedly. Anna said, 'Daddy I will open the door and get hold of Bruno. He has not met BJ and I do not know how he will react.'

'I like dogs.'

'Bruno is very protective and does not like strangers. Even after he got to recognise our visitors, he would not let them touch him. He would get up and walk away.'

BJ helped the Major unload the suitcases and guitar case and followed him through the enclosed entrance porch and the inner door into the hall. The dog was a huge black long-haired Alsatian and he looked like a bear. He was on his hind legs straining against the lead barking frantically and threateningly as Anna held on tightly.

Anna said, 'Bruno, sit.'

Bruno sat, still barking aggressively. BJ got down on his haunches resting on his toes. He said softly, 'Easy Bruno,' slowly extending the back of his right hand. 'Easy boy.'

Bruno hesitated and then slowly quieted. He turned his head sideways, while still looking uncertainly at BJ. BJ continued to extend his hand towards his muzzle and after further hesitation, Bruno first sniffed it tentatively and then started to lick it. Anna had squeezed both hands at various times so he would have smelt her. He had accepted BJ. But that was not all. Anna relaxed her grip on the lead as Bruno now licked his face. BJ rubbed his hands on the top of his head and sides of his neck. What happened next stunned Anna and the Major, who were transfixed throughout. They looked at each other in amazement. Bruno turned over on his back exposing his vulnerable stomach. BJ rubbed his neck and then the underside of his leg where it met the shoulder. His leg started to twitch and Anna said, 'You have found his tickle spot.'

'Tickle spot?'

'See how his leg is twitching? He likes it and you obviously. He would not expose his under belly otherwise. Apart from us he never did that with anyone else before. It is as if he is giving you his blessing and accepting you as a member of the pack.'

Then suddenly, as if remembering who he was, Bruno turned his attention to Anna and the Major greeting them excitedly with his tail wagging frantically. He was one happy dog. He ran up and down the hall barking. He stopped and moved around them slowly rubbing his body against each in turn.

The Major broke the moment. 'Anna, take BJ to his bedroom and show him around the house and the gardens. I'll take our suitcases up.'

They went up the stairs and Anna led BJ to a room on the left hand side at the back.

'This is your room.' It was a large one with a double bed and a bedside cabinet on either side, two-three foot cupboards, a four foot five-drawer chest, a single easy chair and a small coffee table. There were two windows, one large facing the back garden and a smaller one on the other outside wall. Plenty of natural light came through the net curtains. 'I will let you have my transistor radio.'

'What about you?'

'I have a spare one.'

'Daddy has the front bedroom the other side of the landing and I am also at the front next to you. Come I will show you the bathrooms and the rest of the house and gardens.'

'Before we leave, now that I am going to be living here, I must give

Chapter Nineteen

you back your mum's bangle. Thank you for trusting me with it.'

'Don't worry about that yet. I know where it is. But as you are now one of us here, let me have your towels and toiletries. There is no need to keep anything separate.'

Out on the landing she said, 'This is one toilet and this is another that has a bath in it. The hot water boiler comes on when you turn on this tap. The other tap is the cold one.

'This is my bedroom,' she said, and led him in. It was tastefully decorated with pink the predominant colour on the soft furnishings and bed linen. He saw two badminton racquets in the corner.

'You play badminton? Can I feel them?'

'Of course. Do you play too?'

Picking up each in turn to feel the balance and test the tension of the strings he said, 'Yes. Love the game.'

'We can book a court and play. I know others that may be willing to make it a regular thing.'

'That would be nice. Swimming and badminton are my two favourite activities.'

She picked up the transistor radio from her bedside table and handed it to him. They walked into his room. 'Which side will you be sleeping?'

'The side nearest to us.'

She placed the radio on the bedside cabinet. 'I'll show you how to tune into the stations,' and proceeded to do so. 'I'll leave it on a pirate station.'

'Pirate station?'

She explained why it was known as that.

They walked back onto the landing into a small room facing the front garden.

'This is Daddy's office.' In it was a chair and desk and telephone, an easy chair and on a bookcase was a reel-to-reel tape deck and two speakers on the wall.

'Le's go into Daddy's room.'

'Daddy can we come in?'

'Of course.'

This bedroom was also tastefully decorated but more soberly perhaps reflecting his maleness and maturity.

'BJ, do you have a dressing gown or a bath robe?'

'What are they sir?'

'Here you are. This is the dressing gown that goes over your pyjamas or night suit if you need to leave your room at night. This is the bathrobe that you use when you go to have a bath. As you can see it is made of toweling material. You take these,' handing him spare ones from a drawer.

'Thank you sir. Now I remember seeing them in the films.'

'Also as temperatures are still low, you will need an outer coat. Here try this one.'

BJ tried it on and while not a perfect fit it was suitable. 'Good, it fits OK. Keep it.'

'Thank you sir.'

'You go downstairs with Anna and I will put them in your room.'

They went down and Bruno came and joined them. He kept gently nipping his hand until he started to rub the top of his head and side of his neck.

The entrance hall, he now noticed, was very wide. There was a cloakroom with a toilet, small vanity unit and access to under stairs storage area. The lounge was a large room with two long sofas, three single chairs, a sideboard, a showcase and a stereo radiogram.

'This one we use when we have family friends over.'

'This is the family room where we spend most time as it has the television. This is my mother and father's wedding photo. I think that dress is lovely. I'd like to marry in one like that.'

There was a third room also used for visitors, mainly Anna's.

She led him into the kitchen/dining room that extended the width of the house. There were big windows and two pairs of French doors. There was an inner narrow hall that led to the double garage and on the other side to the utility room and through that into the indoor heated swimming pool. It was 24 feet by 12 feet. At one end there was a toilet and shower area and some bathrobes hanging on hooks.

BJ knelt down to put a hand in the water and test the temperature. It felt warm.

'We try to keep it at around 72 degrees.'

'So this why you are such a good swimmer. You can swim everyday.'

'You can too. We can do what we did at sea; go running. We can take Bruno along. He will love that. We can then have a swim so we don't have to change our routine. This is now your home and we want you to be comfortable.'

'Thank you. With running, badminton and swimming it will keep us fit.'

They walked through to the outside onto a graveled patio with a wooden table and fixed bench seats. Bruno ran onto the extensive lawn and played with a ball. The garden was huge and completely secluded. It was bordered with tall shrubs and a hedge. There was an abundance of flowerbeds and borders that were still bare because of the time of the year. But there were several rose bushes, which had started to show signs of having woken from their dormancy.

'This is an apple tree and the other one is pear.'

He teased her, 'No mango?'

She laughed nudging him in the ribs. 'No. No mango.'

'We get a lot of birds that take food from the feeders. You see those things hanging from the branches of the trees? In summer we have lots of songbirds. The robins come quite close to take bread pieces.'

At the foot of the garden was a shed and greenhouse in which there were a number of trays with seedlings.

They walked back inside and the Major was now downstairs.

'Sir, Anna you have a massive house; like a mansion. Thank you for having me.'

'You are welcome.'

'I need to make a few calls. Anna why don't the two of you take Bruno for a walk and you can show BJ around the area a little. There is no hurry. Sandra has made us a beef casserole with dumplings for dinner and an apple pie for dessert. I will pop around later to thank her and Keith and give them their presents.'

As soon as Bruno saw the lead, he became very excited. They walked out of the house towards the main road. She had a routine with Bruno so they always crossed the road at the zebra crossing. Bruno sat at the edge of the pavement until Anna stepped off it. There was a gap in the railings and hedge that led down a few steps to the riverside. It was cool and there were plenty of walkers strolling and feeding the ducks. They walked over a bridge to the wooded area on the other side. Anna unleashed Bruno and he wandered off to sniff around and relieve himself. Anna and BJ continued walking along the footpath. Birds were twittering in the trees and grey squirrels scurried up and down the trunks and along the ground.

BJ took it all in. So this is Blighty, he thought. He liked what he was seeing. He could not have wished for a better first day here.

'I come here regularly with Bruno. Sometimes we go to a field about half a mile away and we play ball. We throw it and he runs and brings it back to us so we can throw it again. He loves it and is good exercise for him.'

'He really is a beautiful dog.'

They strolled stopping from time to time to stare out at the river as rowing boats went past.

'They are members of a rowing club. From time to time they have regattas and we come and watch them.'

'You live in a very nice house and area.'

'We like it. It is a pity my mother is not here to meet you. She would like you.'

With that they turned back and headed home. Bruno knew the routine and as soon as they got to the bridge he sat while Anna put the lead back on.

'Do you want to take him?'

'Will he be alright with me?' he said, and Bruno was. He walked to heel on a slack lead.

When they got home he took the lead off Bruno and Anna said, 'Go

Chapter Nineteen

into the television room and I will bring you a drink. Tea or coffee?'

'Tea please, thanks.'

Bruno followed him in and lay down at his feet with his head resting on them. The Major was still in the neighbour's house but he had seen them walk by. Within a few minutes he arrived with Sandra and Keith. Bruno heard them and barked twice though not in a threatening way.

Anna said, 'It's OK, it's probably Daddy. That is Bruno's way of telling us someone is coming.' She went into the hallway just as they coming through the door.

'Hello Sandra, hello Keith,' and to the Major she said, 'BJ is in the TV room.'

'Tea everyone?'

'That will be nice,' Sandra said. Anna went into the kitchen.

'BJ I want you to meet our neighbours.' Respectfully, BJ got up. Bruno did too.

'Keith, Sandra, this is BJ, our friend and guest, who I told you about.'

Keith shook hands and said, 'Pleased to meet you BJ. I have heard a lot about you. All good, I hasten to add.'

'Pleased to meet you too sir. And you ma'am.'

'Oh please call us Keith and Sandra.'

'I am not used to addressing my elders by their first names so bear with me please when I don't.'

Anna came in carrying a tray with a pot of tea and five cups and saucers a sugar bowl and a milk jug.

The Major said, 'Let's all sit down.' Keith sat on a single chair, Sandra one end of the large sofa and the Major sat on the second easy chair. BJ sat at one end of the smaller one. Anna served everyone and then sat close to BJ shoulders touching slightly.

'Sandra comes in and helps us out daily. She makes sure Bruno is ok and takes him out for a walk. It was Sandra that prepared our dinner for tonight. Keith is a landscape gardener by profession and he looks after our garden. In the summer it is very colourful. We are very lucky to have them as neighbours.'

'It's a pleasure and we are glad to help.'

They drank their tea and chatted generally. BJ listened respectfully, keeping silent.

After a short while, Sandra and Keith got up. 'Thank you for the tea. See you again BJ,' and they left.

Time had flown. BJ said, 'I need to unpack. Will you excuse me please? Also, is it alright if I have a wash?'

'You don't have to ask. This is your home now. There are towels in the bathroom.'

He went upstairs and unpacked. There was plenty of storage and hanging space for all his clothes. He washed and then filled the basin with cold water, burying his face in it for as long as he could hold his breath. He came up for air and felt completely refreshed.

He put on clean clothes and bundled the dirty ones neatly, placing them on the chair.

When he went downstairs, Anna said, 'You have changed. Let me have your dirty clothes and I will put them in the laundry basket.'

'Do you have a laundry man or woman?'

'No we have a washing machine and we have to do our own laundry and ironing like on the ship. But Sandra helps. She puts the clothes in the machine and when I come home I put them on the line.'

'Dinner will be ready soon.'

The Major was in his den, so BJ lingered in the dining room and kitchen. 'Can I lay the table?'

'The crockery and glasses are in the dresser and the cutlery is in the right drawer. Set them at this end of the table. Daddy can sit at the head and I will sit opposite you.'

He had just about finished when she said, 'It's ready. Can you call Daddy please?'

BJ knocked on the door, which was open anyway. 'Sir, dinner is ready.'

Chapter Nineteen

They sat down and ate in silence. Initially, it was a warm dinner, but suddenly it became heavy. The Major and Anna looked at each other sensing BJ was troubled. And he was.

When they had finished, the Major asked, 'BJ are you ok? You look troubled.'

He looked at each in turn and answered 'No sir. I have something on my mind. May I have a word with you in private please? Anna is it ok with you? I am not being rude.'

'I know you are not. Go into the den and I will bring you hot drinks.'

They went into the Major's office. He sat on the chair at the desk and turned it around to face the easy chair. 'Please sit down BJ.'

BJ sat and settled himself.

To put him at ease, the Major said, 'This is my den and office. When Anna's friends are over I sometimes sit here reading in the quiet and solitude. It is my bolt hole.'

'Bolt hole?'

'It is a place to where one escapes to get away from others. Not that I want to escape from Anna and her friends. I just take the opportunity to enjoy my own space as I do not want to cramp Anna's style. She is young and needs young company. You will be that for her now you are here.'

Anna knocked on the door and came in with two cups of coffee. She left, shutting the door behind her.

They sat awhile sipping their drinks. BJ asked, 'May I put the cup down please?'

There was a daily newspaper on the desk and he said, 'Put it on this.'

BJ did so, and settling into the chair again, he leaned forward, arms on its rests and looking straight into the Major's eyes he asked, 'Sir, will you have me as a son-in-law please?'

The Major had his cup to his mouth and was taking a drink as BJ spoke. He spluttered and sprayed coffee towards him. 'Sorry, you took me by surprise. Here use this paper hankie.'

'Sir, it is me that is sorry. You have only known me a couple of weeks.

I had no right to ask you that. I hope you will forget what I said and not hold it against me.'

'Don't be sorry and no I will not forget. Your forthrightness surprised me. You don't waste time cutting to the chase. But to answer your question, I would like nothing better. I would be happy to be your father-in-law. Does Anna know what's on your mind?'

'No sir. As I have said before I do not have your social and financial status. I know Anna is comfortable with me. Beyond that, I dare not think. I have to find work as I have to pay you for staying here. I must build a financial base. I hope that in time Anna will feel the same way as I do. Until I have that base and am sure of where I stand, I will not commit to her. She deserves more than I can give her presently.'

The Major handed BJ his drink. There was a lump in his throat and he needed the time to get a hold of himself. 'You are a very honest and humble person.'

'Thank you sir,' he said and drank his coffee.

'Sir you have accepted I am a product of the country in which I was born and its culture. I will make mistakes now that I am here and learn to adapt. I will never do or say anything to deliberately offend you, Anna and your friends. I am starting a new life in a new country. Please help me to adjust.'

'Just be yourself, BJ and you won't go wrong. Nothing about you causes me concern. You are a well adjusted person and very respectful and well mannered.'

'Come, let's go and join Anna.'

She was in the TV room seated at one end of the sofa. As they entered, Bruno rose and came and rubbed himself against BJ's leg. BJ sat on an easy chair and the Major on the other.

BJ said, 'Anna, I am asking you what I asked the Major. Please help me to settle into living in England and the new culture. Inevitably, I will make mistakes but you know I would never do anything to offend you.'

'I know that and I told you that at sea. And of course I will help you.'

'Yes you did and thank you.'

'Now sir, Anna, the last two days, a whole gamut of emotions has assailed me. The last night, end of the sail, Mr Sullivan not turning up and not being home and now here I am. Suddenly it is all so overwhelming. Would you mind if I just went to my room?'

'Not at all.'

'Goodnight sir, goodnight Anna. And again thank you for everything.'

BJ got up and rubbed Bruno's head and neck before leaving and going upstairs. He stripped off and lay on top of the bed for a while. He then got his bible and read his mother's message and a few chapters and said his prayers. He now felt more relaxed. He put out the bedside lamp and went to sleep.

Chapter Twenty

Meanwhile after he had gone, the Major said, 'I like him. I like him very much.' He continued, 'He is very humble. To make things as easy as possible for him we need to make him feel wanted and welcome.'

They were silent as they mulled things over and then Anna said, 'Tomorrow I will contact the Personnel Director at the office and see if there are any vacancies. BJ has experience in banking so surely it could be used in finance.'

'And I will take him to the bank to check whether his money has come through and also to register for a National Health Insurance Number; he will need it to work. We will make an early start and meet for lunch at O'Grady's. If you have good news, you can tell BJ, otherwise we will just get the local Gazette and see what jobs are available. Hopefully all will go well for his sake.'

She agreed. After a while she said, 'Daddy, today has also been an emotional day for me too. You know how I feel about BJ and I am so happy he is living with us. Thank you for that. He feels so helpless and indebted to us.'

'You love him. I like him. Bruno loves him and you know that is most unusual. If your mum was alive I know she would have been impressed with him too.'

'I will have a soak and go to bed. Goodnight Daddy,' kissing him on the top of his head.

As she lay in the bath, allowing the hot water to relax her body, she thought about the day's events. Because he was let down, he was here and she could not be happier. Fate had intervened. She thought about BJ getting a cancellation at five weeks notice, her father falling, him being on hand to help and them being on the sail together. The last two weeks had been the happiest of her life.

Relaxed, she dried off and returned to her room. She climbed into bed and before long was sound asleep.

The next morning BJ woke more or less at his usual time. He looked around to get his bearings and realisation dawned with the new day. He tried to keep as quiet as possible as he did not want to disturb the others. He washed and dressed. Returning to his room, he pulled the easy chair by the garden window. He read the bible and said his prayers after which he went down the stairs. Bruno heard him and came to the foot of the stairs to greet him. He went into the TV room and sat in the silence.

Though he had tried not to disturb the others, they were in fact awake and heard him go into the bathroom. Because all was quiet in his room while he was engrossed in his morning meditation, they thought he might have gone back to bed. They then heard him go down the stairs. The Major went to the bathroom. Washed and dressed he joined BJ who immediately got up. 'Good morning sir.'

'Don't get up. Good morning BJ. Did you sleep well?'

'Yes sir, I guess I was emotionally and mentally exhausted.'

'I trust you no longer feel troubled and overwhelmed.'

'No sir, thank you. Today is another day. However, I am still apprehensive about finding work and not behaving properly in your house. I will just take it moment by moment.'

'I know you are concerned but Anna and I will do all we can for you. So please trust us and try not to worry.'

'Thank you sir.'

Just as he finished talking Anna walked into the room. 'Good morning Daddy, good morning BJ.' Again BJ got up. 'Good morning,' both men said simultaneously.

She sat while Bruno made a fuss of her. 'Daddy what would you like for breakfast?'

'Cornflakes and toast will be fine.'

'Same for you BJ?'

'Yes please.'

Anna left to go into the kitchen.

'Later on, Anna has some personal business to attend to. You and I will go to your bank and check whether your money has come through. Then we will go to the Department of Health and Social Security so you can register. You will need a National Insurance number for when you start work. What bank is it and where?'

'It is the Oriental Bank in London. I was told to contact it and give them my Indian account number.'

The Major, having been in a similar situation when he left India, knew what to do. He left the room and came back with a telephone directory. He found an address and telephone number for the bank. 'I will call them after nine o'clock, when they open.'

They breakfasted. Conversation was easy and the atmosphere relaxed, quite different from the previous evening.

'Can I help clear the dishes and wash up?'

'Thank you. Help me clear the table and you can join Daddy. I will wash. There is no need to dry as I just leave everything to drain and dry naturally.'

After he had done so, he asked, 'Can you excuse me please? As we are going out I will need to change.'

At ten past nine, Anna went into the office and telephoned her place of work. She asked the receptionist, 'Emily, this is Anna McLeod. Can you put me through to Margaret Waters please?'

'Anna, good to hear from you. Margaret, I have Anna McLeod on the line for you.'

'Put her through thanks Emily.'

'Anna, you're back. Is everything OK?'

'Yes fine. Margaret, can I have an appointment to see Mr Baker please, as soon as possible today?'

'Can I ask what the purpose is?'

'I cannot tell you Margaret. It is a private matter.'

'You are not resigning, are you?'

'Absolutely not. I am home and looking forward to returning on

Monday and catching up with all the news.'

'Can you hold the line please, and I will speak to him.'

Margaret buzzed Mr Baker, 'I have Anna McLeod on the phone. She wants to see you this morning about a private matter.'

'OK, make an appointment.'

She looked at the diary and said 'I'll make it for half past ten. Is that alright?'

'Fine.'

'Sorry to keep you on hold. He'll see you at half past ten.'

'Lovely thanks.'

She rejoined the others and nodded to her father. 'I've got an appointment at half past ten. I'll go and get ready.'

The Major then went and called the bank. He explained the position and provided all necessary information. After being transferred to the correct section and repeating himself, he was kept on hold. The speaker returned, 'Yes sir, the money is here.'

'We will be in later. Who do we ask for?'

'My name is Simon Porter.'

'As we are travelling from outside the city we do not know how long we will be.'

'That is alright. I will be expecting you. Go to the Service counter when you arrive. I will tell my colleague you are coming.'

'Thank you Mr Porter. I appreciate your help.'

'You're welcome.'

'BJ, can you get your passport and bank passbook and any other details you have. Your money is in and we will go there first. We will sort out your National Insurance afterwards.'

BJ did as instructed. The Major shouted, 'Anna, we're off. Best of luck.'

'You too. I'll see you later,' she said, and he and BJ left the house. 'Because it is a working day, there will be parking difficulties. My office is not in the vicinity of the bank so there is no point in taking the car. We

Chapter Twenty

will travel by train and tube, the underground, to get to the bank. Now do not worry, I will buy the tickets.'

'Thank you sir.'

The Major pointed out certain buildings during the ten-minute walk to the station. He bought the tickets, and arriving at the platform did not have to wait very long before the train arrived. As the rush hour was over, it was not crowded and they were able to find seats away from the other passengers.

'This is a fast train making one stop, so we should be at the terminus in about twenty minutes.'

The train sped along through mainly built-up areas and stations. The journey ended and he was in a huge station with numerous platforms. The Major had their return tickets clipped and they entered the concourse. It was massive. He took in the shops and restaurants as they walked to the underground. They went down the escalators into the bowels of the earth. He heard the rumble of the train in the tunnel and saw a speck of light that became bigger and eventually the train was there. The doors opened automatically. BJ was fascinated by it all. Another part of English life, he thought.

At the other end, they went up the escalator. Soon they were out in the open and he saw daylight. But it was now drizzling. As the bank was a few minutes walk away, the Major said, 'We will wait here in the dry. The clouds are not rain clouds and hopefully the drizzle will stop soon.'

'Everything is so different, the cars, the buses, taxis, buildings, road markings and signs.'

'I found things different in India when I first got there.'

It stopped drizzling and the sun was warming and drying the ground as the wind gently nudged the clouds away. They headed off. BJ noted that this was clearly a business area. There were a number of apparently office buildings. He saw the bank sign and they entered. The Information counter was to the right.

'Good morning, madam. This is Mr BJ Conway, the account holder who has just arrived here and I am Mr McLeod accompanying him. I spoke to Mr Porter earlier and he is expecting us.'

'Yes, sir. I will let him know you are here.'

She returned saying, 'He will be with you in a minute. Take a seat please.'

It was less than a minute and a side door opened. 'I am Mr Porter. You must be Mr McLeod and you, Mr Conway.' Well it had to be obvious who was the one from India. 'Pleased to meet you both,' he said, shaking hands with each. He winced slightly at BJ's firm grip.

'Come this way please,' he said and led them along a short corridor to an interview room. When all were seated, he opened a file that was on the desk. 'May I see your passport and passbook please Mr Conway?'

BJ handed them across. Returning them, Mr Porter said, 'Thank you. After commission and the rate of exchange on the day it was received here, there is a net balance of £182, 15s, 04d. What is your current address?'

BJ looked at the Major who answered, 'He is staying with me. The address is 15 Primrose Avenue, East Kington.' He wrote it down. 'Do you wish to transfer the money into a current account or do you wish to retain the passbook?' BJ looked at the Major who advised, 'Keep it as a passbook for the present.'

'No problem. Excuse me while I go and get your new passbook. Oh, do you want to withdraw any money? I will do it all at once.'

BJ had no idea of how much he would need. The Major said, 'Get £22, 15s, 04d leaving a round balance of £160.'

Mr Porter left. After a while he returned. 'Sorry to have kept you waiting.' He opened the passbook to show BJ all the details and entries, counting the money as he placed it on the desk, 'ten, fifteen, twenty, twenty one, twenty two pounds and ten shillings, fifteen shillings and four pence; £22 15s 4d.'

BJ picked it up and put it all in his inside jacket pocket. 'Thank you.'

Mr Porter opened the door for them and led them to the front entrance. 'If I can be of help with anything please contact me.' They shook hands and BJ and the Major left the building.

They arrived back in East Kington at a quarter to noon. 'We are not going home just yet.' He led BJ to a restaurant and entered.

Meanwhile, Anna had driven to the office for her appointment at half past ten. In the foyer, she pressed the button for the lift. The doors opened and a colleague said, 'Anna. You're back but you're not supposed to return till Monday. What are you doing here?'

'I am just visiting on a private matter.'

'I'll see you on Monday.'

'Yes.' She pressed the button for the fifth and top floor where the directors and top management had their offices. 'Good morning Margaret.'

'Good morning Anna. My, you are glowing. It must have been a good holiday and sail.'

'Yes it was. The ship was lovely and the sail very enjoyable.'

'I'll tell Mr Baker you are here.'

She buzzed him. 'Anna McLeod is here.'

'Send her in.'

'Go in please Anna.'

As she was about to knock on the door it opened. 'Good morning. Come in Anna. Take a seat.'

'How was the break? You look well.'

'The wedding was spectacular, the reception lasted days and the hospitality was second to none. It was as well that we sailed back. We needed the time to relax and recover.'

'How did you find India? Has it changed much?'

'It was nice to visit. But in the five years since I left, things have changed. Unfortunately, not for the better. The indigenous people perhaps have not noticed it as much as it has crept up on them. So while it was enjoyable I am glad to be back.'

'Margaret tells me you want to see me about a private and personal matter. I hope all is well.'

'Yes Mr Baker, very well. But I am not here for myself. We have a guest from India staying with us. He does not know I am here seeing you.

You are often looking to recruit experienced staff and I wonder if you will consider interviewing him.'

'Tell me about him.'

'He is twenty-one and worked in the corporate section of the Oriental Bank for five years after he left school. He handled business loans and finance and I think he also did some debt management.'

'How long have you and your father known him?'

'Properly? Less than three weeks. But I knew of him when I was in India. As you know I went to a convent when my father was based there. In the same town as my convent was a boys' boarding school. BJ was in the orphanage attached to it. We went to each other's concerts and sports days and some special events, otherwise there was no contact. But he boxed for the school in the annual inter school tournament. Also, in the latter years he was a successful runner. So we got to know who he was as he was announced before his fights and presented with his trophies.

He also appeared in the school concerts. At the quayside before embarking, I went to the bathroom and when I returned, BJ was helping my father who had tripped and fallen. I saw him before he saw me. We recognised each other. My father was grateful for his help and we all got friendly on the sail.'

'His experience could be useful to us'. He buzzed Margaret. 'Margaret can you bring me an Information pack and application form please?'

She knocked and entered handing him the folder.

'What is his name?'

'Bryan Conway but he is known by his initials; BJ.'

'Get him to fill in the application form and bring him here tomorrow at half past ten. He should bring his passport and all other papers also.'

'Thank you Mr Baker for at least agreeing to see him. He will be surprised. I hope you consider him suitable. My father and I do believe he has something to offer any employer.'

'You obviously do, otherwise you will not have spoken to me. Both of you must have great faith in him.'

But to him it was more than that. It was not just the holiday tan. It

Chapter Twenty

was in her eyes; they were aglow. The girl was in love. She looked like his teenage daughter did when she found her first boyfriend.

'Bye Anna,' and opened the door for her.

'Bye Margaret.'

She was elated. If Mr Baker was prepared to see BJ then she was sure he would be taken on.

She drove home and as there was still time before she met her father and BJ in the restaurant, she made herself a cup of tea and relaxed, thumbing through a women's magazine. When it was time, she dabbed her face with a moist flannel and combed her hair.

She strolled leisurely to the restaurant and going in, she saw they had not yet arrived. She went to a corner table and studied the menu. While doing so, she heard the door open and looking up saw them. They headed straight for her and sat down.

'Get everything sorted out?' she asked.

'Yes, how did you get on?'

'Favourably. I will explain once we have ordered.'

She knew what she was ordering but waited for them to see what the fare was.

The waitress arrived, 'Good afternoon. What would you like?'

The Major asked BJ, 'What are you having?'

Being polite, he said, 'I will have whatever the two of you are.'

Anna said, 'I will have a ploughman's please.'

'Is that ok with you BJ?' the Major asked.

'Yes fine thank you.'

'Three Ploughman's please and coffee for three. May we have some water also please?'

'Certainly.'

'BJ, on the ship you said you hoped to get work where you could use your financial experience. Last night you also asked us to help you settle in to life in England.'

BJ merely nodded.

145

'Well, I have some good news for you. I work in finance too. I have just seen my Personnel Director and he wants to see you tomorrow at half past ten. I have an Information pack and application form. Is that ok? I do not know whether he will offer you a job but at least he is prepared to interview you.'

'I feel I am dreaming and will wake up still in India. Words fail me. I don't know what to say other than thank you both again.'

'We know you mean it son. We know you mean it. After we have eaten, I will go and get the car and meet you both at the far end of Acer Road. We will then go to the DHSS office to register you BJ. You will need a NI Number especially for tomorrow. We also must get you registered with a doctor. We will go the surgery we use. The doctor will want to meet you so they will make an appointment. Perhaps it will be tomorrow as it is not a medical consultation.'

'Can I just say something please? On the boat an elderly couple made a comment that it was a shame you, Anna, were getting friendly with an Indian. You both have opened your house to me. Now there is a chance I could be taken on by the company that you work for. If I am, your colleagues will find out we know each other and I am a guest in your home. As I am an Indian what will they say? I do not want to bring you both down. I would not be happy if people spoke and thought unkindly of you because of me.'

The Major said, 'We were not bothered on the ship. We are not bothered here. And if people who we know say anything bad about you then they are not worth knowing. Our friends will be your friends too. Don't worry. Right Anna?'

'Daddy is right. Besides we spent so much time together at sea you must know we are not worried what anyone thinks. If I was, I would not have spoken to my director about you.'

'Put like that, I understand. But you must know why I am worried. I never expected what happened on the ship. It upset you, it upset me too.'

'Trust us. We will support you every step of the way.'

The drinks arrived and the food shortly later. BJ had not taken in what a Ploughman's lunch was when he saw the menu. But he liked what was

Chapter Twenty

before him. Crusty bread and butter, cheese and salad and pickle.

They ate in silence and then drank their coffees.

'Please excuse me. I will go and get the car. I will be about fifteen minutes. Are you ok for the bill Anna?'

'Yes of course.'

And he left.

'I hope you don't mind my taking it upon myself to speak to my boss and get you an appointment.'

'Of course not. I am grateful for your help. Also I would love to work in the same place as you.'

'I do not know if it will lead to an immediate offer of a job. But if it does although we will be in the same building we may not be in the same section or on the same floor.'

'How many floors are there?'

'Five. I am on the second, and the directors and top management are on the top floor.'

She attracted the waitress' attention. 'Bill please.'

She paid, including a tip. The waitress said, 'Thank you.'

Chapter Twenty One

They left and walked past a cinema. The posters indicated it was showing a Western film.

'You said you like the pictures particularly the Westerns. Would you like to see this one?'

'Is it expensive?'

'I will treat you.'

'You can't do that. The man pays.'

'We are friends aren't we?'

'Yes.'

'Then let me do this for you, your first film in England. You can return the favour next time.'

They were where they should be, and the Major pulled up. They had to go into the next town, which was much larger, where the DHSS office was. They parked the car and entered the office. The receptionist said, 'Good afternoon. How can I help you?'

'Good afternoon. Our friend arrived from India yesterday and he needs to register for National Insurance purposes.'

She took out a form from her drawer. 'Can you complete this while you wait. Do you have your passport and birth certificate?'

'I have a baptism certificate; that is all we have in India.'

'OK. I will let someone know you are here.'

They sat down and the Major helped BJ fill in the form. 'I will have to remember your address.'

A woman approached. 'Mr Conway, I am Mrs Seth. Come with me please.'

The Major and Anna remained seated. 'We will wait for you.'

The woman sat at a desk. 'Sit down please.' She took the form, checked the details on it and the baptism certificate and passport. She noted on the form that his parents had died in 1950. He must have been only seven then, she thought. 'Please remain seated while I go and copy your documents.'

She was some time but when she returned, she had his NI certificate. 'What sort of job are you after?'

'I have an interview tomorrow?'

'Tomorrow? That's quick. According to your passport you only entered the country yesterday.'

'My friends outside arranged it for me this morning.'

'Best of luck. You will now need to register with a doctor.'

'My friends are taking me to theirs after seeing you. Thank you for your help.'

He rejoined the others and out they went. They got to the surgery.

'Good afternoon. I am Mr Alfred McLeod. My daughter Anna and I are registered with Dr Lamarr. Our friend BJ Conway arrived in the UK yesterday and wishes to register with the practice. Will Dr Lamarr take him on? He has registered with the DHSS and has a NI number.'

'The doctor may wish to see him first. I will call him. Doctor I have two of your patients. Alfred and Anna McLeod with their friend BJ Conway who wishes to register with you. Do you wish to see him first?'

'Has Mrs Denton arrived yet?'

'No doctor.'

'Send him in then.'

'A patient has missed her appointment, so he will see you now. His room is third on the left.'

BJ knocked. 'Come in.'

'Good afternoon. I am Dr Lamarr,' he said, extending his hand.

BJ shook it, 'Good afternoon doctor.'

'Have you had any major illnesses? Measles, mumps, smallpox, cholera, malaria?'

'No doctor.'

'You look very fit. Let me check your pulse and blood pressure.'

Chapter Twenty One

The reading showed 110/68. 'Yes you are very fit. Open your mouth and say ah.'

'OK, that's fine. Give your details to reception.'

'Thank you doctor.'

'The doctor agreed to accept me as a patient.'

'Please fill in this form and questionnaire.'

Again, the Major helped him do so. He handed them in and she said, 'The Health authority will send you a medical certificate in a few days.'

'Thank you.'

The Major said as they were leaving, 'That's it. You are now well and truly an UK resident.'

'Daddy, you know BJ likes the pictures particularly westerns. There is one on at the Regal. Would you mind if BJ and I went tomorrow night?'

'Of course not. I may pop into the pub for a while.'

They got to the car and were home by 3 o'clock.

'Tea?'

'Yes please,' they both replied.

'So what do you think of your first day in Blighty?'

'If it is a dream, I don't want to wake up. I appreciate all you and Anna have done. Both of you have given me a lot of time and been very patient.'

'You asked for our help. We are glad to give it. But you must learn to accept we are doing it because we want to not because we have to. Our home is your home now so don't feel you are intruding or a nuisance.'

'Thank you, I will try.' He continued, 'I noticed wherever we went the majority of men were in suits and ties. It must be the normal way of dress for work.'

'For office staff, yes. Non-office workers dress according to the work they do.'

'Then tomorrow I must wear a suit for my interview. May I use your iron please? Also may I borrow some black shoe polish please?

'I am sure Anna will do the ironing for you. I will get you the polish later.'

151

'Thank you. But I cannot allow Anna to do the ironing for me.'

The Major did not pursue it but he was sure Anna would not only volunteer, but insist.

After a short silence BJ said, 'As Anna got me the interview, I do not want to let her down with her boss.'

'You won't. Just be yourself and you'll be ok. I have no doubt he will want to offer you a position.' And he meant every word he had spoken. After some seventeen days, he felt he had judged BJ correctly. He had a lot to offer whoever took him on. It was a question of getting a foot on the first rung of the employment ladder in this country.

Anna came in with the drinks and some biscuits.

'BJ wants to borrow the iron to iron his clothes for the interview tomorrow.'

'I'll do it. I do ours.'

'You can't do that.'

'Why?'

'I am a guest in your house and besides you are not my servant.'

'Daddy tell him.'

'BJ I can understand why you consider yourself a guest but we welcome you as one of us. After all even Bruno took to you immediately.' At the sound of his name, Bruno looked up and went to the Major who rubbed and patted his head. 'We do things for each other and we want you to feel comfortable so you can do things for us too if you feel inclined to.'

'Thank you again, both of you. Oh I forgot. About doing things for you, I have some money now. I need to pay you for letting me stay here.'

'Wait until you start work and know what salary you will get. In India, I imagine you were paid monthly.'

'Yes.'

'Office workers are paid monthly here usually on the last working day of the month. When the position becomes clearer we will discuss it.'

'I won't forget sir.'

'I know you won't. Meanwhile relax and rest easy.'

Chapter Twenty One

They drank their tea. Anna said, 'Daddy, before I start the dinner shall we have a swim to wind down?

'No girl, I will read the paper. You two go ahead.'

'Doesn't Bruno need to go out first? We can swim afterwards.'

'Good idea. We'll do that. There is plenty of time. It is only just after half past three.'

Bruno as always got excited when he saw the lead. 'You put it on him. He is well used to you now.'

BJ did and they walked out.

'Do you feel more comfortable with us after what has happened today?'

'Very. I would never have thought of these things myself. While I wish Mr Sullivan's father survives, him falling ill has allowed me to be in your home. It has turned out very well. I cannot believe it.'

'Nor can I. But I am glad.'

They walked in a different direction along the river and Anna said, 'There is a sports field further along on the other side of the road. We will go there and let Bruno have a good run around and play ball.'

Bruno was in his element. There were a couple of other dogs he knew and they frolicked together.

'Hello. Have not seen you for a while. Have you been ok?'

'Yes, thanks. I have in fact been abroad and only got back yesterday. This is BJ my friend. He is staying with my father and me.'

'Pleased to meet you both sir, madam.'

'You too,' he said as he took BJ's hand and shook it. They walked a while around the perimeter of the field and Anna chit-chatted generally with them. BJ just listened. When they got to one of the entrances, the others said this is where we must leave you. The man shouted, 'Lua, come.' A brown Labrador come bounding up and they said, 'Cheerio. See you again soon.'

Anna called Bruno and showed him the ball. She threw it and he ran to retrieve it, returning to drop it at her feet. He backed off some steps

153

looking at her. She threw it again.

The next time she said, 'Here you throw it.' BJ made as if he was going to throw it in one direction but passed it to his other hand and threw it in another. As he was a spin bowler in cricket in school he bowled off and leg breaks and Bruno seemed to relish this. Anna was pleased to see BJ enjoying himself with Bruno. But time was getting on. 'We need to get back.'

When they got home they got their swimming costumes and went to the pool. Bruno followed them but only as far as the entrance where he lay down. There were two cubicles with curtains and they changed. They walked to the pool and dived in at the deep end. As on the ship they swam a few lengths, rested against the sides, stood up at the shallow end and enjoyed the water. 'Is Bruno allowed to come in?'

'Sometimes, when it is only Daddy and me. Only family and very close family friends are allowed to use the pool but he won't swim with anyone else. That is why he surprised Daddy and me yesterday. He took to you immediately. He showed he trusted you when he rolled on his back and exposed his belly to you.'

They climbed out, dried off, changed back into outer clothes and went back into the house.

'Nice, was it?'

'Yes, thanks. You should have come too.'

'Next time perhaps. I see that Bruno is dry so you did not let him in.'

'Do you want the TV on while I make dinner?'

'I am happy either way.'

'Why don't you have a read through the Information pack and when you are ready, Daddy will help you complete the application form?'

BJ went upstairs to collect them and started to study the material. The company was The Aegis Financial Services Co dealing in loans and insurance. The loans section provided the bulk of their work as it mostly involved hire purchase. There was also a debt management section for defaulting debtors. This very much interested BJ as he was experienced in loans and debt recovery.

Chapter Twenty One

He looked at the application form. 'Excuse me please. I need to get my certificates and character references so I can complete the form.'

He was desperate to get this right, so he said, 'Sir would you mind helping me with this? I want to answer the questions in the best way possible and also do not want to make any mistakes. I will draft the answers first. May I have some blank paper please?'

The Major got some from his den and put it on the table. He sat opposite. 'Can I have a look at the form?'

Having run his eye over it he said, 'It is the usual type of application. Would you mind if I had a look at your certificates and references?'

BJ passed them over and began drafting his answers.

The Major interrupted his train of thought saying, 'Very impressive. Without exception they all speak very highly of you as a person. I noticed from your Examination Certificate you sat ten subjects and apart from Hindi and Bengali, in which you got top Cs, you got mostly As and the rest Bs and therefore earned a First. With those marks it has to be a very good first.'

'Sir, being in an orphanage, I studied during the holidays when the boarders were away. The Anglos were emigrating to the UK and I had to give myself the best chance possible to earn a living among the Indians.'

'These papers will stand you in good stead. I will leave you to do your drafts. When you are finished if you like I will have a look at what you have written.'

'Yes please.'

He had just about finished when Anna called that dinner was ready to be served. 'I need to set the table. Don't move your papers. We will eat at the other end.'

After they had dined and drunk their coffees, Anna said, 'You finish what you were doing. I will clear and wash up.'

'Sir this is my draft. It is a bit untidy with all the crossing outs.'

'That's what drafts are for son. Don't worry.'

It was untidy in places but overall they were good answers. 'Would you mind if I made some amendments to emphasize important points?'

155

'Not at all sir. I want your help please.'

'Have a look at this. What do you think?' he said, handing back the draft.

BJ studied it. 'It does read better. Thank you.'

'Now you can complete the form.'

'Just one other thing, please. There is a section asking for the name and address of my next of kin or person to be contacted in an emergency. As I do not have any blood relatives would you mind if I gave your and Anna's names?'

'Not at all.'

'I will get a manila folder for you so you can keep everything in it.'

When done, Anna said, 'Let me have your suit and shirt for tomorrow and I will iron them.' While she did they sat watching television. A programme finished at nine o'clock and Anna said, 'Bruno needs to have a last walk. Coming BJ?'

The night was cool and cloudy. They just walked around the streets for a while and returned home.

BJ said, 'Would you mind if I went to bed?'

'No, you carry on, I will be going up myself. I will bring your clothes up. Daddy, can he have some polish?'

'Oh yes, I forgot.' They went upstairs.

'Which wardrobe has the most space?'

'That one is empty.' She took the pants of the hanger and placed them over the back of the easy chair. She hung the shirt and coat on the rail making sure there was plenty of space between them, so they would not crease.

The Major came in with the shoe polish kit. It had a cloth, two brushes and polish all inside a pouch.

'I do not want to dirty your carpet. May I have some old newspapers please?'

Anna went into her room and got a magazine. 'Here you are. Use this.'

'Thank you.'

'Do you want to do the same as we did on the ship before breakfast?'

'Yes if you want to.'

'I would not have asked otherwise. We can take Bruno with us. He will enjoy it.'

'If that is all, we will leave you in peace.'

'Good night BJ,' they said simultaneously.

'Good night sir, good night Anna. Thank you again for all your help today.' They left, shutting the door.

He laid out several double pages of the magazine covering about a 30 sq in area. He polished his shoes, making sure they had a good shine. Satisfied, he carefully folded the pages into a small packet and put it in the waste paper bin.

Chapter Twenty Two

The next morning he awoke to hear someone was already up. It was Anna. He changed into his shorts and went downstairs. She was in the TV room in her tracksuit and running shoes. They greeted each other and after calling Bruno, left the house. She had the lead in her hand and allowed him to run free. Bruno seemed in his element with this new experience. They went to the riverside, which from end to end was about a mile and a half. But they entered through a walkway some 400 yards from one end. The air was fresh and cool. They ran up and down a few times before heading home. They got their swimwear and towels and went to the swimming pool. Bruno joined them in the water.

They showered and in their bathrobes, went upstairs. Anna said, 'We will need to leave at ten o'clock for the office. I will not be getting dressed properly until about a quarter past nine.'

The Major was in the TV room reading the paper drinking a cup of coffee. 'Good morning both.'

'Good morning Daddy, I hope we did not disturb you.'

'Not at all. Good run and swim?'

'Lovely. It makes a good start and really sets one up for the day. I realised that when I first did it with BJ on the ship.'

'We will get dressed and then I will make breakfast.'

She opened her door when she was ready so she could listen for BJ. Hearing him on the landing, she came out and they went downstairs together.

They breakfasted and chatted and relaxed while passing time. Just after nine o'clock Anna said, 'Shall we go and get dressed?'

In his room, BJ lay on top of the bed praying quietly and meditating. He felt a sense of peace, got up and dressed. Picking up the manila folder he went on the landing calling softly, 'Anna?'

'Come in.'

She was finishing combing and brushing her hair at the dressing table. She turned around and said, 'As always you look very smart.'

'So do you.'

'Both of you look very nice. BJ would you like a red hankie to match your tie?'

Without waiting for a reply, he left to get it. Returning, he took the white one out of BJ's breast pocket and replaced it with the red one. 'There that is much sharper.'

'Thank you.'

As they were about to leave, the Major said, 'Best of luck.'

'Thank you sir.'

Anna drove to her office. Entering the building she went to the Reception desk. 'Good morning, Emily this is Mr Conway. He has an appointment with Mr Baker at half past ten.'

'Good morning Anna, Good morning Mr Conway. I have you down in the diary. I will tell Margaret you are here.'

She rang through. 'Margaret, Mr Conway is here.'

'Send him up and I will meet him by the lift.'

'Go up to the fifth floor and Mr Baker's secretary will meet you.'

Anna walked with him to the lift and pressed the button. When the doors opened, she said, 'Good luck BJ. Remember, don't worry. Just be yourself and you will be OK. I will wait for you here.'

As he got out, a woman greeted him. 'Good morning, Mr Conway. I am Margaret, Mr Baker's secretary. Come with me please.'

'Good morning.'

She led him into the office. 'Please sit down. I will tell him you are here.'

She buzzed him 'Mr Conway is here.'

'Get his papers and keep him seated while I peruse them.'

'Can I have your application form and references please? Mr Baker will call you in when he has read them.'

She took them in.

Chapter Twenty Two

He opened the envelope and looked at the form. He noted the dates of death of his parents. So he was orphaned when he was seven years old, he thought.

He also noted the ten GCE 'O' level passes mostly A's and B's. This guy was no mug.

He looked at the school leaving certificate, the employer's and character references and he was most impressed. He was eager to meet this applicant for whom Anna had stuck her neck out.

He went to the door, opened it and walked towards BJ. 'Good morning, I am Mr Baker the Director of Personnel.' He shook BJ's hand noting the firm grip and the personable man in front of him. His first impression was a very good one; tall and very smartly dressed.

'Good morning sir. Thank you for seeing me.'

Polite and well mannered too, he thought.

'Come in and sit down please.'

BJ undid the buttons of his coat and moved the chair for no reason before he sat down.

'I have been looking at your references. They are excellent. However, I would like you to tell me about yourself. Before you do, relax. I will be making brief notes from time to time but I am not ignoring you. I will still be listening. Take your time.'

BJ spoke deliberately and easily. 'I was born in India. When I was seven I was sent to a Catholic orphanage upstate. After I finished school, with the help of the physical and boxing trainer, I got a job with the Oriental Bank dealing with corporate loans. Having no family, I never thought I would leave India. But when I became twenty-one, to my surprise, I inherited some money from my father's office. I decided immediately I would use it to make a fresh start in the UK and here I am.'

He scribbled on the page in front of him: Good diction. Elocution.

'When did you arrive?' He already knew but he wanted to hear what BJ said.

'The day before yesterday.'

As BJ was talking, he ticked certain boxes on a form in front of him

161

and made further written comments. He was impressed by BJ's articulation. 'You are very clear and concise and do not waste words. Did you take elocution lessons?'

'Not in school. In the lower classes we had reading lessons and recited poetry. We were taught pronunciation, diction and intonation. We sat tests and exams and it counted towards our average mark. In the last two years at the concerts, I did Mark Anthony's funeral speech and Abraham Lincoln's 1863 speech at Gettysburg. When I left school a teacher gave me elocution lessons.'

'Tell me about the Empire club.'

'It was considered to be the best one for Anglo Indians and had a waiting list for membership.'

'You were the singer.'

BJ fidgeted as he usually did when he was embarrassed. 'Yes. It was because of that the teacher offered me the elocution lessons.'

'The manager states in his character reference that you are a quiet and unassuming person, that despite your popularity as a singer you remained humble and were always polite and courteous to everyone.'

BJ fidgeted again. Baker noticed writing down: Is embarrassed when paid compliments and fidgets in his chair. Is not boastful.

'How did you meet Anna McLeod?'

'The orphanage was in the same town as the convent she went to. We used to go to each other's sports day and concerts. She was a successful runner winning trophies. So I got to know who she was. We met by accident at the quayside just before embarking in India. We recognised each other and she and her father befriended me.'

'How did she recognise you?' The same must have applied to him but as before, he wanted to hear what he said.

As usual, he fidgeted before answering. 'I boxed for the school and also appeared on sports days.'

'You are being very modest,' Mr. Baker said, causing BJ to fidget again. 'You represented the school in the inter school boxing tournament for seven years and was undefeated. You also are described as an all round sportsman

Chapter Twenty Two

having been successful in the 880 yards, one mile, hop step and jump and long and high jump events. You were also in the gymnastics team.'

'Yes sir.'

He did not pursue the point as it was clear BJ was uncomfortable.

'Anna tells me you are staying with her and her father.'

'When we landed the person who was to meet me at the docks was not there. Her father drove me to the address I had for him, but the house was in darkness and there was no answer. The neighbour said he had gone to India urgently two days before as his father was seriously ill in an oxygen tent and not expected to survive. I was stranded but Anna's father invited me to stay at their home. At the outset, they had anticipated a problem and had discussed it while still at sea. They have been a great help.'

'What are your hobbies? How do you unwind and relax?'

'The bank's workers were allowed to use a hotel's facilities. So I did a lot of swimming and used their exercise and weights room. Also I trained with the Orientals mostly Thai in martial arts and played badminton with them. I went to the pictures a lot too.'

'What style of martial arts did you do and what grade are you?'

'It was a mixture. Some were into karate others into Thai kick boxing. Latterly, I never entered for a grading. I got to fourth kyu but after that the free sparring and grading became increasingly more contact orientated. Fronting the group, I could not risk injuring my fingers and hands or getting marked. My appearance was of paramount importance.'

'Understandable. You certainly look very fit and healthy,' he said, causing another fidget.

'Thank you.'

'Did you have a look at our Information pack?'

'Yes Sir.'

'What can you tell me about our company.'

'It has been in business for twenty years initially as a loan company. It changed it's name from the Delta Loan Co to its present one of Aegis Financial Services eight years ago when it amalgamated with Mercury

Financial Services and expanded into insurance and mortgage services. A lot of your business is hire purchase but I do not know what that means. You now have over four hundred staff, about thirty of which are general maintenance and utility staff, the balance being clerical and executive. The company's annual net income is just under £$\frac{3}{4}$m.'

'You have done your homework,' Mr. Baker said, and made further notes.

'Hire purchase. As you know we are a financial institution. When people wish to buy an item for which they cannot pay in full they pay a deposit usually of 10% and the balance with interest either weekly or monthly for a stated period. Until it is fully paid, the item is the property of the company. If they default we can repossess the article or take them to court. For instance if a customer falls behind with payments on his car, we repossess it. Basically that is what hire purchase is.'

'Thank you.'

'What do you believe you can offer this company?'

He had to think on his feet and gave himself some thinking time. He remembered what the Major had said. 'Be yourself.'

So he said, 'Generally I believe any employer wants their staff to be reliable and honest, doing the job they are paid to do to the best of their ability. They should be able to be trusted to work on their own and also be part of a team. They should be able to get on with people though inevitably with some the chemistry will be wrong. But that should not stop them from working together for the sake of the team and the company. We all need to complement one another. I know that I can bring these qualities to the company. I just need a chance to prove it.'

Mr Baker made further notes, giving him thinking time. He had already decided very early on in the interview what he was going to do. He looked up and said, 'Your references and whole demeanour impress me. You have loans experience and you will be a valuable member of staff. I will offer you a position. Are you interested?'

'Yes, very much so, sir and thank you.'

He buzzed Margaret. 'Can you come in please?'

Chapter Twenty Two

He handed her BJ's personal papers. 'Can you copy these for our file please? Mr Conway is joining us.'

'Congratulations.'

'Also can you make us a drink please? What would you like Mr Conway?'

'I'll have whatever you are having.'

'Coffee?'

'Fine, thank you. Just a little milk and one sugar please.'

She went out.

'I feel you will do well in the Repayments and Debt Recovery section. With your experience you will only need to be trained in our procedures, so you won't have any problem with that. Because of company policy that applies to all new recruits you will be on a year's probation. Your appointment is then confirmed. Is this ok?'

'Fine sir.'

'Now your salary. I do not suppose you have a figure in mind?'

'Not at all sir. I am used to Indian salaries. I have only been here two days and don't know anything.'

He paused a while. 'The national average weekly wage is in the region of £19 which equates to just under £1000 a year. But in the financial sector salaries are above average especially for good quality staff. I have interviewed hundreds of applicants over the years and you are certainly one of the more impressive ones.'

As he expected, BJ started to fidget.

'Because of your experience and qualifications, I will start you on £1250 a year. In six months, subject to satisfactory progress, I will increase it to £1350. On the first of January, everyone gets an annual increase and on each anniversary of their start date they get an increment based on the job they are doing. Is this OK?'

'I have no doubt you are being very fair and I am grateful for the opportunity.'

'We work Monday to Friday nine a.m. to five p.m. with an hour for lunch between noon and two p.m. We have a staff coffee lounge and a restaurant offering subsidised meals. However, a number of staff bring a packed lunch and eat at their desks. Some go out if the weather is nice and the women do some grocery shopping. Your annual leave entitlement will be twelve and a half days. Which leaves us just one question. When can you start?'

'Monday, sir please, if that is not too soon for you.'

Margaret knocked on the door and entered handing him the papers. She then brought in the coffees.

'Thank you, Margaret. Can you call Alistair Slater please?'

'Alistair Slater will be your section manager. You will be one of about thirty staff there.' He returned BJ's papers inside the manila envelope.

We have a sports and social club. So you will be able to continue with your badminton. Once a week we hire a local swimming pool for an hour. And our resident group and Master of Ceremonies will be interested in the fact you are a singer-guitarist. They are always interested in new talent especially for the special evenings.'

The phone buzzed. It was Margaret. 'Mr Slater is here.'

'Send him in please.'

After knocking, Mr Slater walked in. Both Mr Baker and BJ stood up. 'Alistair, this is Bryan Conway. He is joining us from Monday and I am putting him with you. Pull up a chair.'

They shook hands each saying, 'Pleased to meet you.' He felt BJ's firm grip.

'Here are his papers. Have a look at them.'

They sat in silence while he did so. BJ drank his coffee. Slater exchanged glances with Mr Baker, slightly pursing his lips and raising his eyebrows nodding his head.

'Very good references. And loans experience too in a bank,' he said, handing back the papers.

'After the necessary formalities I will bring him down to you on Monday. No doubt you will tell the others they will have a new colleague.'

Chapter Twenty Two

Mr Slater got up and BJ arose too, out of courtesy. 'See you on Monday Bryan.'

'Well I think that is everything from me. Do you have any questions?'

'Yes. If one does a good job and their conduct is satisfactory, what are the chances of progressing, of being promoted?'

'Very good. We hope to continue to grow as a company so opportunities are created for good quality staff. We have our own in-house exams at various levels every April after Easter. Passing each level will put you on a different and better salary scale and you will get increased responsibility. We encourage ambition.'

'Thank you.'

'If there is nothing else, on Monday, come to my office at nine in the morning.' He got up and shook BJ's hand.

'Thank you. I appreciate it.'

Anna for some while had looked up each time she heard the lift. All kinds of emotions assailed her. She so much wanted BJ to get the job.

The doors opened and there he was all smiles. She beamed with relief. She did not need to ask. His facial expression said it all. 'I start on Monday.'

She grabbed hold of and squeezed his arm. 'Oh I am so pleased for you. You will like it here. It is a good company and the people are very nice. Aren't we Emily?'

'Pardon? I am sorry, I did not hear that.'

'The people here are very nice. BJ is joining us on Monday.'

'Congratulations BJ. I am Emily. And yes, we are all nice people.'

'Emily can I just use the phone please?'

'Daddy, BJ starts on Monday,' she said excitedly into the phone. 'We are leaving now.'

Alastair had an office of his own in the middle of a large room. There was a lot of glass so he was able to see and be seen. His staff were divided more or less equally on either side supervised by a team leader/line manager. He called one of them, Gilbert and asked him to go with his staff to the other side. He wanted to speak to them all.

He said, 'We are getting someone new on Monday. He is an Anglo Indian with very good references and five years corporate banking experience. He is also well educated. His name is Bryan Conway and he is twenty-one.'

With a teasing smile he continued, 'Now colleagues, I would advise you to watch out. Not only is he is very personable, he is an undefeated boxer and a martial arts exponent. When you see him you will know what I mean. That's all.'

The women were now very interested in this new guy. 'I wonder what he looks like.'

When they got home the Major asked, 'Well it was obviously successful. Happy?'

'Very. Everything is working out so well thanks to you and Anna.'

'We are both glad.'

'Sir as I now have a job, I must pay you for putting me up.'

'No hurry. Wait until you get your first month's salary and then we will discuss it.'

'Sir I do not want to take advantage of your generosity.'

'You are not.'

That evening, Anna and BJ walked to the cinema. They sat by the aisle on the balcony. Seeing vendors selling confectionary etc., BJ asked, 'Would you like anything?'

'Not now thanks. We will have an ice cream during the interval.'

The lights dimmed and she leaned towards him resting her arm alongside his. It was a good western, which both enjoyed. The fact they were together added a lustre to the evening out. At the end he was about to leave his seat when he felt a tug on his sleeve. Some music started and all stood still in silence. When it stopped the audience shuffled out.

Outside she said, 'I forgot to tell you that after the films they play the national anthem. That is why everyone stood still.'

Chapter Twenty Three

The next morning they went shopping. As they walked around, he noted the shop window displays and the prices chalking it up to memory for future reference. She entered the grocers and some of the staff greeted her by name. 'This is our guest BJ. He arrived here on Wednesday.' He carried one basket and she, another. Again, he noted prices. He very much wanted to offer to pay but decided against it. He needed the money to see him through until he got his first salary.

In the greengrocers, she asked, 'Is there a particular veg. you like?'

'Cucumber. In India we used to cut it into long strips and eat it. It was very cooling.'

'I remember. We used to have it also with our meals as a side dish. Beetroot and salad stuff?'

'Yes please?'

A while after lunch, Bruno started to bark. It could only mean he was warning of someone approaching the front door. It was three of Anna's friends, Tony, his sister Kay and Anita. She took them into the visitors' sitting room. BJ said to the Major, 'I will take Bruno for a walk.' It was just 2.40 p.m.

'You don't have to leave. Anna will want you to meet her friends.'

'Sir, she needs time to catch up with them. I do not want to be in the way. I can meet them when I come back—if they are still here.'

The Major did not argue. BJ got the lead and Bruno went out of the door with him and it was only when they got to the pavement that BJ put the lead on.

Anna had seen BJ through the window and left the room to speak to her father. 'Where has BJ gone?'

'He wanted to give you time to catch up with your friends. He said he did not want to get in the way.'

'Oh? I wanted to introduce him to them.'

'He was only thinking of you. He said he could meet them when he got back by when you will have had some time on your own with them.'

A little disappointed, she went back to her friends.

BJ took the lead off Bruno and sat on a bench. To his right and behind him was a small building. An elderly couple were sitting on the next bench several yards away the other side of it. A man appeared from behind and sat next to him. He said after a short while, 'I have not seen you here before. New to the area?'

'Yes.'

'Where are you from?'

'India.'

'It's nice sitting by the river. It's so peaceful. I come here often.'

They sat a while in silence and then the man touched his knee saying 'I will see you again sometime perhaps.' As he spoke his face changed. He quickly got up and hurried away. BJ, in his innocence did not think anything.

He heard a voice behind him, 'Hey wog. Are you queer?'

BJ did not respond because he did not know the voice was for him.

'Hey wog, I am talking to you.' By this time the voice was closer and the speaker was now a few feet in front of him. 'Are you queer?'

'I don't know what you mean by "wog". And I am not odd or strange.'

'You're a Paki aren't you?'

'If you mean am I from Pakistan, no, I am from India.'

'So you are a wog then.'

BJ sensed trouble. He called Bruno who was in fact close by growling with tail up and hair on end. BJ put the lead on and held him tight. He got up to leave saying, 'Leave me alone I don't know you. Why are you talking to me like that?'

As he turned his back, the youth shouted, 'I'm talking to you. Come back here!' Then, he pushed BJ in the back.

Bruno was about to defend him. 'Easy boy,' he said, easy gently scratching the top of his head. 'Sit.' He tied the lead to the metal armrest

Chapter Twenty Three

of the bench.

'Leave me alone will you.'

But the youth, who had been drinking, found false courage in BJ's defensive attitude and threw a punch. BJ parried it and resorting to his boxing skills, jabbed him in the face three times and then uppercut him in the stomach with each hand.

He went down, winded and groaning.

'Now leave me alone,' he said, and turned to walk away.

'Get him.' In the nick of time, BJ saw another youth come aggressively towards him aiming a kick. It was clumsy and BJ easily caught hold of the foot, slightly twisted it to inflict some pain and pushed upwards causing the youth to fall backwards over the first youth increasing both their discomfort. Now there were two on the ground.

BJ shouted, 'Leave me alone will you. I don't want any more trouble.'

BJ naively turned to Bruno and heard a voice from the direction of the elderly couple 'Look out'. He remembered no more as he fell to the ground unconscious. One of the other two had thrown a brick hitting him on the head. He was close enough to Bruno who started to lick his face and bark. BJ came to momentarily and felt for the collar. He weakly released the lead and just as weakly muttered, 'Bruno home, Anna. Go.' He blacked out again.

Bruno made as if to go, hesitated, turned around, barked a few times and then ran off.

Meanwhile the youths themselves ran away in the opposite direction. Two were not very quick, lagging behind, hurting from the punches and the indignity of being floored.

The elderly man said to his wife, 'Go and see if he is OK. I will go to the petrol station across the road and phone for the police and ambulance.'

There was nothing the woman could do. By now a few others had gathered round. Fortunately, the station was not far away and the police were there in minutes, the ambulance following shortly after.

The police asked, 'Anyone see what happened?'

'Yes, my husband and I did. We were sitting on that bench there, and this man was sitting on this one here. Four youths racially abused him; he twice tried to walk away, saying he did not want any trouble. Two attacked him and he dealt with them but he turned his back to go and a third threw a brick at him hitting him on the head.'

Meanwhile Bruno ran to the zebra crossing and trained as he was, sat at the edge of the pavement barking furiously. A bus stopped and Bruno ran across continuing to bark. Anna and the Major heard him before they saw him. He jumped the gate, but stayed on the drive barking frantically. Anna got up from her chair saying alarmingly, 'Oh no, not BJ. Please God, not BJ.'

She rushed out of the room shrieking 'Daddeee, something's happened to BJ!' She opened the front door but the dog would not come any closer. Anna grabbed a light jacket hanging over the stair rail and Bruno turned jumped the gate again and ran, pausing a while to look round and make sure she was following him.

The Major said to the visitors. 'Something has happened to our guest. I have to find out what happened and make sure he and Anna are ok. Please see yourselves out and shut the door after you.' And he too was gone hurriedly.

When Anna saw the ambulance and the police her heart sank. She started to sob. The ambulance men were placing a body on the stretcher. 'That's my friend. What happened? How bad is he? He's not dead is he?' she pleaded. Bruno was now by the stretcher, whining, clearly distressed.

'No, he's not dead but he is unconscious. He was hit by a brick. We are taking him to Casualty.'

'Please let me come. Please.'

They nodded.

The Major arrived, 'I am the girl's father and the boy is our guest. Which hospital?'

'The General.'

'Anna, I will find out what happened from the police and meet you there. Bruno.' And the dog came.

The ambulance left and the Major went to the small group and the

Chapter Twenty Three

police who were taking statements.

'Good afternoon officers. I am Mr McLeod, and the boy in the ambulance is my house guest. What happened?'

'What is the boy's name?'

'Bryan Conway.'

'Witnesses say the boy was racially abused. Also the attackers asked if he was queer. Apparently, he did not know what they meant at first but then it became obvious they were addressing him. He tried to avoid confrontation, told them he did not want any trouble and walked away. They would not let him. He can obviously look after himself because he took out two of them. But he made the mistake of turning his back on the others to walk away a third time. That is when one threw a brick at him knocking him unconscious. This is the brick.' It was in his hand.

'We need to get his side of the story. Meanwhile, another squad car is searching for the attackers in the direction they went. Hopefully they will get them.'

'He was racially abused on the ship twice and only arrived in the UK on Wednesday. Now this happens. It is a poor advert for this country. I did not fight the war so immigrants could be treated so badly.'

'I can understand the way you feel. Sorry.'

'Bruno.' The dog barked once in answer. He was now sitting beside his lead still attached to the bench. They returned home.

The Major got the car out of the garage and drove to the hospital. Entering Casualty, he looked for Anna, who was crying away from the others in the waiting room. She sensed her father approaching and said, 'They have taken him for examination.' After a pause she asked, 'Did you find out what happened?'

He told her what he knew.

'Why did they not leave him alone like he asked?'

'Apparently they were drunk. The time would suggest they had just come out of the pub at closing time. The police are looking for them in the area.'

They sat in silence.

173

It was some time later that a man approached them. 'How is he, doctor?' Anna asked.

'We X-rayed his head and the good news is there is no fracture. However, he is concussed and as a precaution we will keep him in overnight. Also we have had to stitch the wound.'

'Can we see him please?'

'You can but we have sedated him.'

The Major and Anna followed him. When they got to the room where BJ lay, the Major held back. 'Doctor can I have a word with you in confidence please?'

'Certainly.'

They walked a few steps and the Major said, 'Doctor, if you are keeping him in overnight can you put him in a private room please? I will pay. My daughter is distraught and may want to stay with him.'

'There is no need for that. He is in an observation room. We are not busy. If it becomes necessary to move him, then we will have to reconsider. I will have an easy chair and a blanket brought in so she will be more comfortable. I finish my shift at six o'clock but I will leave instructions for the night staff. I am back on duty tomorrow at eight o'clock and I will make it a point to come and see him as soon as possible. If all goes well, I will release him but he will need to take it easy for several days. He will have to come back anyway on Thursday to have the stitches removed.'

'Thank you doctor for your help.' They shook hands and the doctor turned away to arrange for an easy chair and blanket to be taken to the room.

'Oh Mr McLeod, his clothes were bloody and dirty. They are on a chair. Can you bring a change tomorrow?'

'Of course.'

The Major went in. Anna was still crying, seated by the bed, holding BJ's hand. His head was bandaged and he was asleep.

They sat awhile. The Major said, 'The doctor is bringing in an easy chair and a blanket for you. He is happy for you to stay as long as you want.'

Chapter Twenty Three

'Can I stay overnight? I do not want to leave him.'

'You will need to eat something.'

'I am not hungry. I just want to be with BJ.'

'OK, girl. I will see if I can get you a drink and a sandwich. You have to have something.'

He went to the reception desk. 'Is there somewhere in the hospital or nearby where I can get a drink and a sandwich?'

'There is a kiosk along the corridor. Go to the far end and turn right. You cannot miss it. Alternatively, you can go to the main road where there is a bakery shop. However, it is Saturday and coming to closing time so the choice may be limited.'

'Thank you. I will try the kiosk first.'

He bought a tea and two sandwiches, one ham salad and one egg salad. He took them to Anna. 'This should keep you going this evening. Any change?'

'No.'

'I will go home and return early tomorrow morning. Ring me if there is any change.'

'Bye Daddy. And thank you for understanding.'

He merely nodded. He took the clothes and left. This whole experience had upset him too. He was surprised how much he had come to care for BJ.

The police arrived at Reception. 'A Mr Conway was brought here by ambulance. I would like to see him please.'

'I will ask the duty doctor.'

She contacted him. 'Doctor the police are here wanting to see Mr Conway.'

'I will be down shortly.'

'I am the duty doctor, Dr. Nugent. I understand you want to see Mr Conway. He is concussed and we have sedated him. I am keeping him in overnight under observation. Please come back tomorrow morning. I may be able to discharge him then. Or you can call at his home if that is more

175

convenient.'

'Thank you doctor,' he said, and they left.

Anna drank the tea and took a bite of a sandwich but found she did not have any appetite so put it back in the bag. She prayed, 'Lord please do not let this experience adversely affect BJ. I love him Lord. I believe the way we met up again was your will. Now please do not take him from me. Please Lord.'

The Major arrived home and made himself a drink. Bruno was lying somewhat listless and disinterested in life generally. His eyes were doleful. The Major finished his drink, fed him and took him for his evening walk. Even when they got to the riverbank and off the lead, Bruno did not venture far. He was not as energetic as usual seeming to sense the Major's mood.

They had not long got back when suddenly, Bruno jumped up from lying on the floor, barking. Someone was coming to the door. He soon stopped however indicating he knew the caller. It was Keith.

'Is everything OK Alfie? We heard Bruno barking earlier on then he and Anna run past followed by you. Where are Anna and BJ?'

'He was racially attacked by some drunks and is in hospital concussed. Anna is sitting with him. He is sedated and they're keeping him in overnight. Would you like a sherry? Or port? I need one.'

'Sherry please.'

The Major sipped his drink set the glass down on the coffee table and said, 'Despite having met him less than three weeks ago, he has made an impact on our lives. He is the epitome of reassuring masculinity with an imposing well-built figure. But he has a very kindly demeanour. And Anna has come out of her shell since meeting him. You know how quiet, shy and unassuming she was. She has noticeably blossomed and is much less diffident especially when she is with him. Its as if his inner strength has rubbed off on her.'

He paused to sip his drink and continued, 'He intervened when an inebriated passenger was manhandling Anna. He was racially abused for his efforts to protect her. Later that same evening a couple made a derogatory comment about Anna getting friendly with an Indian. But both times he responded with remarkable dignity and exercised supreme self-control despite the provocation.'

He took another sip of his sherry. 'When I saw him in hospital, I was profoundly saddened that the country I fought for in the war had created such a society. I knew how much he had come to mean to Anna, but surprisingly I realised this afternoon how much I care for him. He is like a son who in his own way fills the void created by Joey's death.'

Joey was the son who died at aged two of meningitis. It was this that prompted him to accept a temporary posting in India. The posting in fact lasted eight years until Anna finished her education.

Keith initially maintained a respectful silence. After a while as they sipped their drinks he said, 'Tell me about him.'

The Major described in some detail how they met at the quayside, Anna and BJ recognising each other, right through to the present moment.

'He must be some kind of man for him to have affected your life so dramatically. You are no fool and have the wisdom that comes with experience and maturity. We only met him briefly but he came across to me as very well mannered and personable.'

'And it is not just Anna and me. You know what Bruno is like with people he does not know and even with those he accepts, he will not allow them to touch him. Even you and Sandra. To our complete and utter amazement, he responded to BJ totally differently.'

He went on to tell him exactly what happened. 'That is why Bruno was barking as he ran back. It was to alert us that something had happened to BJ.'

When Keith was sure that the Major was more relaxed, he left. 'Thank you for coming. You have helped. I feel better for having talked.'

'It's a pleasure. We are just next door if you need us. Bye, and take care.'

Bruno was still missing BJ and Anna in his canine way. But he sensed a change in mood for the better in the Major who called him and stroked his head and neck. The last few hours had been emotionally draining so he decided to retire early.

But he did not settle down immediately. He was thinking about BJ in that hospital room with Anna by his side.

Chapter Twenty Four

Time passed and Anna did not leave the room, other than to go to the toilet. At times, she walked around to stretch her legs and get the circulation going again. Mostly she sat holding BJ's hand kissing it from time to time. A nurse popped in occasionally to check on him and offer her a hot drink.

Darkness had long since closed in and now the lights in the room dimmed automatically. She settled herself in the chair, laying her head on top of his hand and closed her eyes.

Some time during the night, BJ half awoke briefly. His eyes still closed, he felt warm flesh against his hand. He slowly opened his eyes and at first he was disorientated. He felt a throbbing pain in his head and reached up slowly to touch it. He felt the bandage around his head. As his eyes focused in the dim light he knew he was not in his own bed. But where was he?

He looked at the warm flesh against his hand. It was Anna's face! Oh my God what happened? Why am I here? he thought. He concluded he was dreaming. The lingering effects of the sedative took over and he fell asleep.

At about six o'clock he woke fully. His head still hurt and Anna was still there. It was not a dream after all. Then he remembered what happened, right up to the point when a voice shouted, 'Look out.' Now here he was, and it was the morrow. At least he hoped it was Sunday.

The nurse came into the room to routinely check his pulse and temperature. 'So you are awake. How do you feel?'

'My head hurts a bit.'

Anna roused. Her hair was disheveled and her eyes puffy from crying and sleep. BJ lifted his hand to put it around the side of her neck and face. She put her hand over his and pressed it to her cheek. 'Anna. I am sorry for putting you and your dad through this.'

'Don't be silly. Daddy is upset too it happened to you.

'While the nurse tends to you I will go and freshen up. I won't be long.'

The nurse did the necessary. Satisfied all was in order she said, 'I will bring you some breakfast later.'

'Thank you.'

She left and BJ was on his own for a while.

Anna returned and sat down again.

'You look tired. I woke up briefly during the night and saw you. I thought I was dreaming.'

'No, it was not a dream.'

'You've been here all night?' But it was a rhetorical question. He knew she had.

'Yes.'

It warmed him to the core.

'You were concerned the night before we docked that I would go my own way and not maintain contact with you. After all that has happened since surely you don't have any doubts anymore.'

'No.'

'The doctor who examined and treated you yesterday will be seeing you as soon as he can after he comes on duty. He may discharge you,' the nurse said.

'I hope he does. I have to start my job tomorrow.'

He noticed he was in a gown. 'Where are my clothes? I will have to get dressed if I am going home.'

'They were dirty and bloody so Daddy took them home. He will bring a change when he comes.'

They sat a while. He asked, 'How did you find out I was in hospital?'

'Bruno ran home barking. We heard him before we saw him. He jumped over the gates, stopping just inside and continued barking. He would not come any further. Both Daddy and I knew something was wrong. As soon as I went out of the door he turned round jumped over the gate and started to run. I followed him. When I got to the river they were putting you in an ambulance. I came to the hospital with you.'

The nurse came in again with a tray. 'Here is your breakfast.'

And to Anna she said, 'Can I get you a drink?'

'Thank you. Coffee, black.'

'You can have part of this. I won't eat it all.' There was cereal and a roll with some butter and what he thought was jam on a plate. Actually it was marmalade.

She felt a cementing of the bond between them as they shared breakfast. It was an intimate few minutes and they savoured their togetherness.

They had just about finished when the Major came in.

He had not slept very well. He woke early, soaked in the bath to relax and, refreshed, got dressed. He went into BJ's room. He saw the crucifix on the chest of drawers and the rosary and the bible on the bedside table. He opened a cupboard and he saw all was neatly folded and hung up. He took out a shirt and jeans and searched for a suitable coat. But they were all too good to wear back from the hospital. The shoes were neatly set out at the bottom. He got a clean pair. Opening a drawer, he found socks and underpants. He went into his room and got a fairly thick cardigan for BJ.

Returning downstairs, he made himself a coffee and some toast. He also made a flask of coffee and sandwiches for Anna and BJ. When he was satisfied he had done all he needed to, he drove to the hospital. He had completely forgotten to take Bruno for his morning walk.

'Good morning girl, good morning BJ.'

'Hello Daddy.'

'Good morning sir.'

'I've brought a flask of coffee and sandwiches for the two of you. Also, here is a fresh change of clothes. He put the clothes at the foot of the bed. How are you son?'

'My head throbs a bit, otherwise I am OK. But sir, I hope I have not damaged your reputation and standing in the neighbourhood. I tried to avoid trouble but they would not leave me alone. I will not hold you to your offer of a home sir. I will leave if you want me too. Just give me time to find a place, please.'

'Daddy?' Anna gasped as tears welled up in her eyes. 'Tell him please he can stay.'

'Son, it is not your fault. And we are not concerned what people might think. There is no question of you moving out. You have only just arrived.'

'Thank you sir for everything.'

He was so engrossed talking to the Major, he did not see the police come in. When he did, he jerked his head forward in surprise. But the sudden movement hurt his head and he fell back on the pillow. Recovering, he exclaimed, 'Oh my God a Bobby. You're not going to send me back to India are you? I have only just arrived? I did not start it.'

Anna was beside herself in anguish. Sent back? 'Daddy it will not come to that will it?' she asked agonisingly.

BJ's head settled down and he slowly sat up.

The police said, 'No you will not be deported. I have witness statements and they are consistent in that you tried to walk away but the attackers would not let you. Take your time, sir, but I need you to tell me exactly what happened. Is that OK?'

'Yes, sir, Mr Bobby.' But at that moment, the doctor came in with a nurse.

'Good morning all. Can you all please leave us while I check my patient?'

The police, Anna and the Major left.

'Good morning doctor. Good morning nurse.'

'How is the patient this morning.'

'My head hurts slightly, otherwise OK, thanks doctor.'

The doctor did his routine examination, noting BJ's responses and eyes. He was satisfied he could be discharged.

'You can go home when you are ready. Just keep the bandage dry and we will see you on Thursday to take the stitches out. Meanwhile take it easy and rest. You've had a nasty knock. Don't stand up quickly. Rise slowly otherwise you might get giddy.'

'Thank you doctor.'

Outside, he said to Anna and the Major, 'You can take him home when you are ready. Make sure he gets plenty of rest and keeps the bandage dry.'

The Major shook the doctors hand. 'Thank you for everything.'

Anna was all smiles. They went back into the room. 'So you can come home. Here is your change of clothes. I have brought you one of my cardigans as your coats were too good for this purpose.'

'Thank you sir. But a Bobby wants to speak to me.'

'Yes, I would like to hear your story before you leave please.'

BJ paused a while to collect his thoughts.

'I took Bruno for a walk along the river and while he wandered around I sat on a bench. I was sitting sideways with my left thigh on the seat and my left hand along the back of it. After a while a man came and sat beside me. He said he had not seen me before. He asked me some questions about myself and if I lived close by. I just felt he was being friendly. But then he touched my knee. As he did so, he looked over my shoulder. His face changed and he got up and hurried away. I thought nothing of it.

Then I heard a voice behind me say "Hey wog. Are you queer?" It did not occur to me the person was talking to me so I ignored it and just sat there. A man appeared in front of me. He said, "Hey wog I am talking to you. Are you queer?" I told him I did not know what he meant. And I was not odd. He said I was a Paki and so I was a wog. He was aggressive and mocking which made me uncomfortable. I decided to leave, got up and called Bruno. I told him to leave me alone. I didn't know him and asked why he was talking to me like that.

But as I turned away he shouted, "I have not finished talking to you. Come back here" and pushed me in the back. I had never been in this position before and did not know what to do. I just wanted to go back to Anna and the Major at home. Bruno was barking and I was worried he may have bitten him if he had not been on the lead. I tied the lead to the metal armrest of the bench. Again, I told him to leave me alone but he threw a punch. I shoved it away and jabbed him a few times in the face and hit him twice in the stomach. He went down. Again, I told him to leave me alone and turned to walk away. I heard him shout "Get him" and quickly turned around. Another aimed a kick at me. I caught hold of his foot, twisted it slightly to hurt him and pushed it up and back. He fell backwards over the first one on the ground. I shouted, "Leave me alone. I don't want any trouble," and turned my back. I heard a voice from the direction of the elderly couple saying, "Look out". I do not know what happened after that. Then I woke up here on a trolley. I cannot remember being brought to this room.'

'You have confirmed what witnesses have said. In fact, one man was in the pub where the men were. They became rather loud and the landlord had to ask them to quiet down. At closing time, they were still boisterous as they walked along the road and down by the riverside. He was going home the same way and saw them throw stones at the ducks so they seemed to be out to cause trouble.

It is unfortunate they chose you as a victim. Not only because you ended up here, but you floored two of them. They were still feeling the effects of being winded because they staggered down the road. We were able to pick them up and kept them overnight in the cells. Hopefully after sobering up and recovering from their bruised pride and egos, they will see sense and admit to what they did. The weight of the witness evidence is against them. They will be formally charged and appear before the magistrates tomorrow. But I will need to get your statement typed and signed.

You are going home so I will call on you later. I will make it about half past two to give you time to have your lunch. Is that ok?'

The Major said, 'Fine.'

'I go off duty at half past four, so that will give me time to get the paperwork in order for the court tomorrow. What is the address please?'

The Major said, '15 Primrose Avenue, East Kingston.'

'Bye, for now. I will see you later on. Thank you for your time.' And he was gone.

The Major said, 'We will go outside while you get dressed.'

BJ got out of bed but felt a little giddy. He leaned against the side of the bed to clear his head. When he felt OK, he got dressed, making sure he did not rush in case he got giddy again.

He tidied the bed, puffed up the pillows and placed the folded gown on it. He went out and the three of them headed home.

Bruno recognised the sound of the Major's car engine. He smelled the three of them in the air and knowing all were back, barked and whined excitedly. He greeted them exuberantly as they entered the house. On the doormat was an envelope. The Major opened it. It was a note from Sandra and Keith. 'Sandra and Keith have invited us over for Sunday lunch at half past twelve.'

'Daddy, I need to go and have a soak in the bath and get changed. BJ, shall I run the bath for you after I have finished?'

'Yes please. I also need to clean my teeth.'

As she went upstairs, the Major asked, 'Would you like a drink?'

'Yes please, thank you.'

'You just sit there and relax. Remember what the doctor said.'

'Yes sir, but I have to start my job tomorrow.'

'Will you be up to it?'

'I have to be. I gave Mr Baker my word I would start. Besides, I cannot let Anna down.'

The Major said nothing going to make the drinks.

While BJ was in the bath, he said, 'He does not look well enough to start work tomorrow but he is determined to make it. He does not want to let you down. Also he says he gave his word and he must keep it.'

Bruno, meanwhile, had grabbed the leash hanging over the banister. With it in his mouth he went to them whining.

'Oh my God. I was so concerned about BJ and you I forgot to take him for his walk.'

'I'll take him. I feel refreshed after my soak.'

Just before half past twelve, they left to go next door.

'How are you feeling BJ?'

'OK thanks.'

'We are sorry for what happened. We are not all like that. They were

185

just drunken ignorant thugs.'

The Major said, 'The police arrested them and they spent the night in the cells. They will appear in court tomorrow.'

'Come let's eat.'

'This is our traditional Sunday lunch; roast beef, Yorkshire pudding, roast potatoes and vet.'

He wondered why it was called Yorkshire pudding and what it was.

Anna sensed this and said, 'It is that yellowish round thing. It is made of batter.'

'I have to get used to English meals.'

He ate heartily.

'Thank you for that. I enjoyed it. And I liked the batter. It was unusual but it was nice.'

'You are welcome. We are having apple crumble and ice cream for dessert.'

Again, he did not have a clue as to what crumble meant in a dessert but kept quiet. But as with the main meal he liked that too.

At quarter after two, the Major said, 'The police are coming at half past two so BJ can sign the statement for court tomorrow. Thank you for lunch.'

'You are welcome as always. Bye all and get well soon BJ.'

'Bye sir, madam. Thank you for the meal.'

The police arrived at twenty-five to three. BJ asked the Major to check the statement over and when he cleared it, he signed it.

Late in the afternoon, Anna was showing signs of tiredness. But she was more concerned about BJ. 'You rest and take it easy. What will you be wearing tomorrow? I will iron it for you?'

'I was thinking of the grey suit.'

She brought it down and setting up the ironing board in the room she pressed his clothes.

He was humbled by her attention.

Chapter Twenty Five

They had both had early nights. Though they woke at their normal time, they did not go running or swimming. But they did take Bruno for his walk.

After breakfast the Major left for work. 'Best of luck son. See you in the evening.'

BJ made sure he had all his papers, checking and double-checking. He was nervous. That he did not feel 100% himself did not help.

Anna drove them to the office and they got into the lift together. BJ did not recognize that his bandaged head attracted attention. Anna took him to the top floor and walked with him to Margaret's office. 'I'll see you during the coffee break. I will come to you.'

She squeezed his hand and left. He knocked and entered. 'Good morning.'

'Good morning. My God. What happened? Are you ok?'

'Not as well as I was before it happened, thank you.'

'I'll tell Mr Baker you are here.'

'Mr Conway is here.'

'Send him in.'

She got up and opened the door for BJ.

'Thank you….Good morning Mr Baker.'

'Good heavens! Take a seat.' He came around to the front of his desk and sat on another chair facing BJ. 'What happened? You do not look well.'

'I was attacked on Saturday afternoon and had to spend the night in hospital.'

'Attacked? By who? Why?'

'Four men picked on me because they said I was a Paki and a wog. I tried a few times to walk away but they would not let me. I had to defend myself but one of them knocked me unconscious. The doctor said I was concussed and he had to stitch a gash in my head. I learned yesterday from the police I was hit by a brick.'

'Did the doctor say you could come in today?'

'No sir. He did not know.'

'When he discharged you what did he say?'

'I had to go back to the hospital on Thursday to have the stitches removed and meanwhile I was to take it easy and rest. That I was to stand up slowly in case I got giddy.'

'But you are here. Anna could have told me what happened and I would have understood.'

'Sir, you asked me when could I start and I said Monday. I gave you my word and I am honour bound to keep it. That is why I came in. Besides I did not want to let you and Anna down.'

'On Friday I told you I was impressed by your references. You also impressed me as a person and that is why I offered you a position at a good starting salary. By coming in today despite how you feel proves I was right.'

'How I feel is of less importance than keeping my word sir.'

Mr Baker noted that BJ understandably was not as sparkling as on Friday. He looked slightly drawn no doubt because of the concussion and head wound. But he could not get over him turning up this morning.

'I see that. But I would not be doing my duty as an employer if I allowed you to work while you are not fit. You say you are honour bound to keep your word. Likewise I am honour bound to keep my word to you. As of today you are on the payroll and payment of your salary starts. But I want you to go home and take it easy as the doctor advised. You can start next Monday. Did you come in with Anna?'

'Yes sir, she drove. I do not know my way around yet.'

'I am going to get her to take you home.'

'Sir, I do not want to get Anna into trouble. She only returned today.'

'She is not in trouble. I am authorising it. The company looks after its staff.'

Chapter Twenty Five

He buzzed Margaret. 'Margaret can you ask Anna McLeod, Joe Whyte and Alastair Slater to come up please. Get the men to bring in two chairs and send them in as they arrive.'

'I am very sorry you were racially attacked. We are not all prejudiced so please do not let it put you off living here.'

'It won't. Anna, her father and the people I have met so far have all been very welcoming and friendly.'

As usual, all were interested in Anna's holiday. They spent a little while catching up with each other. Anna settled down to do some work and was barely into it when Joe came to her. 'Anna, Mr Baker wants to see the two of us.'

Her face dropped immediately sensing it concerned BJ. Was he OK?

Margaret said, 'He is expecting you. Please go in.'

Alastair Slater was already there.

BJ got up. Mr Baker also arose, saying to Joe Whyte, 'This is Bryan Conway, who was to start in Alastair's section today. But he was racially attacked on Saturday, was concussed and hospitalised overnight. As you can see he is not in a fit state to work so I am sending him home. I called you here because Bryan is a guest of Anna and her father. Though she only resumed work today, I want her to take him home. Also, he needs to go to the hospital on Thursday to have the stitches out. I am also allowing her to take him there.'

'Yes, of course.'

'Anna take him home please. Make sure he takes it easy.'

'Thank you sir. I appreciate it.'

'Yes thank you too Mr Baker. My father and I tried to dissuade BJ from coming in today but he said he gave his word and he had to keep it.'

'I know, he told me the same thing.'

Joe, Anna and BJ left. As they entered the lift, BJ said, 'I will wait in the foyer for you Anna.'

Anna and Joe went into their office. She got her coat and handbag and said, 'An emergency has arisen and I have to go home. I will see you all later. Bye.'

Joe said nothing to anyone though they were dying to know.

Meanwhile, Mr Baker said, 'No doubt you told the staff on Friday that Bryan was starting today. To stop any speculation I will come down and tell them myself what has happened.'

As they walked in, Alastair said, 'Gather around everyone please.'

When they had done so, Mr Baker said, 'Good morning all. Alastair told you on Friday you were getting a new colleague today. He only arrived in the UK on Wednesday and on Saturday afternoon he was racially attacked by four men. He was knocked unconscious by a brick, was concussed and had to spend the night in hospital. He has also had a gash in his head stitched.

He did come in but he was clearly unwell and I have sent him home. He will start next Monday by when he should have fully recovered. Now, you may be wondering why I felt I had to tell you myself. It is because I want you to know of the calibre of your new colleague. I do not know what Alastair said on Friday but Bryan Conway has excellent character references and credentials. More than that, he is very humble and of great integrity. His integrity was proved today.

The doctor told him to take it easy and rest. Anna McLeod and her father, with whom he is staying, tried to talk him out of coming in and do you know what he said to them and to me? He gave his word and he was honour bound to keep it. He further told me how he felt was not important; keeping his word was. Yes, how he felt was not important, keeping his word was. That, ladies and gentlemen, is the quality of man you will work alongside.

Now, because the police are involved and it was a racial attack, it will probably be reported in the local paper at the weekend. He may or may not see it so when he starts please refrain from referring to the attack. It can't have been a nice experience more so as it was just three days after he arrived in the UK. That's all.'

They dispersed returning to their desks. Alastair said, 'Compared to how he was on Friday, he did look ashen and a bit weak.'

'That is why I could not let him work. He needs to rest as the doctor told him. However with his physique, I have no doubt he will recover sooner rather than later.' Then he left.

Anna took BJ home. She said, 'I will make you a drink while you get changed. I will bring it up to you.'

She brought the tea and some biscuits. She sat on the easy chair while he sat on the bed. 'Now BJ, please rest. You have to get your strength back. I will go and tell Sandra who will be coming in later. I will also come back lunch time to check on you but I will not be able to stop long as I will have to get back within the hour.'

'Don't rush. I'll be ok. You need to have your break.'

'I would not relax, worrying about you. It will be OK. I have an hour.'

'Thank you. I appreciate your concern. But I am sorry to put you and your father through this.'

'Don't be silly. You did not ask to be attacked. We do not let Bruno upstairs but I know how well you get on. I will call him up and he can stay with you. Bruno.' He came bounding up to her. She rubbed his head and neck and he then went to have the same from BJ.

'Do you want the radio on?'

'Yes please.'

'Now rest please. Do you want any magazines?'

'No, thanks. I will just doze a bit.'

'You do that. It will do you good. I will give you some magazines anyway. I will also keep the door open so Bruno can go down and get a drink if he wants. If he does not recognise the sound and smell of anyone coming up the drive, he will bark aggressively and run to the door.'

'OK.'

'I'm off now. I'll see you later.'

She was on her way out when he called, 'Anna.' She stopped and turned round. 'You really do look after me. Thank you.'

'Do you remember what I said when you asked me on the ship if I had a boyfriend waiting for me?'

'Yes. You were a real relationship person and would only spend time with someone you liked.'

'We spent a lot of time together on the ship. We ran, we swam, we danced. In fact we spent almost all of our time together. And I sat with you overnight in hospital.'

He nodded 'Yes.'

'That should tell you something. I do it because I want to. I like being with you. I want you to be happy and comfortable living with us.'

Then she was gone, leaving him to his thoughts. He was warmed by her concern and words. But he would not allow himself to get carried away. He knew he was not in their social and financial class and had nothing to offer her.

She went next door to Sandra's and Keith's. 'Hello Anna. I thought you were going back to work today.'

'I did, but I have just brought BJ home. The Personnel Director has told him to start next week when he is better. Bruno is upstairs with him and he is going to rest. Would you mind checking up on him please and making him some lunch? Knowing him, he would rather go hungry than presume to help himself to the food. I will try and visit for a while during my lunch break but I will not be able to stop long.'

'Don't worry. I'll look after him. I have to do some shopping. Do you want me to get anything especially?'

'No, thanks. I have already shopped. Oh! Perhaps you can get some painkillers and a suitable tonic to build up his strength.'

She opened her bag to hand over some money but Sandra said, 'Don't worry about that. You can pay me later.'

'Thanks. See you later. Bye.'

She returned to the office. Joe said, 'That was quick. You were not gone long.'

'I am less than a fifteen minute drive away. I just made a drink and left him to rest. I will go home lunch time to check up on him. Meanwhile, I have asked my neighbours who have met him to go in and give him some lunch.'

'Don't rush. If you go over for the hour, it will not matter.'

'Thank you but not only have I been away this morning but I will also be away part of Thursday morning to go to the hospital.'

She went to her desk. Some had heard what she said but refrained from pressing her.

Thursday morning, they went to the hospital. He had to wait about thirty-five minutes before he was called. The nurse was very gentle and considerate. She soaked the pad over the gash with warm water to soften any congealed blood. Even so, despite her best efforts, when she gently pulled the pad away, it was uncomfortable and a little blood seeped. She cut the stitches. 'It's healing well. I will just smear some antiseptic ointment on it. Keep it dry and dab it every night with cotton wool soaked in warm water and Dettol.'

'That looks a lot better. Did she tell you if you have to do anything?'

'I have to clean it with warm water and Dettol every night.'

'I will do that for you. You cannot see what you are doing.'

She dropped him off at home and headed to the office.

'Everything OK?' Joe asked.

'Yes thanks. The wound is healing nicely and he looks and feels a lot better without the bandage around his head.' That night after dinner, she washed and cleansed the wound.

Chapter Twenty Six

On Saturday there was an article in the local paper:

'Immigrant racially attacked.

An Indian immigrant, Bryan Conway (21) was racially attacked on Saturday, three days after he arrived in the UK. Four drunken men abused him and despite walking away several times, they pushed him in the back and tried to punch and kick him. He winded the leader, Colin Morris (22), with, as one witness said, 'the speed and skill of a boxer' and flipped the kicker, Leslie Jones (22) backwards over the first. As he turned to walk away for the third time, a brick knocked him unconscious. He was concussed and was hospitalised overnight. He also had to have a head wound stitched.

As the two assailants that were winded could not walk properly, they, with their accomplices, were easily picked up by the police less than a half a mile away. They were charged and appeared before the magistrates on Monday. With the evidence against them, they pleaded guilty. Morris and Jones were sentenced to six months probation and each fined £50 and costs for racial abuse and violence.

Mick Taylor (20) who threw the brick was sentenced to 12 months probation and fined £100 plus costs for actual bodily harm and racial abuse. The fourth Clive Leigh (19) was given a conditional discharge for six months as he had not been involved in any violence or racial abuse.'

The Major said, 'BJ you are in the local paper.'

'Oh! My goodness. I did not want to attract adverse attention to you and Anna.'

'It is just a court report. The attackers pleaded guilty and were placed on probation and fined.'

The report was seen by Messrs Baker, Slater and Whyte and others, with whom BJ would work alongside. They were particularly interested in the part about him taking out the first with the speed and skill of a boxer and then also flooring a second.

On Sunday, the Major, Anna and BJ went to mass and BJ was introduced to the parish priest Father Daniels.

The next day he entered Margaret's office. 'Good morning.'

'Good morning Bryan. My! You do look so much better.'

'I am better thanks.'

She buzzed Mr Baker, 'Mr Conway is here.'

'Send him in please.'

She knocked and opened the door. Mr Baker was on his feet walking towards them.

He held out his hand. 'Good morning. Good to see you looking the way you were the first time we met. Sit down please.'

'Thank you sir for your concern and kindness last week.'

'Don't mention it.'

He had the file in front of him. 'I need you to sign your Contract of Employment. It is the standard one for all employees. It sets out the terms and conditions that apply to both sides.'

After the formalities, he said, 'I will now take you to your room.'

As they entered, the others looked up and round. He was taken to Alistair's office. 'I will leave him with you.'

'Sit down BJ. How do you feel?'

'Better thanks.'

'Now don't put yourself under any pressure. Relax and give yourself time to settle in. Everything will fall into place sooner rather than later because you have the experience. Come and I will show you your work station and introduce you to your colleagues.'

He actually took him into the area where he would not be working. 'Colleagues, this is Bryan Conway whom I told you about.'

To Brian, he said, 'You will get to know their names. There are too many to mention now.'

He then took him the other side and to his desk. 'This is where you will sit. Adrian, who has been with us twelve years is sitting opposite you.

Chapter Twenty Six

He will help getting you settled.'

Adrian stood up and shaking hands said, 'Pleased to meet you.' He felt the strong grip and was reminded of what Alastair told them about his boxing and martial arts. Indeed he did strike an imposing figure, was tall, good-looking and sartorially elegant.

There was everything he needed on the desk. Adrian said, 'This is our instruction manual. Perhaps you can spend a while reading through it. There are also a few files to look through so you can familiarise yourself with procedures. Your telephone extension is 2307. All calls go through the operator so you will need to ask for a line to call out or the extension if internal. If you have any questions, please ask.'

'I do not know if there is a notebook. If not, may I have one please?'

'There should be one. If not I will get you one. The clerical staff are responsible for stationery so if you need anything just ask them.'

'Also, where are the gents?'

'Turn left at the door and it is on the right at the far end of the corridor.'

BJ took off his coat and put it over the back of his chair. Those discreetly eyeing him up noticed his presence, smartness and broad chest. The bald patch at the side of his head showing the healing wound was plainly visible.

BJ settled down at his desk and busied himself studying the manual. Time passed and Adrian said, 'We have a drink and a short break about eleven. Also we each subscribe a shilling every week into a kitty to buy the tea, coffee, milk, sugar and biscuits. What would you like to drink?'

BJ took out a shilling from his pocket and handed it over. 'Coffee with one sugar and just a little milk please.'

Just then, Anna came in. She looked around and seeing him, walked to his desk attracting further attention. His back was to the door so he did not see her. She leaned against his desk. 'Hello BJ. How is everything?'

'Hello Anna. Fine thanks.'

The coffee came. 'Hello Anna,' the lady with the tray said.

'Hello Yvonne.'

'Biscuits, BJ?'

He took a couple saying, 'Thank you.' He handed one to Anna. 'Have some of my coffee.'

As with the shared breakfast in hospital she drank some of it as she ate the biscuit. All this aroused the interest of the others. Anna was known to be a quiet one who showed no interest in boys despite being asked out often. Spurned suitors sometimes unkindly referred to her as the nun as she was known to be a devout Catholic who attended mass regularly. She also had a 4-inch wooden crucifix on her desk. A few with bruised egos and hurt pride cruelly wondered if she was a lesbian. Now, there she was, sharing a drink with BJ.

'What shall we do for lunch? Go to the restaurant? You will be able to see what it is like for the future.'

'Fine. Whatever you wish.'

'I will come for you about half past twelve. See you then. Bye for now.' Then she left.

BJ finished his drink. 'Adrian, I will go and wash the mug but where do I return it?'

'I will show you but can you bring your own tomorrow? How do you know Anna?'

'I was in a Catholic orphanage run by a boarding school. The boys' school and her convent were in the same town and we used to go to each other's concerts and sports days. She was a successful runner and also appeared in its concerts so we got to know who she was. But we only met properly before we boarded the ship when we recognised each other. In fact, as it happens, I am now a guest in her and her father's house. The person who was to meet me at the docks had flown back to India urgently two days before. I would have been stranded but for them.'

He was surprised but tried not to show it. Others within earshot picked up on this and were intrigued. Interesting, they thought. Anna had never shown any warmth or encouragement to the males before. Now she had come to visit BJ, have one of his biscuits and share his drink. And, they would be lunching together.

Chapter Twenty Six

Around half past twelve, Anna came for him. The restaurant was on the fourth floor. Several colleagues noticed them as they walked in. Who's that with Anna? some thought. The nun with a guy and a coloured one at that aroused interest. Also, there was something about BJ. Smartly suited with an easy gait. He walked tall and did not swing his arms; they just dangled and moved rhythmically with each step. He would have attracted attention even if he was on his own but having Anna alongside was something else.

However, he did not notice and even if he had, in his naiveté and being the modest person he was, he would not have thought they were looking at him with Anna.

One who had read the article in the paper, seeing the bald patch on his head and the wound, said, 'That must be the bloke who was racially attacked. The case was reported in the Chronicle on Saturday.'

Another said, 'Oh yes I saw it too. So he is the Indian that dealt with one of the attackers with the speed and skill of a boxer. At least I think that is what they reported. He certainly looks as if he can look after himself.'

Others who had seen the article in the paper put two and two together.

Often Anna lunched with a few colleagues. Now here she was with a new face and a male at that. Well! Well! they thought, Anna with a breed she had shown no interest in before.

They joined the queue and looked at the menu board. 'Do you want to have a full meal or just a snack?'

'We will have dinner at home won't we? I will be happy with just soup and some bread.'

'They do hot pies and sandwiches. Shall we just have a sandwich?'

'That will do fine. I will get them. What would you like?'

'Shall we share egg salad and ham salad sandwiches?'

He ordered and paid for them.

'We will need to get the hot drinks from the other counter. I will get them.' She got their drinks and Anna looked for the colleagues she normally ate with. Seeing them, she headed their way.

'Hello everyone this is BJ. He started today. BJ, this is Janet and Gill. We often lunch together.'

'Pleased to meet you both.'

They sat down. The others knew who he was from the office grapevine. But they said nothing. They ate and drank and made general chitchat as BJ listened. After they had eaten, Anna said to BJ, 'I am going to have another tea. Shall I get you one too?'

'OK thanks.'

'Anyone else?'

'No thanks,' they said.

She got up to go to the counter. It aroused the others' curiosity. Anna buying a bloke a drink?

While Anna was away, BJ asked, 'How long have each of you been working here?' As they talked generally Anna returned with two mugs of tea and a slice of cheesecake. The others excused themselves and left as they had to go to the shops.

Anna said, 'Try this,' and taking a piece off with a fork she fed him.

'It's very tasty. What is it?'

'Cheesecake.'

'Cheesecake?'

'Yes. It is made of biscuit crumbs, cream cheese and double cream. I'll make it for you at the weekend,' and proceeded to feed him a piece alternately.

Throughout, others were discreetly watching them. They were amazed by Anna and her behaviour.

'Thank you for your company and support today. Colleagues will not have failed to see us together and will talk.'

'I don't care what they say,' putting her hand over his and leaving it there.

'But I cannot stop thinking of what that couple said on the ship. I do not want anyone to think unkindly of you because of me.'

This time she picked up his hand and held it to her lips kissing it. She did it spontaneously, oblivious of their surroundings. He too was caught up in the moment.

'I am not responsible for what people think only what I am.'

'Thank you.'

She kissed his hand again before releasing it.

'Let's go. I will show you where I work.'

As they walked out, he put his hand gently in the small of her back. It did not go unnoticed. Anna behaving this way with a guy had really captured their attention.

She led him into her office and to her desk. 'This is where I work.'

He noticed the crucifix on her desk as he leaned against it and looking straight ahead caught the eye of some as they looked up.

Anna was behaving perfectly natural. She loved BJ and being with him. Being a sincere person, it did not occur to her that her behaviour and actions were a statement. But to her colleagues it certainly was. Without realising it, she was nailing the lie that she may be a lesbian. She was just principled, knowing what she wanted out of a relationship.

He left to return to his desk as she said, 'I will come up for tea.'

When the Major got home, he asked, 'Well how was your first day?'

'Good, thanks. Anna was very supportive and spent her morning and afternoon coffee breaks with me. We also lunched together in the restaurant.'

Chapter Twenty Seven

The days passed and became weeks. Their lives fell into a pattern. They ran. They walked Bruno. They swam. They played badminton. They went to the pictures. And then it was the end of the month.

All staff were paid in cash. That evening before dinner, BJ said, 'Sir I have received my first salary. I cannot continue living here for free; I must pay my way.'

Anna looked at her father, who insisted on him paying just £15 a month.

'Sir I have seen what Anna pays for the shopping every week. £15 won't buy the food for a month.'

'You want to build up a financial base. Save. £15 is fine and that is the way I would like it.'

BJ looked at Anna for some guidance and reassurance. It was forthcoming. She nodded and reluctantly he said, 'Sir, Anna, you are being very generous. Thank you,' and handed over £15.

He, in turn, passed it to Anna, 'Put it towards the shopping.'

On Saturday, they did the usual shopping together. He had noticed the range of shops previously and seen berets displayed on the mannequins in a ladies dress shop window. This time he stopped. 'Have you got any of them?'

'No. I have seen women wearing them and they looked nice. I had toyed with the idea of buying one but I did not have the confidence to wear it.'

'You would look nice in one. Shall we go in and see?'

'Good morning. Can I help you?'

'Good morning. Yes please. We would like to have a look at the berets.'

'Try the red one,' he said. 'It will go with your dark hair.'

She did and looked in the mirror. She felt good. 'Is it OK?'

'You look lovely. Do you like it though? If you are not comfortable wearing one I do not want to pressure you. I want you to be happy.'

'And I want to make you happy too. I have wanted one but as I said I did not feel confident enough to wear it.'

'I will get them. What colours would you like?'

'Colours? I only need one.'

'You can wear different ones to match your outfits. How about the cream, white and red?'

'The red and one other will do.'

'We'll take all three,' he said to the sales assistant and paid for them.

'You can put on the red one now.'

'Thank you.' She was somewhat overwhelmed.

'You look great. If you let me, I will help you become confident.'

With him, she already was.

On Monday, she wore the red beret to work. BJ was pleased she did and said, 'You look very nice. I wonder what your colleagues will say.'

When she walked into her office, her colleagues noticed it. 'Anna that is nice. You've never worn it before.'

'I never had one to wear. BJ suggested it and bought me three on Saturday.'

'BJ? Are the two of you involved?'

Anna went a bright red. 'No.' But her face betrayed her true feelings for him.

His wound healed and the bald patch disappeared as his hair grew. They did increasingly more together.

Anna was always a smart dresser but wore mainly pastel shades. But she became more adventurous with colours generally.

Barry invited them to an Anglo-Indian club dance. There, Anna met several former convent girls but more recognised BJ from school and his subsequent public appearances. They were made quite a fuss of and inevitably he was asked to entertain. Anna was very comfortable with the community having lived and been educated within it.

It was one of many they went to. They were also often invited to spend the day with Barry and his family once they had settled into their own home. And they met others with whom they exchanged addresses and maintained contact widening their social circle.

They went to live concerts, the office social club, dances and on outings. She never danced with anyone else, refusing many requests to do so. She just wanted to be and dance with BJ and he was more than happy with that.

One such outing was to a seaside funfair. It was a novel experience and BJ was in his element. The incessant noise of the rides and people screaming, the general buzz, everything fascinated BJ. He enjoyed watching the people enjoying themselves and Anna enjoyed watching him, as he seemed awestruck with the experience. The big wheel and big dipper provided panoramic views in the late evening glow. They went on the ghost train, Anna gripping his arm several times along the way and the tunnel of love. He was fascinated by the Wall of Death. She could not tear him away but she did not mind. Not only was she infinitely patient she was sharing his childish enjoyment.

She took him to the promenade and they walked on the beach. On the coach, going back, others had had a few drinks too many and were rather noisy having a sing-along at the back. Anna just leaned against BJ and they rested easy, keeping to themselves in the front.

With the passing of time, the Major resumed going to his bridge club in the evenings and played more golf at the weekends. He took them to his golf club social events. These helped BJ's confidence tremendously, because the Major did not shy away from introducing him to everyone.

In September, the new badminton season started at Anna's private club. They went and Anna showed him the routine. Each player had a clothes peg with his or her name on it. The ladies were in red and the men in blue. They were hung on a board as they came in and BJ had to use a guest's one. She said the first on the board chooses any three of the next five and places the four pegs under the court number below. The winners then replace theirs in the queue in front of the losers.

Anna, being known, was selected before him. BJ was the next one to choose from one red and four blues. He selected the first three blues, one of which was David's. He usually partnered Peter, leaving BJ and the fourth, Eric on the other side of the net.

David had the reputation of being very competitive and a bad loser. He was very vocal and liked to dictate the play and proceedings. As he always did, he called for two shuttles to warm up. He faced BJ and lobbed the shuttle to him. BJ in accordance with protocol lobbed it back half court but David smashed it back grounding it. BJ, using the edge of his racquet scooped it up and without handling it flipped in the air lobbing it again half court. Yet again it was smashed back and grounded. BJ recovered the shuttle as he had before but this time took it in his hand and served it low over the net. David returned it low also but BJ was up to it and more accurate in his net return causing it to be netted. David now had to serve to BJ who lobbed it deep into the back court, forcing a defensive return. BJ smashed it straight back, aiming for the neck and head of his opponent causing him to duck to avoid being hit.

Several non-players were watching this particular scenario. They wanted to see how good BJ was and how he coped with David. What they saw brought a smirk to some of their faces. David decided to play safe and serve deep to BJ's backhand but to his chagrin, found that he was strong on that side and had to back-pedal himself to return weakly. BJ summarily smashed it into his body. David did not like being bettered; he had lost the battle of wills so decided to start the game.

He spun his racquet, 'Rough or smooth?'

BJ called, 'Rough.'

'Smooth,' taking the shuttle, meaning he would serve first.

BJ asked, 'Are you serving?'

'What does it look like?'

'Just making sure. In that case we will change sides.'

David was surprised. By changing, he would be facing the non-players and they could be a distraction. Again, BJ had got the better of him.

Chapter Twenty Seven

He served to Eric and after a short rally won the point so he had to serve to BJ. He served low, which BJ attacked. The game continued and it became clear that BJ was the best player on court with Eric being the weakest. They were 1-6 down when BJ decided to take charge his side of the net. He spoke to Eric. 'We can win this. Just let me call the shots and follow.' He scrambled for everything to prevent Eric from playing a weak shot and giving away the point. BJ played the percentages to frustrate his opponents and succeeded. David's frustration turned to annoyance and then anger.

BJ played shots under his right thigh and backhanded around his back. During one rally, David lobbed deep over BJ's head. Caught off balance he turned his back to the net. He watched the shuttle as he scurried to the baseline. With good timing he jumped and hit the shuttle between his legs. His opponents had relaxed somewhat, reasonably believing they had won the point. They recovered too late and lost the point instead. David threw his racquet on the ground as Eric said, 'Excellent shot.' The non-players were stunned.

They leveled at 12-12 and went ahead 14-13 with their two serves to come. Eric lost his serve, leaving BJ to serve for the game to David. In his cocky way he fully expected an attacking low serve. BJ made as if to do so but at the last moment flicked the shuttle over David's head as he moved forward to attack it. The game was won. As they shook hands at the net, David said to BJ, 'You had some luck there.'

'Yes, you are right. The more I play the luckier I get. You should try it.'

David walked off court in a huff and said to no one in particular, 'Who brought that foreign bozo along?'

Anna had come off court some while earlier and had been watching BJ's game. 'If you mean the guest that bettered you, his name is BJ and I did. Why?'

'What gutter did you drag him from?' he asked cuttingly.

BJ heard this and stepped in front of him. 'Don't talk to Anna like that.' There was no mistaking the menace in the tone of his voice. 'Besides if you want to know anything about me, ask me not Anna. I speak and understand English. Now repeat your question.'

There was a hush. David was getting his comeuppance. And not before time.

David hesitated momentarily, not liking the look on BJ's face. But his ego would not allow him to back down so he decided to bluff it through.

'I asked what gutter did she drag you from.'

Immediately BJ replied, 'The same gutter as you. Only you live in it; I tripped and fell in and Anna - that is her name - helped me out.'

There were gasps and sniggers from several of the women. Some men simply smiled. David was not popular.

There was a pregnant pause, during which BJ glared into David's eyes, whose demeanour had changed. His resolve weakened and he was now bereft of bravado. BJ sensing this did the honourable thing to diffuse the situation. 'I am new to the club. Let's just forget it and shake,' he said, extending his hand. David's face relaxed and he shook hands.

BJ turned to Anna, 'Are you OK, princess?'

She nodded. She took a drink from the water bottle she had brought and passed it to him. 'That was a good close game especially coming from behind.'

After that, BJ never had to wait before being selected to play. He later found himself partnering Anna in a mixed doubles. Having played regularly with her at weekends, he knew she was a better than average player being particularly good at the net. They complemented each other and proved too strong winning comfortably.

Arriving home, the Major asked, 'How was it? Good?'

'Yes sir, thanks, I thoroughly enjoyed it. I love the game anyway.'

Anna said, 'He showed he is the best player in the club. One arrogant and loud man is very unpopular because he is full of himself. BJ put him in his place. He got the better of him in the warm-up and came from behind to win. He did not like it and got nasty with me because I took BJ along. BJ stood up to him and he had to back down. But BJ was very dignified. To save the other's face he suggested they forget it and start again and offered to shake hands.'

'Just like on the ship with that drunk. Well done son.'

She made them a hot drink and BJ excused himself. He wished them goodnight and went to his room.

As a statement of fact, the Major said, 'You really love him.'

'Daddy, I love him with all of me. And I know he loves me too but he is holding back. We started to become very close that night with the drunk on the ship and then that couple referring to him derogatorily as an Indian. But really what sealed everything was the day he was attacked. When he awoke to find me sitting beside his bed and realised I had been there all night he was very affectionate. We shared his breakfast and it was very intimate. Also, when we are out, he is a thorough gentleman and very protective. I feel safe with him. He gets a hold of my arm before we cross the road and always gets me to walk on the inside. In a crowd, he either takes my arm or puts a protective hand on my back.'

'That is how the Indians are generally. The men get up on public transport and offer their seat to a woman. They do it here too.'

After a short pause he continued, 'Girl, remember what he has said more than once. He feels he is beneath our financial and social status. The orphans were referred to as poor boys. Also I am sure he feels so strongly because of what that couple said and his attack. You can't blame him. I don't. I understand the way he feels. And that is why without doubt I want him for a son-in-law. I am very fond of him. Very fond.'

'I am sure you are right.'

They sat a while. He closed his eyes, clasped his hands together resting his pointed index fingers against his lips. It was his pensive mode. She knew the signs, so kept her silence. After a great deal of thought and deliberation he said, 'Daughter, maybe you should think of taking the initiative and telling him you love him. He needs to know that to reassure him it is not how much money he has got or that he is of a different culture. You love him for who and what kind of person he is.'

She was surprised. 'Daddy the first time I suggested we went to the pictures and I would pay he was shocked. He said the man pays. However, I persuaded him and he was ok about it. Every time we have been anywhere we took it in turns to pay. Often he insisted he paid anyway. I do not know how he would react to my taking the initiative. I do not want to spoil what we have already.'

'You will not know until you do. And you won't spoil it. Of that I am sure. In any case, I have no doubt he will be delighted. You just need to give him some encouragement.'

'I will have to think about it. Also how to go about it and then choose the moment.'

After a while she said, 'Anyway, I must go to bed myself. Goodnight.'

Chapter Twenty Eight

On Friday, the Major went away for the weekend for a club bridge match. That evening Anna and BJ went to the pictures. When they arrived home, Anna said, 'Thank you for a lovely evening. Do you want Horlicks or some other night-time drink?'

'Any if you are having one.'

They drank and went up together, each to their own rooms. He heard her go to the bathroom. He stripped off, put on his dressing gown and waited for her to finish her ablutions. He then went to the bathroom himself and washed and cleaned his teeth, a habit he had developed noting the Major's and Anna's routine.

He lay on top of the bed, taking his rosary and bible he was about to read and pray when there was a knock on his door. 'BJ?' Before he could answer Anna walked in. She was naked.

He had never seen a naked girl before. Shocked and taken completely aback, he swung his legs over the side of the bed stuttering, 'Anna, you're naked! What are doing here?'

An onlooker would have found the situation absolutely hilarious. He had forgotten he was naked too!

She knelt sitting on her heels in front of him quite unabashed. She took his hand and placed it over her left breast. 'Can you feel my heart beating?'

'Yes.' It was racing. But then so was his!

She clenched her other hand into a fist saying, 'It is as big as my fist and it all belongs to you. I love you BJ. I love you with all of my heart. I've loved you since my sports day when we both turned around to look and smile at each other.'

'Anna, at the quayside I knew why I had not been interested in any girl before. On the ship I did not dare hope you felt anything for me. And then you stayed with me all night at the hospital and I felt you must care.

But I am of a different culture. And I am not rich like you and your dad.'

'Money is not important. The gospel of Luke says, 'A man's life does not consist in the abundance of his possessions.' Nor is the fact you are an Anglo-Indian. All that matters is I love you.'

Rising to her feet she said, 'Push over.'

Realisation dawned with the new day and he remembered the previous night. Shock and shame initially overcame him but Anna loved him.

They took Bruno for his morning walk. Things could not have been better. The sun was shining, giving them its blessing as its warm rays gently caressed their heads. Even Bruno seemed to catch the atmosphere. He bounded here and there catching thin air as if he was warming up in anticipation of the real event. It was the ball game.

They were in a glade on the common. Anna handed BJ the ball and he threw it back and forth as Bruno ran, fetched and dropped it at their feet. His canine instincts sensed the aura of love they exuded. It wasn't just the sun that was warm.

It was some time before they returned home.

The sun continued to shine on their day. That afternoon they played their usual session of badminton. At home they had a light lunch relaxing in the back garden soaking up the sun. The flowers were still in bloom and it was nice and peaceful. The odd bird fed at the feeders and on the bits of bread they threw on the lawn.

Anna asked, 'What do you want to do this evening?'

'I don't mind. As always I am happy just being together. But would you like to go to the New Orleans?' It was a disco dance venue with live music and restaurant. 'Or would you rather dine out? You don't want to be cooking a meal.'

'Let's do both. We can go for an Indian and then go dancing. We can celebrate being a couple.'

They drove into the city's entertainment centre and went into a restaurant her father had told her about. However after coffee, she said, 'BJ would you mind if we did not go dancing? I'm stuffed and feel like going home and relaxing.'

Chapter Twenty Eight

He was content just being with her no matter where. Life had taken on a new meaning and purpose so he was happy to agree.

They took Bruno for a walk and sat for a time by the river as he enjoyed being off the lead. It was a nice night. Ducks swam, creating ripples in their wake.

Returning home they had a night-time drink after which she said, 'Tonight we will sleep in my bed.'

The next day, as usual, they left early for the nine o'clock mass so they could go to confession. At home, after breakfast and later, she prepared a picnic lunch and filled flasks. She got Bruno's bowl and a bottle of water. She drove some way to a woodland lake. At one end there was a gentle waterfall. The sound of the water was soothing and the whole scene idyllic. They found a secluded spot away from the walkers' path but still within sight and earshot of the waterfall, albeit in the distance.

She handed BJ the air mattress to inflate and they sat down to eat. BJ said, 'This is lovely. The sound of running water, the ducks and swans, the birds twittering in the trees. If this is lovely what must have the Garden of Eden been like?'

Finished they loaded the car but did not drive home immediately. They walked for some time by the lake, under the canopy of trees, besides shrubs and bushes. There was always bird song serenading them. BJ thought, 'My whole life has completely turned around.'

All too soon they returned home. He was not looking forward to facing the Major and became a little subdued. She sensed it and kept squeezing his hand and kissing him.

'Don't worry. He will be OK. You'll see. Trust me.'

The Major returned about a quarter after six. As soon as he walked in through the door, he instinctively sensed a change in the atmosphere.

Anna greeted him asking, 'How did you do?'

'We won overall. It was a very enjoyable weekend and the Welsh Club want to visit us for a return match. How was yours?' The answer was in her sparkling face and eyes. He knew there had been a development in her and BJ's relationship but kept a discreet silence.

213

'Excellent. Have you eaten? We waited for you so we could have our main meal together.'

'We had a big lunch before we left. The two of go ahead and eat. I will go and unpack and change.'

They had just about finished when he came back down. She told BJ, 'Go and join Daddy and I will clear the table and bring the drinks.'

She brought them in and the Major asked, 'So what have you been doing with yourselves?' He looked at each in turn and BJ answered.

'Sir I have betrayed your trust. I am sorry. Please forgive me. Anna and I slept together.'

He was shocked. Not only at the confession but BJ's forthrightness.

Anna chipped in. 'Daddy, yes we did sleep together but the truth is I took the initiative and went into his room. BJ has always been a thorough gentleman and never took anything for granted. He was very reluctant because he did not want to betray your trust but I persuaded him. You could say I seduced him. We love each other. I convinced him that money and status was not important. Us loving one another was.'

The Major was in fact relieved and reassured BJ, 'I do not consider you betrayed my trust. I am relieved you have committed to each other.'

Anna asked, 'Relieved? Why?'

BJ answered, 'It is my fault. I asked your dad something the first night I was here. Sir, have you at anytime regretted your answer? Does it still apply?'

Anna was intrigued. 'What does still apply?'

'I asked if your dad would have me as a son-in-law.'

She was shocked. 'You what? You asked Daddy that that first night?'

'Yes. He affirmed and I went on to say that I would not commit to you unless and until I had built up a financial base and felt you reciprocated.'

She started to cry tears of joy. To her father she said, 'All this time and you said nothing.'

'I could not for the same reason I could not tell BJ what you asked me.'

It was BJ's turn to show surprise. Anna said, 'Remember when the ship set sail and I came to look for you?

He nodded.

'I asked Daddy the same question; would he have you for a son-in-law?'

BJ's mouth opened in amazement. He tried to speak but no words would come out. The Major intervened. 'I have carried that knowledge of what you both felt about one another with difficulty. I saw the chemistry between you and the closeness that was developing. I knew it would be a matter of time but knowing you BJ because you were determined to save money I thought it would be later rather than sooner.'

They sat in silence for a while as all these confessions sank in.

BJ broke it. 'Sir will you allow me to marry Anna please?'

'Son, nothing would make me happier.'

Anna's face was alight. If she emitted any more watts she will have blown up. Or burnt her face.

BJ got up and kneeling on one knee before her took her hands in his. 'Anna, part of a verse in the New Testament is "Silver and gold I have none but what I have I give to you." I am not rich, cannot buy you diamonds and jewels. All I have is my love. I love you with every cell of my body. Please, will you marry me?'

She stood up pulling him up with her. 'BJ, yes. I will marry you!' and they embraced kissing briefly. When they sat down again, they realised they were alone. The Major had gone upstairs to control his emotions and fetch something he had planned for this moment.

One Saturday when Anna and BJ were out, he had gone into the loft brought down a suitcase and put it under his bed. He now took it downstairs and placed it on the floor between Anna and BJ and himself. He opened it and took out his late wife's wedding dress holding it up. 'This is your mother's. She kept it for you in case you wanted to marry in it.'

It was all silk and lace. There was a tiara and veil too.

'Daddy, I have always liked it in the photo.'

'You can have it altered to suit.'

Anna took it and put it against her looking at BJ who said, 'It is a lovely dress.'

The Major took three small boxes from the pocket on the inside of the lid. 'These are her wedding and engagement rings. This one is my wedding ring. Again it was her wish you decide whether you wanted them. Her rings have been in the family for three generations.'

Anna tried them on and held her hand out to look at them on her finger. She said, 'Thank you Daddy. This has been such a lovely weekend I do not want it to end. I just wish mummy was here to share these moments.'

'I am sure she is happy, nodding her approval and giving you both her blessing.'

The rings also can be altered to fit and can be cleaned and polished as good as new.

He put the dress back in the suitcase.

BJ felt an overwhelming desire to tell all about himself. 'Sir, Anna, I want to tell you about my parents and how I was orphaned.'

'You don't have to son. It is past.'

'But I want to. I have not told anyone else but you are the two most important people in my life. I want you both to know everything about me.'

They sat down and BJ took some time to gather his thoughts and find the words. Anna sensed it was painful and got down on the floor resting her arms on his thighs. She held one of his hands looking up at him. With the other he played with her hair and the back of her neck.

'You both know I was orphaned when I was seven. It happened on my birthday.' Both were shocked.

'My father was a marine engineer and originally a merchant seaman. A few months before, he had become home based in charge of the river dredgers. He used to drink a lot, getting drunk and physically abusing my mother. That evening he had been playing bridge at a friend's house. I had gone to sleep but woke up to shouting. My father was standing over my

Chapter Twenty Eight

mother who was cowering on the floor against the wall. He was threatening her with a bicycle security chain. I got a hold of his arm, saying, 'Daddy please don't hurt mummy again!' He backhanded me and I went backwards hitting my head against the corner of a wardrobe and falling unconscious. When I came to, my mum was slumped against the wall with blood pouring from her head. She died in my arms as I cried myself to sleep on her shoulder. When the servant arrived the next morning we found my father hanging from the ceiling fan in the front room.'

Anna gasped loudly. 'Oh! no, BJ!' She got onto her knees and with watery eyes held his face in her hands. After a few moments she settled down into her original position sitting at his feet.

He paused not to allow this to sink in but to cope with the memory of that horrible and painful night. His lips were quivering and he had to fight hard to control tears that were welling up.

He continued, 'Everything, all the memories that had made up the golden fabric of my life in those formative years had been taken from me. Overnight I had no one around who loved me and I never felt more alone or afraid. Three weeks later I left the only life I had ever known to go to the orphanage. I grew up emotionally insecure and even after I left school never gave any thought to falling in love let alone getting married.

But then we met at the docks. Seeing you Anna ignited feelings within me I had not experienced since we turned around and smiled at each other on your sports day. On the ship, you both made me feel wanted, that I belonged. But I was afraid to let go of my emotions. I was scared I would lose you too. Yes my culture and status had a lot to do with it. I believed I could not fit into your lives.'

Both Anna and the Major were now in tears. She arose and sat on the arm of the settee. She put her arm around his neck and kissed his head. Neither could believe what they had heard. What a way to be orphaned. That he had turned out to be the kind of person he was was even more remarkable. He showed no outward signs of being psychologically affected.

The Major was profoundly moved. Here he was a company director who in the war had killed and seen men killed. He had been injured himself in battle and medically discharged and now he was overcome with emotion.

He arose, 'Come here BJ,' holding out his arms as he took a few steps towards him. He embraced him saying, 'Thank you for telling us that. It must have been very painful. But we are now your new family. No longer are you alone with no one to love you. Put it all behind, close the book on it and look to the future. Today is the first day of the rest of your life.'

Anna joined in the embrace as the three of them hugged each other in physical confirmation of their loving pact.

The Major took control. 'Phew! We have all had an eventful weekend. BJ you have really impacted our lives. Me crying! I fought in the war. And you reduce me to tears.'

He meant every word but tried to make it light-heartedly to ease the atmosphere.

Chapter Twenty Nine

Neither Anna nor BJ said anything to anyone the following day at the office. But increasingly, over the previous months, it had become evident there was something between them.

They returned from work at twenty past five. A few minutes later, Bruno warned of a known visitor. It was Sandra.

'Hello Sandra. Come in. Tea? Coffee?'

'No thanks, I just want a quick word. This afternoon while I was cleaning, a man came to the door. Bruno went frantic and I had to keep the chain on the door. He asked if I was Mrs Conway? I asked who he was and where from. He gave his name as Mr Inglis but would not say where he was from. I said I was not Mrs Conway and he should come back at seven o'clock tonight. I said seven o'clock because your father should be home by then.'

'Thank you Sandra. I wonder who it could be, especially as he obviously wanted BJ personally.'

The Major was home after six o'clock and Anna told him what Sandra had said.

At five to seven, Bruno went berserk. He sat when told but was still very much in guard mode. The Major opened the door.

'Mr Conway?'

'Who's asking?'

'I am Mr Inglis. Are you Mr BJ Conway?'

'Who do you represent?'

'I can only reveal that to you if you are in fact Mr Conway.'

'Can you wait here a moment please?'

The Major went into the sitting room and asked, 'BJ do you want to see the caller? I do not know what it can be about as he won't tell me who he represents.'

'Yes, I will see him.'

The Major invited the caller in and introduced him to BJ and Anna. Bruno sat on the floor watching him suspiciously. If Mr Inglis had any bad intentions, he would have been attacked. BJ saw this and called Bruno, putting his hand around his neck, rubbing it.

'Mr Conway may we speak privately please?'

'You can do so with Anna and the Major here. It is their house.'

Anna asked, 'Would you like a drink?'

'Coffee please with milk and two sugars.'

Mr Inglis extracted some papers from his briefcase and handed over a business card with his photograph on it. BJ, without looking, immediately handed it to the Major.

The Major's face registered pleasant surprise but it was lost to BJ who was looking at Mr Inglis.

He handed it back to Mr Inglis who said, 'I am the Finance Officer for Lighthouse Pools. Did you check the football results on Saturday?'

'No.' He had had other and better things on his mind!

'Well Mr Conway I have good news for you; very good news. You are the sole 1st dividend winner and initial estimates suggest you have won about £150,000.'

Anna returned with the drinks and having served everyone sat down herself shoulder to shoulder with BJ.

'One and a half lakhs? That is a lot.'

The Major said, 'In rupees it is 3 million.'

'What? I am sorry. Pardon? Rs3m?' He was stunned.

'There may be more. Also, obviously the company would welcome the publicity but I see you showed on the coupon you did not want any. We will increase the sum a little if you change your mind.'

As always, BJ looked at the Major. 'What does publicity mean in this context?'

'Son, it is up to you but I would not agree to it. I will explain later.'

'Then, no thanks. No publicity, absolutely none. I do not want to disturb Anna's and the Major's lives. Or mine for that matter.'

'I respect your decision. Subject to confirmation, I will personally call on Wednesday at the same time to give you the cheque.'

'Are you in a marked company car?' asked the Major.

'No. Mr Conway wanted no publicity and it would not have been prudent to do so. No marked car on Wednesday either, I assure you.'

After he had left, BJ took a few moments for the news to sink in. He rested his forehead on his hand and shut his eyes. He had gone from being a poor boy to rich man. When his heart had slowed down to normal, he said, 'Sir, Anna I will share this good fortune with you equally.'

Both were left speechless. Anna started to cry.

BJ put his arm around her. 'I am sorry Princess. Please don't cry. I did not want to upset either of you. What did I say wrong? I really do want to share the money with you.'

She said, 'No you did not say anything wrong. It is a lot of money. It's yours.'

'Princess, sir, on the ship you knew I could not afford to buy you any drinks in return. Yet both of you insisted. Anna, you paid the doctor's bill when I was seasick. You also took me in and fed and sheltered me taking just a nominal sum monthly and then only after I had got my first month's salary. Does it really matter how much it is? Isn't a good deed a good deed? Also a gift, a present is not one unless it is accepted. How does one value a kindness or a gesture of gratitude? I am simply doing for the two of you what you have done for me all these months.'

'We are very touched.'

The Major knew he had to ease the atmosphere. 'Son, I too feel like Anna. I'll tell you what I think you should do. You and Anna are getting married. Share it with her. I don't need it. To maximise your returns, I will ask our stockbroker and company accountant for advice. I feel that you should buy properties in the city and other prime locations and rent them out. There is always a market for good quality lettings. Also perhaps he might recommend a shares portfolio and high rate savings accounts, probably in building societies. Invest in your future life together and your children. When they are born, you can set up trust funds for them so when they reach the age of maturity, they will have a start.'

'Sir if that will make you happy then I will abide by your wishes.'

'My wish is for you and Anna to be happy. That will make me happy. I have seen you together and the relationship developing from the first day we met and I could not be happier for the two of you.'

'Thank you sir. Are you OK now Anna?'

She had her head on his shoulder and nodded squeezing the hand around her.

'Sir, what did Mr Inglis mean about publicity?'

'Oh yes. What happens is that the company holds a presentation party. They may lay on a finger buffet. That is, eatables you pick up with your fingers like sandwiches, cocktail sausages, nuts, crisps, sausage rolls and food like that. Also hot and cold and alcoholic drinks are provided. The press are invited and they take photographs of the pools representative presenting you with the cheque. The next day the photo is published in the papers and everyone will know who you are and the area where you live. Previous winners have been known to get sacks of begging letters and proposals of marriage. Unless you want your face to be known and enjoy being in the public eye, I would not advise it.'

'No. That is not what I want for myself, apart from the marriage proposals,' he said, grinning mischievously. The Major laughed and Anna dug him in the ribs, 'You dare,' but she saw the funny side and the grin on his face and laughed too.

'Seriously more so for Anna and you, I do not want outsiders interfering and disrupting your lives.'

'Sometimes the local press pick up the story and call at the winner's home.'

'No, definitely not.'

The next day after dinner, they were in the lounge with their hot drinks when Anna said, 'On Sunday you told us about the loss of your parents. Daddy and I want you to know about how Mummy died.'

BJ said nothing.

Chapter Twenty Nine

The Major continued, 'As it turns out the final year in school was very significant for both of you. Not just because of the exchange of looks on Anna's sports day but because of my wife and Anna's mother. As you know her name was Senga. After the summer holidays, she became very ill and lost weight. We had a European staff doctor who after various tests diagnosed leukemia. It is a blood cancer. And it was terminal. Because of Anna's exams, we kept it from her but knew that we would have to return to England. We arranged everything in readiness for the end of term. When Anna got home we still kept it from her. We flew back a couple days later. We did our best to have a normal Christmas and enjoy Anna's birthday. God helped because he strengthened Senga during that time.

But not long after Anna's birthday she deteriorated rapidly and died on 18 January. We also had a son. But he died of meningitis and that is why we took up the posting in India. We were only to stay a couple of years but we liked it and Anna was doing well in the convent so we decided to stay until after her final exams. So it was a family death that took us to India and an imminent one that brought us back. Now son, we all know about each other's bereavements.'

Chapter Thirty

The cheque was actually for £152,000, 11s, 7d. On advice, they put it into a new joint bank account. Then they opened a few building society accounts so they could transfer money into them for easy access.

The following Saturday, the three of them went into the city to a jewelers that the Major knew of. Ring sizes were determined and the three family rings handed over for adjustment and cleaning and polishing.

BJ was knocked back when Anna pointed to a tray of men's signet rings and said to him, 'I will have an engagement ring. I would like you to wear one also. I will buy it.'

The salesperson brought it out and laid it on the counter.

'Which one would you like?'

He had never worn a ring. All were very expensive and any of them would have been fine. 'They are all nice ones. You choose as you are giving it to me.'

'I want you to be happy wearing it. Remember what you said about the beret?'

'What about this one,' he said pointing to a plain one that was also relatively speaking, the cheapest in the tray.

'It is too plain.'

'How about this one?' It had an onyx inlay with a diamond in the corner and was in the mid-price range.

'I like this one,' she said, pointing to a thick heavy one with a large square ruby stone and diamonds on either side of it. It was the most expensive in the tray but he did nor demur.

The assistant took it out but it was not the right size on either the left or right finger. 'I will wear it on my left until we marry then I will transfer it to the right as I will have a wedding ring.'

'We can adjust it.'

225

'BJ? Do you like it?'

'Yes very much.'

And she paid for it.

On the way home, BJ said to the Major, 'To celebrate our official engagement may the three of us go out for dinner tonight please?'

'Thank you for asking but I do not want to cramp your style. The two of you go.'

'Sir, I want to share this with you. Please.'

Anna chipped in. 'I would like that too Daddy.'

'OK then.'

When they got home, Anna and the Major agreed the venue and she telephoned to reserve a table.

The evening was intimate. The Major toasted their future happiness and while they waited for their first course he asked, 'Have you yet talked about a date for the wedding?'

Anna looked at BJ to answer. 'Yes sir. We are thinking of next June if you have no objection.'

'No I do not have any objection.'

'Of course it depends on the availability of the people that matter to all of us. I only have a few; my best friend and his parents who live in Bangkok. I want him as my best man. The parish priest who arranged for me to go to the orphanage and when I finished school allowed me to live in the presbytery for two years. We will pay their air fares. Perhaps Father Daniels will put up Father O'Shea. We will also pay Li's and his parents' hotel fees. But I think Mr Leung has friends or relatives in the UK though I do not know where. And finally Barry and his parents. The rest will be whom Anna and you want.'

They chatted generally about the wedding plans and by the end of the evening most of the guest list had been determined. The Major found himself getting quite excited at the prospect.

When they got home, Anna reminded BJ, 'We need to ask Daddy if we can continue to live here after we are married.'

Chapter Thirty

'Oh yes. Are you sure he won't mind?'

'I am sure but we need to ask anyway.'

When all three were seated Anna said, 'Daddy, BJ and I want to ask you something,' and nodded to BJ.

'Sir, you know there is enough money to buy our own house outright but we wonder if you will allow us to continue to live here with you. We want us to live together as a family.'

'I don't want you to leave either. Nothing will make me happier as I cannot imagine life without you both in this house.'

Two weeks later, the rings were ready and on the Monday, they both wore theirs to work. Neither said anything but it was very soon that colleagues noticed Anna's.

'Anna you're wearing a ring. When did you and BJ get engaged?'

'We actually became engaged three weeks ago but we only got the rings on Saturday as they had to be adjusted to fit.'

As girls do, they looked at the ring and were impressed. News spread and it reached BJ's colleagues who had not noticed his ring.

The next Sunday, they saw Father Daniels after the mass and asked if they could see him one evening. 'Come into my office and we can talk now if you like.'

'Father, Anna and I are planning to get married sometime in June next. We have not fixed a date as my best man and his parents live in Bangkok and also we want to invite the parish priest in India to whom I owe a lot. We hope he can come and if so we will be happy to pay for a hotel. But we are wondering whether you might let him stay here in the presbytery so he will be more comfortable.'

'Certainly. Just let me know if and when he can come and we will discuss it further.'

'Thank you very much Father.'

That afternoon BJ wrote to Li and Father O'Shea. He emphasised that he and Anna wanted them there and would pay their airfares and all other expenses. A few weeks later they replied congratulating both and confirming their availability.

They started to slowly put things together. The Major telephoned his sisters to tell them the news and the month of the wedding. BJ asked, 'Anna what colour of dress do you want for your bridesmaids? It will determine the colour of my suit.'

Over a period of time, they purchased three three-storey houses with self-contained basement flats and bedsits. They were all within a two to three mile radius, in fact two were on nearby roads. They also purchased a couple of terraced houses and two adjacent semi-detached houses. As they were paying cash, they held the aces and therefore negotiated good prices. The sales went through very quickly.

Two substantial properties were also purchased in the city, the rentals of which were put in the hands of management agents that the Major's company used for short and long term corporate visitors. The total income generated was more than their joint salaries. After expenses and tax, it was still a substantial sum that they saved in a separate rentals account. They intended to use the money to increase their property portfolio.

Chapter Thirty One

One Saturday, a few weeks after their commitment, the Major and Anna were going to the hairdressers. He also had some personal business to attend to after that, so BJ was on his own. He had been wondering what to buy Anna for Christmas and her twenty-second birthday on 1 January. He had learned that the new registrations came out on that day, so he was inclined to buy her a new car, even though her present one was just coming up to three years old. She had been given driving lessons for her eighteenth birthday and the car for her nineteenth.

He walked to a showroom he had seen often about fifteen to twenty minutes walk away. As he entered, a salesman saw him and greeted him, 'Good morning, can I help you?'

'Yes please. I am interested in one of those cars,' pointing to a couple of models of a mini. One particularly caught his eye. It was white with a black roof and black trim along the sides. The showroom lights reflected off the highly polished body. But BJ did not show his interest to the salesman. Walking towards the cars, BJ seeing the prices on the windscreens, asked about the cheaper one first. It was red and a basic model. He listened attentively, being shown the inside in which he sat, the boot and the engine. According to the salesman, it was the best value car on the road with excellent petrol consumption and acceleration.

BJ then pointed to the white one. 'And what about that one? What makes it more expensive?'

'It has better a quality interior and finish all round. Also, it has extra features. It is the top of the range.' Again the salesman went through the whole spiel.

Then BJ asked about a large car that was similar to the one the Major had. It was a Jaguar. Going from the smallest range to the biggest surprised the salesman but as his commission depended on it, he again went through the routine. Satisfied after what seemed a long time, BJ asked, 'How much for the two; the white mini and the white Jaguar?'

The salesman thought, Is he serious? but in fact asked, 'I take it you will want hire purchase. What is your job?'

'No, cash. My job does not matter therefore.'

Now the salesman was convinced BJ was not a serious enquirer and wasting his time. But he decided to see it through and humour him.

'The Mini is £699 and the Jaguar £1299, a total of £1998.'

'I will give you £1800.'

'What? Where do you come from?'

'I live not far from here.'

'No, where were you born?'

'India.'

'You may bargain there, we don't here. You've been wasting my time,' he said impatiently and sarcastically.

BJ just looked hard and long at him but said nothing. He said, 'Thank you,' and walked away.

When Anna returned, she asked what he had done.

'I went for a walk.'

When the Major returned and he had settled down, BJ asked, 'Sir may I have a word with you please in your office?'

There he told him where he had been and what had transpired. 'Sir I wanted to surprise you and Anna but being unfamiliar with the way things are done here, I handled it badly by offering less than what they cost.'

The Major was very touched.

'Son, not for the first time I am touched by your thoughtfulness. But my car cost me nothing. It is a company car that is replaced every two years. However Anna will be very pleased. Let's go and see the showroom manager.'

'Anna we are going to see someone.'

She knew better than to pursue it.

When they got to the showroom, the Major drove onto the court and parked the car. They entered the showroom and BJ said, 'There he is. The one I spoke to.'

Chapter Thirty One

The salesman saw them and approached. 'You're back.'

The Major said, 'I would like to speak to your manager. What is his name.'

'Guy Williams. Come with me please.'

They followed him to the manager's office the door of which was open. 'Guy, this gentleman wants to have a word with you.'

'Good afternoon. My name is Guy Williams.'

'Good afternoon. This is Mr Conway and I am Mr McLeod.'

Turning to the salesman he asked, 'What is your name please?'

'Ralph Carlton.'

'Would you mind staying please? It concerns you.'

'Please sit down.'

When they were seated, he continued, 'How can I help you?

The Major said, 'BJ, tell Mr Williams what happened when you called earlier.'

He explained all, from time to time looking directly at the salesman who was clearly uncomfortable asking, 'Am I right so far?' to which he merely nodded.

When it came to the part about India and, 'Here we don't bargain,' the manager was most displeased.

'Did you say that? And impatiently and sarcastically?'

'Yes. I was out of order and am sorry.'

'And that Mr Conway was wasting your time?'

He nodded.

'OK you can go now and I will take it from here. Of course we negotiate especially in a cash sale. Are you still interested in both cars?'

'No. The Jaguar was for the Major here but I did not know the car he had was a company one. So I am only interested in the small white one.'

'He is my future son-in-law and it is his birthday present to my daughter.'

'When is her birthday?'

231

'New Year's day, the date of the new registration.'

'I am deeply sorry for the way you were spoken to Mr Conway. There was no need for it, absolutely no need. Let me show you the car again. And if you have any questions Mr McLeod, I will gladly answer.'

'Sir I don't know anything about cars so will you mind asking the questions? If you feel another car would be better for Anna I will accept what you say.'

The manager was very helpful answering all the Major's questions and knowing how good the Minis were, he agreed on the choice.

The list price is £699 without tax and petrol. However, what happened is not good for the company's image and I want to redress that. How old is your daughter and what no-claims bonus has she got?'

'On the first of January she will be twenty-two and has been insured since she was nineteen. What no claims will that be? 45%?'

'Yes. As a goodwill gesture and by way of apology I will let you have it for £630 all-in. That is tax and insurance and a full tank of petrol. Is that ok?'

BJ looked at the Major who nodded.

'Normally we open the showroom for customers from eleven forty-five on New Year's Eve. We provide a finger buffet and drinks and after midnight customers drive their new cars away. Do you want to pick it up then or in the morning? Whatever time, I will put a ribbon round the car with happy birthday and the lady's name on it and also have a bouquet of red roses all thrown in.'

BJ looked at the Major? 'I don't think Anna would like the fuss in public. She is a very private person.'

'Yes, I agree.'

'We could drive it your home and prepare it in the drive if you can keep your fiancée away, out of sight.'

BJ said, 'That's a good idea.'

Looking at the Major he asked, 'Shall we do it that way?'

'Yes. It will be more private and she will prefer it I am sure.'

Chapter Thirty One

'Good. That's how we will arrange it. To make sure nothing goes wrong, I will be there myself and give her the flowers. Shall we go and complete the paperwork?'

They went back into the office. All the details were taken, and the manager asked, 'I know you don't need hire purchase. Will you be paying by cheque or banker's draft?'

BJ looked at the Major. 'What is a banker's draft?'

'It is effectively the bank's guarantee of payment. A cheque can bounce.' Seeing the puzzled look on his face, he explained, 'The bank may not pay out on the cheque so to avoid the dealer losing money they wait for it to clear before they release the car. But there is plenty of time so you can come back later with a cheque.'

The manager did not demur and passed the paperwork across. The Major checked the details before handing it to BJ to sign. The deal completed they all stood up and shook hands. 'Thank you for your custom. I hope we can wipe the slate clean.'

'Just one thing please, Mr Williams. I personally would appreciate it if you did not deal harshly with Mr Carlton. Certainly for the benefit of other customers, he needs to be spoken to but I am prepared to forget it.'

'As the manager, I have to act but I understand what you are saying and I will in fact tell him of your feelings.'

As they left the office, Mr Carlton approached them. 'I'm sorry I was not very helpful and for saying what I did.'

BJ extended his hand shook his and said, 'Thank you, I appreciate it.'

As they walked back to the car, BJ said, 'Thank you sir for your help. Because of you, we got a good deal I think.'

'Yes I think it is a good deal and arrangement. Anna is going to have a lovely surprise. She will have to get rid of her present car.'

'Can she give it to someone who needs it? What about the priest? Are they allowed to have cars?'

'I don't know but we can leave that until after Anna's birthday.'

Chapter Thirty Two

Anna trusted BJ and his judgement implicitly. This was manifested at the annual office sports championships in December. They entered the badminton mixed doubles. They won fairly comfortably in straight games through to the semis where they lost a close second game 18-17 but won the deciding game 15-11. In the final, they were to meet the previous year's winners.

They lost the first game 15-17 in which there were plenty of rallies making the spectators vocalise a lot as it progressed.

The second game they won 15-13 taking them to the decider. At the changeover, BJ whispered, 'Don't look surprised at anything I decide. Trust me. We will win this.'

She simply nodded.

The other side had first serve. As all were moving into position, BJ said to Anna, 'I will receive.' Immediately, without betraying any emotion, she walked to the left court while BJ prepared to return the serve. The opponents were visibly surprised but the lady served anyway. Perhaps the unexpected switch had unsettled her because her serve was higher than it should have been over the net and was summarily attacked.

It was now BJ's serve and he took advantage of the lady's discomfort. Play ebbed and flowed thereafter with points having to be fought for and won rather than lost. The opponents were not champions for nothing.

BJ and Anna were leading 14-12 but the scores became 14 all with their opponents still with one serve to come, the lady's to him from the right court. BJ, without batting an eyelid, said, 'Straight through.' This surprised all but Anna. Normally, any sane person would have set three, i.e. first to 17. The spectators gasped in disbelief and there was a loud buzz as they exchanged looks and comments with each other. This was for the championship and they were sure BJ had had a mental aberration and thrown it away. The umpire called for quiet and all settled down.

As with the first serve of the game, the lady erred on the side of caution. They just needed to win one more point and she had to make BJ play the shuttle. Again, she served a little higher than she should and BJ attacked it hitting down. But she was prepared and ducked holding her racquet above her head. The shuttle bounced back but Anna killed it. It was then BJ's serve to the lady and there was Anna's to follow. Each knew they had to win this final point on their serve otherwise all was lost.

The lady was unnerved. She had lost her serve and they might now lose their championship. She prepared to receive and BJ, at the last instant, flicked the shuttle over her left shoulder to the back of the service court. Caught off balance, she could not make the return and netted the shot. Anna leaped in the air and squealed with delight. But BJ, apart from a beaming smile, was his cool and calm self. He hugged Anna and kissed her. The spectators were on their feet beside themselves. An excellent match had ended in an unorthodox way, but Anna and BJ were worthy winners. BJ's tactic had worked.

The four players shook hands and the gentleman opponent sportingly said, 'That was an amazing decision you made. I could not have been that brave, especially when it was championship point. But well done.'

'Thank you, it was that close we had to try something different. Fortunately it worked. But I can tell you I cannot see me trying that again.'

The Major was in the crowd and he climbed down to put an arm around each as they came off court. 'Well done the two of you.'

After showering and changing, they met the Major in the bar lounge where the presentation was to take place. There was warm applause when BJ and Anna were presented with their trophies. As BJ accepted his, the presenter asked, 'What prompted you to call it the way you did at match point all with the serve against you?'

BJ answered, 'To unnerve them. We had to break the pattern and do the unexpected. We were lucky it worked.'

BJ's birthday followed shortly later. The Major had agreed with a local, reputable Driving School for him to have as many driving lessons as was required to pass the test. As a general rule, a novice required an hour for each year of their life so initially he paid for six two-hour lessons.

Chapter Thirty Two

Anna gave him a watch and gold bracelet. At the office, his colleagues gave him a card and he bought cream cakes for them.

That evening, Anna treated him, the Major, Sandra and Keith to an à la carte meal in an expensive restaurant. By this time, BJ had become familiar with English and European cuisine. There was gentle music provided by a pianist, violinist and drummer and with the soft lighting and plush décor the ambience was very intimate.

At the end of the evening, BJ said, 'Thank you Anna for the meal. And thank you Major, Keith and Sandra for helping make this the happiest birthday since before I was orphaned.'

'It's a pleasure. We've had an excellent evening too,' Keith said.

The day of the office Christmas party arrived. At previous ones, Anna had only stayed for a while, eating some nibbles and having a couple of soft drinks. But she used to leave early to avoid the silliness that everyone talked about afterwards. Behaviour became loud and uninhibited.

This time, she and BJ stayed for some time dancing and enjoying the party. But inevitably the effects of the free drinks kicked in and lewdness and innuendos increased. It was time for them to leave.

They spent most of the evening on their own as the Major had gone to his golf club celebration after spending some time at his own company's party.

Christmas dawned. Over the months, especially since that eventful weekend in September, BJ felt loved and wanted. He was like a little boy eagerly anticipating opening his presents. And he was not disappointed.

Anna gave him an electric guitar in a hard protective case and her father an amplifier with built in echo chamber.

He gave her a Swiss multi-jeweled watch and gold necklace with matching earrings. He gave the Major a gold fountain pen and pencil set, cufflinks and tiepin.

Late morning, they visited Harry and Ruth for the day. Other members of their family were also there and they were excellent hosts. BJ was very comfortable now and had a good time gaining the respect of those he had only met that day by his behaviour and demeanour. It turned out to be the best Christmas since he lost his parents.

On Boxing Day, so that Bruno was not left on his own all day for the second day running, they had already decided to stay in and have Keith and Sandra over.

On New Years Eve, they went to the Major's golf club dinner dance. It was a black tie event. The Major wore a dress suit, BJ a white tuxedo, and Anna a white Grecian style evening gown with a chain belt. BJ said, 'You look absolutely stunning.'

The Major chipped in, 'Both of you are a lovely looking couple but tonight you look particularly nice together.'

Sandra and Keith, who the Major had invited, arrived and they set off.

At the venue, Harry and Ruth were also there and they all sat together. BJ was reminded of previous such New Year's Eve events when he sang at the club and there was no one in his life. Now he was seeing out the year with his new found family and friends. And next year he would be married. As midnight approached, he shared these thoughts with Anna. He was very much looking forward to the rest of his life.

Anna similarly shared how she was feeling. The old year was in its dying throes and a new one was opening its door to them and their future. On the stroke of midnight they hugged each other and Anna said, 'I love you with all my heart. I cannot wait for us to be husband and wife.' BJ echoed the words adding, 'Happy birthday.' The guests had already started to sing Auld Lang Syne and they now joined in.

Having been to the club before, they had become known to the members. One got an opportunity to speak to the Major in the bathroom. He was a psychologist and psycho-analyst.

'Alfie, you have a lovely daughter and BJ is a smashing person. They make a lovely couple. They are ideally suited and talk to each other with their eyes and smiles. Each has emotional intelligence.'

'Emotional intelligence? I have never heard that before. What does it mean?'

'They know their own and each other's feelings and emotions and use this information to guide one another's thinking and actions. It is just my

Chapter Thirty Two

tentative clinical opinion.'

'That is rather profound. But then I am not a psychologist. I am very fond of BJ and am delighted Anna has found him. They are great together.'

'Yes I see that.'

The next morning, the Major and BJ wished her happy birthday again and gave her their cards. The Major said, 'We have not forgotten your presents. We will give them to you later.'

After breakfast, which BJ cooked, he and Anna took Bruno for his usual walk. He tried not to make it obvious but kept them away for some time. After all, they did not have to go to work. But Anna did not think anything untoward anyway. They were happy. She loved being with him and Bruno was always in his element because of the attention he got from BJ.

Around nine o'clock, BJ suggested they head home. As they turned to walk through the gate, she saw the car. It had a ribbon with a bow and the Major had attached lettered bunting spelling, 'Happy birthday Anna. Love, BJ'

Anna gasped, 'BJ', started to cry and hugged him. She rested her head on his shoulder for a time to compose herself. When she looked up, the Major and Guy Williams were beside the car. The manager handed Anna a bouquet of roses.

He opened the driver's door for her to get in. BJ took the bouquet off her. The manager told her everything about the controls and dashboard pointing out that it was taxed and insured with a full tank of petrol and the documents were in a folder on the passenger seat.

The Major had already checked them and the car, which was in showroom condition. The manager had himself given it the once over. After what had happened, he did not want anything to go wrong. He asked BJ to sign for the car, shook hands with all wishing them, 'Happy New Year' and left.

Anna was still overcome with emotion as they went into the house. The Major gave her his present and said, 'You two stay here and I will make a drink.' As he was doing so, Bruno barked softly alerting them to known visitors. They were Sandra and Keith.

'Happy birthday Anna. I see you have a new car. It is lovely. Our gift is small compared to it.'

'A few months ago BJ asked Daddy and me how does one measure kindness? He went on to say a gift is a gift and is not one unless and until it is accepted. So thank you. I appreciate the thought.'

She opened it. It was the French perfume she wore which Sandra would have seen on her dressing table. The Major offered them a sherry, port or martini and they sat awhile enjoying the fellowship.

The next day some colleagues noticed Anna pull up in her new car. They knew from the registration letter it was only twenty-four hours old. 'Nice shining new car!'

'BJ bought it for my birthday.'

Some girls were envious and as they walked to different rooms one said, 'I wish my boyfriend would buy me a new car.'

Chapter Thirty Three

The Major had arranged for the three of them to visit his family in Scotland for Easter. They had Maundy Thursday and Easter Tuesday off. On that Thursday, after breakfast they were about to leave and BJ asked about Bruno.

'He is not coming. It would not be fair to him as it is too long a journey. Also we cannot expect my aunt and uncle to have him in their house.'

'But he will be on his own.'

'Sandra and Keith stayed here while we were in India. They will do the same this time. So he won't be on his own. Living next door, they pop into their own house during the day.'

'I am glad.'

Bruno sensed they were going away. He lay on the floor looking up at them dolefully. BJ was equally sad to leave him behind, giving him a lot of attention.

It was a long drive, which had to be broken regularly for nature breaks and refreshments. They arrived tired but the warmth of the greeting warmed them to the core, particularly BJ, who they were meeting for the first time. The Major said, 'Wayne and Sheila, Norman and Margaret, this is BJ,' adding with pride, 'my future son-in-law.'

'We've heard a lot about you BJ, all very good, we hasten to add. It's a pleasure meeting you. I hear even Bruno who is naturally aloof with everyone including us took to you immediately.'

'Sit down boy and feel at home.'

Anna sat sideways at his feet with her arm on his thighs. She proceeded to tell them about Bruno's reaction on meeting him. As the evening wore on, BJ experienced the kind of hospitality that was on a par with all that he had experienced with Anna and the Major, Harry and Ruth and Keith and Sandra.

They dined and about half past eight, the Major excused himself. 'It's been a long drive and I would like to have an early night.'

Anna and BJ were staying with Wayne and Sheila, the Major with Norman and Margaret. After they left, Sheila said, 'Come I will show you to your room BJ. Anna you know where yours is.'

'This is the bathroom and toilet. And this is your room. Make yourself comfortable.'

'Come back down when you are ready.'

They asked BJ about himself and because he tended to hold back, Anna elaborated often. There was no mistaking the pride and her love for him.

In the following days, Wayne and Sheila would not let BJ do a thing, even to stoke the open fire or get in the coal. In fact Sheila said, 'You sit down. We Scots lassies take care of our men.' And looking at Anna, 'Don't we hen?'

Anna who was on the sofa beside him, laughed saying, 'Aunty, don't tell him that, otherwise he will expect me to be at his beck and call.' They all laughed and although he had seen the funny side of it, Anna took his hand and held it to her lips reassuring him 'I did not mean it. You know I will always look after you.'

'And I you,' he said, playing with her hair.

They took him to a loch where they went on a boat ride, and to some beauty spots. He had never seen anything like it. On Saturday, they held a party and he learned how the Scots partied. As each one arrived, they were given a bowl of hot soup. During the evening, each had to sing a song. Some were pretty bad but it did not matter one iota. They were having fun and no one was trying to win points over the other.

On Tuesday, he was sorry it had ended. He had enjoyed the break, particularly the hospitality.

'It's been a pleasure meeting you BJ. We will see you at the wedding.'

'Thank you for everything.'

Bruno greeted them on their return in his canine way. His whole demeanour had changed from that on the day they left.

Chapter Thirty Three

By this time, plans for the wedding were complete. The church, reception at an exclusive hotel, a suite at another for two nights had all been arranged. On the day before the wedding, BJ would take their suitcases there in readiness for the flight to Canada for the honeymoon on Sunday. They had also organised everything for Li and his parents and Father O'Shea.

Ten days before the wedding, Anna and BJ met Fr O'Shea at the airport. 'Father, this is Anna. Anna Father O'Shea whom I have told you about. I have a lot to thank him for.'

'Pleased to meet you Father.'

'And you Anna.

Thank you both for inviting me to your wedding and paying my fare.'

'After all you did for me it is the least we could do.'

BJ had passed his driving test the first time after eight two-hour sessions and was a named driver on Anna's insurance. He drove to the Our Lady of Lourdes Church presbytery where Father Daniels awaited their arrival.

After the necessary introductions and cup of tea, Anna and BJ left.

On Sunday morning, the Major, Anna and BJ went in both cars to meet Li and his parents. Li's and BJ's faces face beamed with genuine pleasure as they embraced.

'Li you know Anna from school. Mr and Mrs Cheung this is Anna and her father.'

'Nice to meet you all,' they all said.

Mrs Cheung kissed her and BJ.

'We have come in two cars. We will put your luggage in Mr McLeod's and Anna will travel with him. I will drive the three of you in Anna's car. You must be tired and jetlagged after the flight so we will go straight to your relatives' house.'

When they got there, it was a Thai restaurant and the family stayed in the two storied flat above.

The Major, Anna and BJ were invited in but declined.

243

'You have a lot of catching up to do.'

Chapter Thirty Four

On the Friday after dinner, BJ took a taxi to the hotel. The next morning, he was excited and nervous. He breakfasted and arranged for his clothes to be valeted. He took his time before getting dressed.

He wore a made-to-measure grey/blue mohair suit and with his white silk shirt, dark blue shirt studs, red bowtie and red breast pocket hankie and matching grey shoes he looked immaculate. He had booked a chauffeur-driven car to take him to the church. There, Li and his family greeted him.

Anna too had been nervous. Sandra helped her get ready and when she went downstairs, the Major said, 'You look just like your mother when she wore the dress. She would have been very proud of you.'

She walked down the aisle with the Major and came alongside BJ, who kissed her on the nose, 'You look lovely.'

The ceremony proceeded, the register signed and photos taken. The sun shone its blessing on them.

The reception was in a high-class hotel. Li, Mr and Mrs Cheung were on the platform with the Major and Anna and BJ. There were table microphones in front of Li, the Major and BJ.

When all were settled down in their allocated seats and drinks had been poured, Li stood up.

'Good evening all. There are no words to describe how my parents and I feel about being here. And it is a particular privilege and pleasure to be best man. As my school and Anna's convent were in the same town, we used to go to each other's concerts, sports days and special events. Because of her success in running and appearing in concerts, BJ and I got to know her by name and sight. And though I only met her a few days ago, she is everything he has written to me about her. I—no—my parents and I are so happy for him. Seeing them together they make a lovely couple.'

Turning to Anna he continued, 'Anna I hope that God blesses me with a wife like you. And I will tell you something else. BJ liked you in school and used to defend you against some boys who used to make school-boy comments about you.'

BJ and Anna looked at each other and she lifted his hand to her lips to kiss it. Her face was beaming.

He picked up his glass, 'I am not used to public speaking and my mouth and throat are dry. Perhaps you will stand please and join me in a toast'

'To Anna and BJ.' The guests echoed the sentiment.

'Now, about BJ, my beloved friend and brother. Yes, brother but I will explain in due course. He is a remarkable person, very principled and resolute. He is also tremendously loyal and I could not wish for anyone better in my life. They say that a friend halves your sorrows and doubles your joys. He does that. And yes we are blood brothers. I do not know how many of you saw a western some ten years ago. The good cavalry scout and Indian Chief came to trust one another and each cut their thumbs pressing them together so their blood intermingled. It made them blood brothers. I suggested it to BJ and he agreed.'

Li continued, 'You may be wondering what prompted me to suggest that. I'll tell you. It was my first year in school and during the lunch break I had been playing marbles with a boy two classes above me, and therefore one above BJ. I won all this boy's marbles and he demanded them back. When I refused, he started to hit me around the head. I was crying. Next thing I knew, BJ was on this boy's back and knocked him to the ground. He pulled his hair and shouted, "Don't you bully him. Pick on someone your size." On reflection, it was laughable as BJ was smaller than him but here he was defending me. He warned the chap, "Don't touch him again." That bully walked away sheepishly and I never had any trouble from him again.

We became friendly and one day I offered him a sweet. He refused. When I asked why, he said he was an orphan. The boarders called them poor boys because they got everything free and did not get any pocket money. I need to add that they often wore the boarders' clothes they had

Chapter Thirty Four

outgrown and mostly had used textbooks. He went on to say he would never be able to offer me a sweet in return. I tried to persuade him but he was adamant. He said, 'I have seen boys fight and call each other names. You may call me a poor boy or say I took your sweets but never gave you any. As young as I was, I knew he meant what he said. A strong bond developed between us and that is why I suggested we become blood brothers. It was our commitment to one another.

Throughout the years he never took a thing of me or indeed anyone else. When he left school and got work he always gave my parents and me Christmas and birthday presents. He never changed even when he became popular as the singer/guitarist in a club resident group and performed in cabaret, concerts and hotels. And the three of us have to tell you that that so called poor boy in school insisted on paying our air fares and all our expenses so we can be here. In school I remember being taught during Catechism certain truths.'

He took a sheet of paper from his inside pocket, unfolded it and read:

'If you plant honesty, you will reap trust.
If you plant goodness, you will reap friends.
If you plant humanity, you will reap greatness.
If you plant perseverance, you will reap contentment.
If you plant consideration, you will reap perspective.
If you plant hard work, you will reap success.

In school, he may have been poor materially but ladies and gentlemen, BJ has lived by these truths. In my opinion it puts him among the richest in humility, integrity and honour.'

His voice broke. He paused to compose himself and then picked up his glass, which signalled the others to stand. Turning to look at Anna and BJ, he said, 'Today is the first day of your married life and from the bottom of my heart I wish you health wealth and happiness,' adding mischievously, 'and many bambinos. To Anna and BJ.'

'To Anna and BJ.' And they remained standing to clap loudly as Li sat down.

They quieted and the Major stood up.

'BJ is tall, he is dark, he is handsome and he cuts a dashing figure. He is better looking than I was at his age. He makes you sick doesn't he?' But there was no mistaking the mischief in his tone of voice. His face, smile and twinkle in his eyes spoke volumes.

'But as the bride's father I must first talk about Anna. She is a lovely daughter, one that any father would be proud of. She has always been there for me after my wife and her mother died not long after she finished school. She took it hard because being in boarding school she was only home for the school holidays. And being a naturally shy and quiet person she then receded into somewhat of a shell.

She was asked out many times but she did not think she was ready. Then after she was eighteen, someone she liked asked her to the office dance. But he was too forward and she never went out with him or anybody again. As a doting father, I was concerned about her. But she maintained that she was not interested in dating just for the sake of it, like other girls. She wanted a meaningful relationship.

Then BJ came into our lives. Immediately he had an impact on us. I noticed while we at sea there was a change in her. In the course of time, in a dynamic way, he brought her out of her shell. She blossomed with him and become a lot more confident. And doesn't she look gorgeous?'

He reached for his glass and all stood. 'To Anna and BJ.'

'To Anna and BJ.'

'Now about this man who is better looking than I was at the same age.' The guests laughed. 'BJ has a powerful presence, is very dynamic and does not mince words. He can appear intimidating to some, yet when you get to know him, he is very kind and gentle and full of human warmth.

As a lot of you know, Anna and I went to a wedding in India last year. At the docks, she had gone to the bathroom. I tripped and fell on my knee on the pavement and guess what? BJ was there to help. He took charge helped me to a bench and asked the coolies to get some ice. He did not

Chapter Thirty Four

order them. He was polite saying please and thank you. He treated them as equals. When they brought the ice he took a Rs5 note from his wallet and gave it to them. As he was attending me, Anna returned and put her hand on my shoulder. But very soon she gasped, 'Oh my God. BJ!' and held her hand to her mouth. But he was so engrossed in tending to me he did not hear.

When she saw BJ, she dug her nails into my shoulder and grabbed a hold of my arm, doing the same thing. I looked at her and she was red with excitement. Her eyes were alight. Only when BJ had finished did he look up and ask if I felt any better. I did and then he noticed Anna. He shot up exclaiming, 'Anna. Anna McLeod!' Turning to me he said, 'Then you must be Major McLeod.' I could not stand let alone walk properly. He then carried our luggage into the Customs hall and supported me onto the ship.

We had to register our preferences for the first or second sitting in the dining room. Anna whispered, 'Please ask BJ to join us at our table.' When we got to our cabin one of the first things Anna asked me was, 'Daddy would you have BJ as a son-in-law?'

There were gasps in the audience as some looked at each other in astonishment.

'Yes, that is exactly what she asked me. And because she is my daughter and I had seen her face and reaction when she recognised him, I knew she was deadly serious. I told her all I wanted was her happiness and if it was BJ she wanted, I would give them my blessing. I asked her to search for him, as I wanted to thank him properly and buy him a drink. He joined us but do you know what he said? He declined the drink for the same reason he would not accept a sweet from Li. He said that travelling on an Indian passport he was only allowed to take out Rs75 the equivalent of £3, 15s. He needed that money until his own small savings were transferred and he found a job. He would not therefore be able to return the kindness.

Now to put things into perspective, he was only allowed to travel with Rs75. Yet he gave Rs5 of that to the coolies. I reminded him of it and he said, 'Their need is greater than mine. It is probably what they earn in a few days if they are lucky. I still have Rs70 left.' I had to persuade him that he did not have to feel obligated in any way. I understood and wished him to accept whatever and whenever we bought him anything. Yes as Li said, BJ is a man of principle.'

He reached for his glass and all stood up to toast him and Anna.

Resuming he said, 'There is a guest here with his family. I have asked Barry to say a few words. Come up here, son.'

The Major stepped aside so he could use his mic.

'Thank you sir for this opportunity. Everything that Li and Mr McLeod have said about BJ is absolutely right. I was only seven years old and it was the first time I was away from my family. I was homesick and crying. BJ thought I had been bullied but I told him that I missed my mum and wanted to go home. He put his arm around my shoulder and comforted me. He reassured me that my family, especially my mother, would be missing me too. Also I would get letters and pocket money and go home for the holidays. But he like the other orphans had no one. For some days after that, whenever he saw me he asked how I was.

I can tell you a lot about how BJ won the respect of his peers and the Christian Brothers and teachers. But believe me, what Li and Mr McLeod have said, I endorse wholeheartedly. BJ is one in a million. Thank you.'

And he returned to his seat.

The Major continued. 'Thank you for that Barry. Barry and I talked on the ship one morning before breakfast. There were other favourable things he had to say about BJ, which enhanced my own impressions of him from the outset. There was something about him. He was a special person. He was a man of kindness and integrity.

One evening a drunken middle-aged English passenger was manhandling Anna and BJ intervened. He coolly stepped between them, politely saying, 'You're upsetting my friend.' Freeing his hand from Anna's arm, he walked her back to our table. As they did so, the man punched him in the back and racially abused him. He cast aspersions on his legitimacy and effectively accused him of having an incestuous relationship with his mother. I am putting it euphemistically but you know the words that were used. I have never seen a man so much in control of himself. BJ's first concern was for Anna and only when she assured him she was all right did he excuse himself and turn towards the drunk who was walking away smugly. I learned later that BJ was an undefeated boxer and a martial arts student. He could have done serious damage to this drunk but in an even voice he told him his mother died when he was seven, nine years after his parents were married. BJ further embarrassed him into apologising to Anna and him. That man told me before we disembarked, other passengers had expressed disapproval of his language and behaviour. He respected BJ for the manner in which he dealt with the situation and had gone on the wagon. He had not had a drink since that evening.'

Several muttered, 'Aah,' and as some started to clap, they all joined in.

'BJ was wounded by the abuse of his mother and went on deck for some fresh air. Anna was now concerned about him and followed. And to add insult to injury someone else made a derogatory comment about Anna being with an Indian. It was now Anna's turn to defend BJ. Yes, the quiet and shy Anna. She gave them a piece of her mind and from then on the bond between them strengthened.

Fate continued to play a hand. The person who was to meet him at the docks and accommodate him had to return to India urgently because his father was fatally ill. We asked him to come and stay with us.

That first night after dinner, he asked to speak to me privately. And you will never guess this. The first thing he asked was would I have him as a son-in-law. I had just drunk some coffee and I spat out a mouthful, I was so surprised. He thought he had offended me. But it was exactly what Anna had asked me. Besides, BJ had cut to the chase immediately. No preamble. We talked about other things and it was not just his forthrightness and honesty that impressed me. There was his humility. After just fifteen days, he struck me as being a man rich in spirit. I told Father O'Shea this and I was then not surprised when he described his mother in the same terms.

But as if the racial abuse and on the ship was not enough, BJ was racially attacked by four drunks. And this happened only three days after he arrived. He took two of them out but made the mistake of turning his back to walk away. He was knocked unconscious with a brick, concussed and was hospitalised overnight.' This surprised everyone. They had never talked about it to anyone. Father O'Shea, Barry and his family and Li and his parents were stunned.

After a short pause the Major continued, 'Anna was distraught and beside herself. She sat with him through the night. BJ though, was concerned that he was damaging our reputation and standing in the neighbourhood and offered to move out to save us any further embarrassment. But we were far from being embarrassed. He did not know it then but that attack made Anna and I realise how much he had come to mean to us in the short space of time since we met.

She and BJ developed a very close bond and spent almost all their time together. They were completely at ease in each other's company. So when six months later, BJ asked if he could propose to Anna, I had no hesitation in agreeing. The three of us were already a family unit.

As I said, they were already close but now their relationship went to a much higher level. It became very intense and they were inseparable. Most of their waking hours were spent in each other's company and they thrived on it. Anna had always been a neat and smart dresser but being with BJ made her more confident. She took a leaf from his book and began to wear brightly coloured clothes a lot more often. She blossomed and she radiated inner peace and happiness.

At my golf club's New Year's Eve function, a fellow member who is a psychologist remarked they each had emotional intelligence. I asked him what he meant. He explained it simply but I have since learned it means they have this innate ability to recognise and understand their own and each other's feelings and emotions, to guide one another's thinking and actions. They communicate with each other with looks and smiles. They are soul mates.

And so here we are today. Their love for one another is plain for all to see and I am one proud man, one happy father. My daughter has found a good man and I have found a son. Indeed I am and have.'

Seeing him reach for his drink the others stood up. 'BJ I am proud to have you as a son-in-law, no, I will go further than that. I am proud to have you as a son. Because that is what you are.' And mischievously he added 'And I cannot wait to become a grandfather to many bambinos.' They all laughed.

As Li said, 'I wish you both health wealth and happiness. To Anna and BJ.' And again there was loud applause.

Things quieted. Anna kissed BJ's hand as he took a drink and stood up. With all eyes focused on him they saw what a dashing and good-looking person he was. He did have a presence and exuded a certain aura. There was an air of expectancy as he looked around slowly. He took another drink as his eyes dwelt on each table mentally photographing each face to store in the archives of his mind.

'Thank you all for taking the time and making the effort to be here. I know some of you have travelled great distances. Father O'Shea from India, Li and Mr and Mrs Cheung from Bangkok and relatives from Scotland.'

He paused and continued.

'Life is a book of many chapters. It consists of numerous possibilities and experiences. Many chances are only available within a short time frame, and if we do not take advantage of them, they are lost. I was very lucky. There were many people who contributed significantly to various chapters. They ensured I never missed those chances, those opportunities. In fact they created them.

The early years of my life made up the first few chapters. The next few were about my schooling and life in the orphanage. Li, and Mr and Mrs Chueng contributed significantly. Their impact on my life continued after I left school as new chapters were written. They bought me new clothes for work, gave me money and got me a job in banking that I could not have otherwise.

Another, a manager of a club and the father of one of the boarders in school, opened a door enabling me to earn more money. When I was twenty-one, to my complete and utter surprise, I inherited a small sum of money. It was my father's provident fund. It is similar to the pension fund here. As I had no family I decided to burn my boats and make a fresh start in England. Talk about fate playing a hand? It was the best decision of my life until then. People helped and because of a cancellation I had five weeks notice to emigrate. And you know now that is how I met Anna and my father-in-law.

When my parents died, I felt all alone. I was only seven. I did not know what would happen to me and I was afraid. I switched off emotionally. Even when the Major and Anna befriended me at sea and later took me into their home I held back. I was afraid they would tire of me and I would lose them too.

I had always been comfortable with myself in India. But as the Major has already alluded to, there were incidents on the ship and shortly after I arrived, that undermined my confidence somewhat. The last thing I wanted was to damage the standing of the two very people who had extended the hand of friendship to me. But I came across some words somewhere and they were the key to the door of my emotions. It went something like this: "Do not hide your feelings from yourself. It is only through your acknowledgment and loving embrace of them that you are able to truly let them go." I imagine this was the beginning of what the Major said about emotional intelligence.

Coming to think of it, Anna is very intelligent in every respect. Me? At least I have some kind of intelligence.' He paused as they laughed. 'Even though I am not intelligent enough to understand it myself.' The humour in his voice was unmistakable and it elicited great laughter. The Major himself laughed aloud.

'They treated me so well that I came to accept that my culture and background did not matter. They taught me to accept myself, an Anglo Indian in the UK, because they accepted me as a person. The Major, sorry, my father-in-law—I must get used to that—may consider that Anna gained confidence with me. I assure you that I gained confidence because of them. I felt so lucky that a pretty girl like Anna and her father would spend time and be seen out with me, irrespective of what people might think and say. Now I have them in my life new chapters begin.

Before I finish, it would be very remiss of me not to mention one particular person. He is Father O'Shea. My mother used to take me to mass every day. He arranged for me to go to the orphanage. When I finished school, rather than see me go to an hostel, he let me stay in the presbytery for two years until I was eighteen and was no longer considered a minor. And he would not allow me to pay him.

I mentioned at the outset about the chances and opportunities that come our way in life. Father provided many of them. When you think of it, if I had not been orphaned I would not have been sent to the orphanage. I would not have met Anna and the others on this platform. I realised a long time ago that God had His Hand on my life. As He closed one door when I was orphaned, He opened another when I went to the orphanage. That is why we are here today.

The past is dead. I will not dwell on it. To do so would bankrupt my tomorrows with Anna. Today is an extra special day. It is a gift to enjoy. A new chapter begins and I look forward to the future with Anna by my side.'

As he said this, Anna started to arise from her chair. He went behind her to pull it further back then returning to her side. He moved the microphone in front of her.

She said, 'You have toasted us several times. Now, my husband and I....' mimicking the Queen, eliciting a lot of laughter, '....want to toast you.'

She and BJ raised their glasses. They turned to the Major, 'To Daddy. Thank you for being such a wonderful father.'

'Amen' said BJ, continuing as he turned to Li, and Mr and Mrs Cheung, 'Thank you for everything. And to you Father, the same.'

Then together, Anna and he said, 'To all of you. Good luck, good health and God bless you with all you would wish for yourselves.'

Many women had tears in their eyes. Others including the men had lumps in their throats. As one everyone stood and spontaneously applauded. As it died down, the Major started to sing, 'For they are jolly good fellows,' to Anna and BJ. And the rest joined in.

The Major then said, 'That's my son.'

Several women exclaimed, 'Aaah.'

He continued, 'We have your food choices and dinner will now be served.'

After they had dined again the Major stood up. 'Hot drinks and cheese and biscuits will be served in the lounge and there is a free bar. The staff will clear the tables and prepare the room for the band and dancing.'

When all was ready the band leader said, 'A lot of you know the groom is an accomplished singer/guitarist. When he and the bride got engaged, he dedicated a particular song to her. The bride's father and maid of honour have suggested he sing it now. Mr Conway, the microphone is yours.'

BJ was caught completely unawares. 'I did not expect this.' But he sang and the band accompanied him having rehearsed it in anticipation. The song was titled 'She wears my ring' the words of which were

'She wears my ring to show the world that she belongs to me
She wears my ring to show the world she's mine eternally
With loving care I placed it on her finger
To show my love for all the world to see

This tiny ring is a token of tender emotion
An endless pool of love that's as deep as the ocean
She swears to wear it with eternal devotion
That's why I sing, because she wears my ring

She swears to wear it with eternal devotion
That's why I sing, because she wears my ring

This tiny ring is a token of tender emotion
An endless pool of love that's as deep as the ocean
She swears to wear it with eternal devotion
That's why I sing, because she wears my ring
That's why I sing, because she wears my ring'

It was clear he meant every word and it went down well.

Chapter Thirty Four

BJ returned to the platform but he was not seated for long. The band leader said, 'The bride and groom have chosen a song for the first dance; The Hawaiian Wedding Song.'

The words of it were:

*'This is the moment
I've waited for
I can hear my heart singing
Soon bells will be ringing
This is the moment
love sweet Aloha
I will love you longer than forever
Promise me that you will leave me never*

*Here I am now dear,
You're my love,
I know dear
Promise me that you will leave me never
I will love you longer than forever
Now that we are one
Clouds won't hide the sun
Blue skies of Hawaii will smile
On this, our wedding day
I do love you with all my heart.'*

The band started to play and the female singer sang. Anna and BJ took to the floor. By arrangement, towards the end, a club official handed BJ a microphone and he sang the final five lines.

There were not many guests if any, that were not moved by the song.

When Anna and BJ returned to the platform, the Major said, 'That was really touching. BJ you really can pull at the heart strings of people when you sing.'

As Anna and BJ mingled with the guests, many said how touched they were by what had been said and his singing. It was a lovely choice of his songs.

Anna said, 'Everything Daddy, Barry and Li said about BJ is true. I am so happy to have him as my husband.'

Time went by and all were having a good time. The Major had arranged for the wedding car to take off the ribbons, take them home to change into day clothes and then drive them to their hotel. It was the first night they had spent together since that eventful weekend the previous September when they committed themselves to each other and became engaged.

The following day at noon, they were on a flight to Toronto. He was flying for the first time. As they were in First Class, the service added a lustre to what were already excellent facilities. The attention they received was second to none and of course he was sharing it all with his beloved Anna, his wife.

They spent the first three nights of the next fortnight in Niagara where they had a hotel suite overlooking the falls with the rainbow over it. There was a balcony that enabled them to enjoy a panoramic view. It was enclosed to keep out the spray. And at night when the coloured lights shone on the cascading water it was a breathtaking picture. They went on the Maid of the Mist boat trip and also the helicopter ride over the falls. They had wanted to cross the bridge to America and go behind the Bridal Veil but because BJ had an Indian passport, the hotel concierge did not think he would be allowed to. But it did not matter. There was enough to enjoy in the short time they were there. They fed off each other's enjoyment and were in their element.

In Toronto they dined out, went to the pictures, the odd show and nightclub and took in the sights both by night and day. After a longish day out and about they had the odd quiet evening in the hotel lounge with the pianist providing mood music in a very nice ambience. There continued the silent communication between them: a look, a smile, a squeeze of the hand, arm or a cuddle.

All too soon it was time to fly home. Arriving early morning, the Major met them at the airport. Bruno was very excited to see them again. He had missed the walks and games with BJ. His tail wagged furiously and he rubbed himself against them, licking their hands and enjoying being petted. The pack was together again.

The Major had missed them too. Now the house was full not just by their physical presence but by the love the three of them had for one another. It was a family home again in every sense and wistfully he thought of his late wife. Shaking himself out of this reverie, he looked forward to becoming a grandfather.

Chapter Thirty Five

BJ and Anna settled into married life and were as inseparable as ever. Apart from each other, they were not themselves. They had an implicit understanding they would enjoy being husband and wife before they became parents. And so against the Catholic Church's rules on contraception, they mastered its art as they had a great time.

As one year became two, then three and then four inevitably questions were asked about when they were going to become parents. But neither would be pressed and then one night spontaneously they just decided without speaking it was time. Each sensed it was what the other wanted and they were ready for the responsibility.

But there was no evidence of Anna becoming pregnant. The months went by and a year later they decided to see the doctor. Tests were done and the day came for them to be given the results.

'Good evening Mr and Mrs Conway. Please sit down.'

'Good evening doctor,' they replied.

'I imagine you are both a little nervous so I will cut to the chase. Mrs Conway you are as fertile as any young woman can be.' This rang alarm bells in BJ's mind and he was preparing for a different result.

'Mr Conway, you are fertile too but have a low sperm count. It may take time but you will become parents. My clinical opinion is that perhaps latterly both of you became a little anxious worrying about why you were not conceiving. Be reassured by what I have told you and be relaxed about it. It may happen tonight, tomorrow, next week, next month, but I cannot be more sure of anything, Mrs Conway, you will conceive.'

BJ smiled and Anna squeezed his arm herself beaming reassurance at him. 'Thank you doctor.'

'My pleasure, I look forward to seeing you again soon Mrs Conway.'

They went home and told the Major about the prognosis. Privately he had been worried but he was now very pleased for them and indeed for himself. They would give him a grandchild; but like them he had to be patient. 'This is good news. Let's dine out together.'

That night, they were relaxed and at peace. And as the doctor had said, it was not long before she missed her period. They were excited but did not say anything to the Major in case it was a false alarm. They arranged to see the doctor.

When he saw them, he read their faces. But he did not want to anticipate anything and asked, 'How can I help you?'

'Doctor I am late which is very unusual. I think I am pregnant.'

'I need to examine you. Can you get on the bed please?' He got up and closed a curtain.

'Do you want me to leave doctor?' BJ asked.

'No. It's OK. You sit there.'

The doctor examined Anna and smiled at her. She saw it but kept her silence. 'You can get dressed.'

He took off the plastic gloves and washed his hands. Anna returned to her seat, pulling her chair closer to BJ gripping his hand.

The doctor smiled. 'You are expecting. Have you calculated the dates?'

'Yes. I think I am five weeks pregnant and our baby will therefore be due on 23 May.'

He checked the dates of her cycle and agreed. 'Good. 23 May it is.'

They got home and could not wait to tell the Major. He arrived and after he had changed and come back down, Anna gave him a cup of coffee.

'Daddy you are going to be a grandfather.'

While he had always been hopeful, it was a surprise. But a very pleasant one!

'We have just seen the doctor and he has confirmed it. The baby is due on 23 May.'

'Brilliant news. I am delighted for both of you. And for myself too.'

The following day at the office, Anna was quick to tell her colleagues.

Chapter Thirty Five

BJ kept quiet, knowing the news would get around. And it did.

'I hear congratulations are in order. Anna is expecting.'

'Yes and we are ecstatic as also is my father-in-law. The baby is not only Anna's and my first but will be father-in-law's first grandchild. So naturally we are all excited and looking forward to the big day.'

'Do either of you have a particular preference for a girl or boy?'

'None whatsoever. It is God's gift to us and we will be happy either way.'

'Maybe you will have twins, one of each.'

'Who knows. If it is God's will so be it.'

As they were financially secure, she finished work at Christmas. They made arrangements with a private Catholic Nursing Home run mainly by nuns for the birth. Father Daniels had recommended it. By this time they had traded in her birthday present car for a newer model and for some while, she drove BJ to and from the office. She prepared a packed lunch and never failed to slip in a note telling him she would miss him, or she loved him or something to make him feel good. Often she also met him for lunch anyway just to be together.

Antenatal visits were reassuring, except for the fact that latterly the baby was in a transverse position. But Anna was told not to worry so she, BJ and the Major did not.

The weeks flew by and as she got bigger they decided to buy another car, a medium sized one. BJ then used the smaller one to travel to and from work.

Because Anna was now heavily pregnant they did not pay the reciprocal visit to Scotland at Easter. So for the second year running, the relatives came down. With each visit they noticed how close Anna, the Major and BJ were. And how Bruno now looked on BJ as top dog, the undisputed pack leader.

On 22 May, at half-past-ten that night, Anna roused BJ. She felt it was time. The Major, who was still up, telephoned the Nursing Home to alert them of the position and they would shortly be on their way. He then drove them to the hospital. The midwife made Anna comfortable in the delivery room and the doctor examined her. 'The baby is not yet in the right position. Do you want to go home Mr Conway and come back in the morning? I will call you if there are any developments. Or you can say here.'

'I will stay with Anna please. Sir, I will call you.'

'I will not be able to sleep myself but I will leave the two of you alone.'

The doctor said, 'You can stay in the lounge if it will make you feel easier. You can then pop in and see your daughter and son-in-law from time to time especially if he needs to go to the bathroom. I am sure neither one of you would want her to wake up and find herself alone.'

The Major felt a sense of déjà vu as he thought about that first weekend BJ was attacked. He kissed Anna, hugged BJ and left. The doctor and midwife also left leaving them alone.

During the night, the midwife regularly checked that Anna was OK. In the morning, the doctor came in and after examining her said, 'The baby is still in the transverse position but it looks like being here inside the hour.' She was by now dehydrating so was put on a drip.

The Major arrived and BJ told him what the doctor had said. They sat together each holding one of Anna's hands. As she looked pale and drawn they maintained a silence so she could rest. However, the two most important people in her life were sharing these moments and she drew a lot of comfort from their presence.

But an hour went by, then two. A team came in and it was clear something was now going to happen. The doctor examined her and told BJ, 'The baby is still in the transverse position. I am afraid we have to assist the birth and must therefore ask you both to go into the lounge. I will call you when you can come in.'

BJ was worried but tried desperately not to show it. He kissed Anna saying, 'I love you. I will see you and our baby soon.'

There was no one in the lounge. The Major made them coffees and another and then another. Neither spoke. As often happened in his life BJ felt his mother's presence. In his mind's eye he saw her and she was smiling saying, 'Everything is OK. You will have a daughter.' And a short while later, he heard a baby crying. He was impatient to go and see Anna and their baby but he had to stay where he was.

It seemed an age before they were told they could go in. But there was no baby. Anna was pale and drawn but she was smiling. The nurses and doctors had sponged her face and she had combed her hair.

'Where is our girl Senga Violet?' BJ asked.

'How did you know it was a girl?'

'I just did. I'll tell you both later.'

The Major was moved. His granddaughter was named after his late wife and Anna's mother.

The doctor said, 'She is fine and weighs 7lbs 3oz. But because it was traumatic for both mother and daughter, as a precaution we have put her in an incubator. We will let you see her in about forty-five minutes.'

He kissed her asking, 'How do you feel?'

'Exhausted but happy.'

'I am sorry for what you had to go through.'

'I will go through anything to make you happy BJ. I love you. I cannot imagine life without you. Now we have the child we wanted so much.'

'You get some rest now. Everything is ok. It's over. We are now a family of four.'

She closed her eyes and lightly dozed. He studied her serene face and prayed silently, 'Thank you Lord for a safe delivery. Help Anna recover quickly, please.'

'You are calling her Senga Violet?'

'Yes sir. Anna and I thought it was the right thing to do. My parents are dead. We felt it would honour you and her mother.'

Anna chipped in weakly, 'Actually Daddy, it was BJ's idea from the outset and he would not have it any other way.'

'Thank you both. It means a lot to me. She would have loved to be here and part of this. But I guess she has been and is still watching and rejoicing in the birth of her granddaughter named after her.'

Anna had dozed again and so as not to disturb her, they maintained a silent vigil. And then a nurse came in carrying Senga swathed in a blanket. She handed her to Anna who had woken. She looked lovingly at her, kissed her forehead and after a while passed her to BJ. 'Our daughter,' she said.

BJ was a proud father and gazed in wonder at his flesh and blood. He was in heaven. He then passed her to the Major, who having witnessed Anna's and BJ's tenderness, had moist eyes. The atmosphere in that room was charged with emotion.

Handing Senga back to Anna, he said, 'I will leave the two of you alone to savour these moments. I'll go home and come back later. I will bring the cameras. Shall I call your office to give them the news and to confirm you will be off until Monday after next?'

'Yes please.'

Keith and Sandra, Harry and Ruth and friends from the office visited over the next five days before mother and daughter were allowed to go home. BJ had brought a change of clothes for Anna and several boxes of chocolates and biscuits for the nuns, nurses and doctors.

The Major was at work so Keith picked them up. 'I wonder how Bruno will react to Senga,' he said.

'Bruno is very clever and has powerful senses. I am sure in his canine way he will know she is the new addition to his pack. He will be OK, you'll see.' And BJ really did believe it.

When they got home Bruno was excited. Sandra was there as she had been preparing some lunch and dinner for them. BJ held Senga to his muzzle and he sniffed and whined tail wagging vigorously. He deliberately laid her on the floor and Bruno lay beside her, tail thumping the floor.

Keith said, 'You really know Bruno. He is a different dog since you came to live here.'

He said jokingly, 'Maybe he felt sorry for me then having no family of my own so he adopted me.'

Keith and Anna saw the funny side but both knew it was more than that. BJ was the genuine article and personified kindness and human warmth. Bruno obviously trusted him.

'Well I am glad you are home Anna. Take care and we will see you. Bye both.'

'Bye. And thank you for the lift and the meals.'

'Think nothing of it.'

Then they were alone. 'I'll just go and change.'

As she departed, Bruno rose and came and lay down at BJ's feet. He sat in silence until Anna returned. 'She is still sound,' as she sat beside him. He put his arm around her as she snuggled up to him. She was glad to be back home with BJ. They had both missed each other. No words were spoken. There was no need.

The Major came home as Anna was feeding Senga. He too was glad they were all together again. He had the photos and they spent some time going through them.

'Tell me which ones you like especially and I will have copies printed. We will all want to have some us.' The Major said.

Chapter Thirty Six

That night and every night for some three months, Senga slept between them. She was a good baby. When she did wake up, Anna fed her and while BJ winded her, she got warm water to change her nappy.

As the weeks passed, sometimes Senga woke before them and started to gurgle and kick her feet and move her arms. She was their alarm clock.

Anna had come to the office a few times to see her friends, who made a fuss of the baby. And BJ could not wait to get home after work. Often he would think how his life had changed. Senga was loved by all and it was one happy home.

When BJ came home, if she was awake, she used to extend her arms and reach out to him. The months went by and she would crawl and then walk to him. She was Daddy's girl.

For her first birthday, they organised a celebration with Harry and Ruth and Keith and Sandra. Plenty of photographs were taken, especially as she had started walking at just over eleven months. She was a happy child and they got some lovely photographs of her smiling face.

They sorted the prints selecting some for a montage. One chose itself as the centre piece. It was of Senga sucking her fingers on BJ's lap on an easy chair with Anna sitting on the armrest with her arm around his shoulders. There was something indefinable about that picture that stood out. There was also another very endearing one. It was of Senga with her wet mouth open over the end of his nose. The Major had caught the moment beautifully by taking several shots. This one was the best.

A week later the extra prints, album and montage were available.

I stared at it, particularly the centre piece. As I did so, once again, I sensed my mother's presence. But she was not alone. I felt another woman's and it was Anna's mother. The two grandmothers were holding hands. There was a strange but very peaceful aura in the room. They both smiled lovingly.

I blinked a couple of times and then they were gone.

Continuing to look at the photo I thought, 'My life has come full circle.'

'I've got a life!'